THE FINAL FRAME

HARMONY REED

THE FINAL FRAME

Chapter One

BEHIND THE WHEEL OF A CAR HE'S JUST STOLEN

SHE WASN'T LISTENING.

She never listened.

Cameron tried again anyway.

"Life itself is meaningless. But art creates meaning by bringing events into focus. Art is the closest we can come to perfection."

"Save it for your Oscar speech," Emily teased as she lowered her window for the security guard and handed over their IDs. She was his agent; telling Cameron to shut up was part of her job.

He usually gave zero fucks about producer meetings, and wished he could tell his nerves to shut the hell up. They went his way or they didn't, and they usually did, whether he wanted them to or not.

But Cameron had been waiting years for this specific meeting.

"Just the two of you?" asked the guard, peeking past Emily.

She nodded. "Cameron Parrish and Emily Egerton, here to see Marshall Jeffries."

The guard swiped a couple of times on her tablet, then nodded and raised the boom. After maneuvering them into the lot's second-to-last available spot, she turned to Cameron. "You're sure you want to take the risk?"

"Are you going to keep asking me that?" It irritated him more than he wanted it to. Every time she said it, he heard *I don't think you can pull this off.* "Isn't every movie a really big risk?"

He opened the car door and got out, hoping that would kill the conversation.

It didn't. "I just want to protect what we've built."

What I've built, Cameron wanted to say. But that wasn't exactly fair. He never would've gotten his first directing gig if she hadn't fought so hard for him.

So he stayed silent until they stepped off the elevator and entered the reception area of Jeffries' office suite — hallowed ground for someone like Cameron.

A bright-eyed twenty-something with bangs and French tips greeted them. "Emily and Cameron, right? Can I get you a bottle of water?"

"No thanks." Cameron shook his head with a polite smile.

"Two, please," Emily said.

The assistant stepped through a door behind her desk, then Emily turned to Cameron. "Always take the water. It gives you something to do with your hands."

"Why are you talking to me like I've never pitched before?"

"Because you've never pitched to someone like Jeffries."

Before Cameron could ask what that was supposed to mean, the producer's assistant returned with water, then ushered them down a short, Zen-themed hallway to Jeffries' office, whispering, "I love your work," to Cameron before she opened the door for them. "Especially *Namaste*."

"Thanks," he replied, with a smile he wished could be wider.

Even if they liked his movies, no one *loved* a Cameron Parrish flick. Thin plots cobbled together by a studio exec and his B-team of writers. Cheap sets. Spectacular action sequences audiences loved because Cameron hired excellent stuntmen and pushed them to try things they'd never done. Viewers admired him and studios hated him for refusing to lean on AI-generated shots like everyone else. He didn't use AI-enhancement at all. Every second of every stunt in a Cameron Parrish film was real. These days that made him an artisan, even while he handcrafted schlock.

His movies weren't meant to be blockbusters; they were made to open big, or at least big enough, then make enough on streaming rights to keep the investors happy. Critics, too. They loved to savage his work, no matter how beautifully shot it might be. If they knew how much rewriting he did to turn what the studio gave him into a passable story, they'd … who was Cameron kidding? They'd still compete for the honor of stabbing him in the back with the wittiest verbal blade they could possibly whet.

He longed to make something for the ages. Something fathers and sons would share, not just on opening weekend or when the movie made its way to streaming, but more than once, and maybe even as tradition.

"Emily, so good to see you," Jeffries said as Cameron followed her into the similarly Zen-themed office, a room of pale beiges and soft creams accented with pale wood furniture. A wall fountain at the far end and *sumi-e* paintings both looked like antiques. A tree in the corner looked shockingly real, even though it couldn't have been, making the entire room appear to blush in its cherry blossom hue.

All it needed was a Japanese businessman lounging on the couch with his mistress, and a couple of tattooed Yakuza about to burst in and threaten to reveal his terrible secret.

A secret that Cameron didn't have to figure out, because after this meeting, he would never have to make another cheesy action flick again.

Jeffries gave him the warmest handshake he'd ever had on a cold meeting like this one, then said, "I've been wanting to meet you for a long time."

He had? "The feeling is mutual. It's an honor."

"I loved *Namaste*. Big fan."

Cameron believed Jeffries could be a fan, but not that he actually was. Not based on the movies he'd made so far. "That's very kind."

"I'm serious. I admire your eye for the perfect shot, same as everyone else, but your films have something to them. Buried too deep beneath the glossy action for critics to notice. But it's always there, especially with *Namaste*."

"Thank you." He should say something else, but what? Cameron had plenty of quips ready for the critics, but it had been years since someone had commented on anything other than the flashy aesthetic that made the films *his*. "I'd really like to bring that something to the surface."

A flash of movement in the corner of his eye — Emily crossing her legs and leaning back in her chair. Was that a signal?

Had he said the wrong thing?

He unscrewed his bottle, took a long sip of water, then said, "You're an uber-producer. You love making movies, but you love making money even more. I have a project I think is perfect for you, even though Emily disagrees."

Emily flicked something off of her slacks, the only sign she might be annoyed that he'd just thrown her under the bus. "I don't disa—"

"She thinks I should stick with the Namaste franchise." Hopefully she'd forgive him later, but Cameron's gut told him that total honesty was the way to this man's heart and mind. "I feel like the timing is right for me to make a change, and if you agree that the project is worthwhile, Fire Marshall Films is the ideal home."

"Why do you think Cameron should stick with the franchise?" Jeffries asked Emily, even though they all knew the answer was *money*.

"Timing," she replied with no hesitation. "He spent the first five years of his career making streamers so he could build up enough of a reputation to land a decent budget, and the ten after that establishing his brand."

"Which is why the timing is perfect," Cameron cut in.

"Which is why the timing feels dangerous to me. You're on top right now. You have a style that others are copying—"

"Which means it's time to try something different."

"—and people are waiting for the next *Namaste*. It makes more sense to finish that trilogy. Make *Bitter Nirvana* before you start something new."

"Unless I change my aesthetic entirely, the third *Namaste* will look derivative. Like I'm copying all the people who've started copying me."

Cameron glanced at Jeffries. He got it, didn't he?

No way to tell from the man's amused expression.

Shit, was this what Emily had meant about never having pitched to someone like him before? Had Cameron already blown it?

Or had Emily blown it for him, knowing that without

this specific producer's support, he'd have no other choice than to make more movies like *Namaste*?

He couldn't get enough air. Something was crushing his chest. It would kill him to lose this chance, but this meeting was already off the rails. The right damage control now might mean he could return alone and try again.

Cameron turned to Jeffries, his expression apologetic. "I'm sorry, we're wasting your time."

"Not at all." Jeffries looked like he was loving every minute. "I agree with Emily."

She set this up. Convinced Jeffries to help her twist my arm.

He should have gone around her. Found an agent who believed in his vision.

But who else would back him on making anything other than the action flicks that made him famous?

"It seems ludicrous for you to do anything other than *Bitter Nirvana* right now. Everyone knows it's going to get made, and you need to be behind the camera. Or they'll replace you with Anderson Wyatt."

"Fuck that guy." Cameron couldn't help it.

"It's the sincerest form of flattery," Jeffries said.

"Fuck that guy," he repeated. "Did you see *Nunchucks*? He rips off everything about my style, and he rips off my stories. He's always in my rearview, behind the wheel of a car he's just stolen."

"Yet you seem perfectly willing to let him take your franchise away from you."

Fuck him that they were having this conversation with Jeffries, instead of the conversation he'd wanted to have. And fuck Emily for putting him in this position.

"It's not my franchise," Cameron replied. "Those movies make me a hack."

"Absolutely not," Jeffries said. "Anderson Wyatt is a

hack. A good one. I'm not gonna lie and tell you I don't like the guy. He knows who he is and what he makes. He's happy with it. Thinks he has the best job on Earth."

"He's smug," Cameron said. "Sorry."

"You've met him?"

"Once or twice." Four times. Wyatt had been completely unrepentant about the fact that he'd aped his every move. Acted like Cameron was his fucking mentor.

He'd given Wyatt a few choice pieces of advice that the man couldn't, anatomically speaking, actually take.

"Sincerest form of flattery," Jeffries repeated. Then, "Tell me about *The Fountain of Truth*."

Cameron might have thought something was wrong if it wasn't so obviously right. He was hot and cold in unison. Clammy skin and a bitter taste in his cotton mouth. His tongue felt wooden. But that was just fear of ruining the pitch.

"For years I've been wanting to tap into our universal sense of—"

"Not why you want to make it, Cameron. What kind of story will people pay to see?"

Had Emily smirked, or had he imagined it?

Cameron wasn't about to let her skepticism ruin his chance to make a film that would shame the critics who'd been panning him for years.

"Of course." How could he be sweating when his hands were so cold they were practically numb? "It's *Hangover* meets *Life of Pi*. A group of college friends reunite for a camping trip in the Dominican Republic twenty years later, and they drink from an ancient fountain whose waters force them all to tell the truth. We learn how each of them altered the course of the others' lives, and for the worse. All while they're being chased through the jungle by drug runners."

"So … it's about secrets and lies?" Jeffries asked.

"Not exactly, but yes," Cameron laughed, warming up but still working to regain his composure. He'd practiced this pitch so many times, but still his heart raced, and his tongue felt heavy in his mouth, as if reluctant to shape the words.

"It's more about the stories we tell ourselves. I don't just mean the obvious ones, about how we look, or how we think others might see us. But the deeper stories, the ones we tell ourselves to excuse our behavior. No one ever wants to be the bad guy in his own story, right? No one ever thinks of themselves as the villain."

"Some people do," Jeffries disagreed.

"Fair enough." Cameron nodded. "But most people don't. If they're the good guys in their stories, they can get away with some pretty awful things, right? As long as they can justify what they've done, not to the world but to themselves. To disavow the consequences."

Cameron paused to make sure Jeffries was paying attention. He absolutely was.

"If we excuse our actions, maybe we can escape the shadows of our worst decisions. We've seen this type of story done on a large scale before. Films that humanize history's villains. *Mongol* from two-thousand-whatever was great. Last year's *Adolf* probably took it too far."

"That should never have been made," Emily cut in, shaking her head.

"Never again," Jeffries added.

"We've also seen this movie done on a small scale. Indie dramas love their antihero. But *Fountain* is neither of those things. It's the kind of film that's never been made."

"You're thinking of shooting on film?" Jeffries asked.

"It's an expression," Emily answered.

"*Fountain* has the balls of an indie and the spectacle of a tentpole. It's a story that's about story itself."

"Tentpole?" Jeffries repeated.

"It's the kind of movie the Oscars will love."

"Maybe," Jeffries shrugged, "but you can't bankroll a film on that."

"Fair. But it's also the kind of movie that can become a classic."

"You can't predict that. There's no cell on the spreadsheet for classic."

Emily had told Cameron almost the exact same thing. But he'd expected the great Marshall Jeffries to get his vision immediately. If Jeffries couldn't see its brilliance, would anyone?

Cameron ignored the stabbing pain in his temples and tried again.

"The stories we tell ourselves define our existence. They're how we understand the relationship between who we are and who we could become. Descartes said *I think, therefore I am*, but I don't think you are until you've told your first story."

Jeffries finally stopped nodding. "So just to be clear, you want a shit ton of money to make an art film."

"No, not exactly." Cameron felt like he was going to vomit. "A tentpole film with the depth of an art f—"

"Let me stop you there," Jeffries interrupted. "You've built a name for yourself. Why throw that all away on such a massive gamble?"

Great, Jeffries too. Cameron hated explaining this part most of all. It felt like begging.

"Everyone is assuming this will damage my career. That I'll be a flop. But I believe in this project. I believe it will show everyone my true value as a director."

"Your name might be a liability on a film like *Fountain.*

People open their wallets to see your single-take action scenes, and they'll be expecting more of the same. Where is the room in your passion project for the thing that makes you bankable?"

"It'll still have single-take shots, and everything else audiences love, and that I do best. Only the context will change."

"No one's asking for it to change," Jeffries said.

"That's what I keep telling him," Emily added unnecessarily.

"We'll have to sell audiences on it. I get that. But it's not like no one has ever made a transition from action to high-budget art. Nolan made *Inception* after—"

"You're not Nolan." Jeffries somehow made the comment sound almost kind, or at least, not like an insult.

"Maybe I could be."

"Maybe." Another shrug. "But it seems to me like wrapping your trilogy would be the best next move."

"It's not *my* trilogy." Why couldn't anyone seem to get that?

Jeffries grunted and smiled. "You said you've been thinking about this for years. Why now?"

"And speak clearly," Emily said. "I'm hoping I'll get it this time."

"I've been trying to ignore this idea and focus on my career. But I've been dreaming for years." Cameron tried to swallow, but his tongue was so dry, it stuck to the roof of his mouth. "When it was time to sign on for *Bitter Nirvana*, I just couldn't do it."

"Cold feet," Jeffries suggested. "You're afraid you've maxed out at the box office and someone like Anderson Wyatt is about to steal your spot."

Cameron shook his head.

"If I said yes, how would you proceed?" Jeffries asked in a disinterested tone.

"We stay away from the usual garbage with all the notes and rewrites and the project changing fifty-four times before the first day of shooting. I'll write the script with Simon Niles."

"Niles is great. That piqued my interest, when Emily mentioned you wanted to pull him in."

It did? "Sounds like she's told you a lot."

"She really wants us to work together."

"Interesting," Cameron said. "It felt like begging, getting her to do this meeting."

"She doesn't want us to work on this, at least not yet."

"Exactly," Emily cut in. "If you're going to not make *Bitter Nirvana* and work with Jeffries, great. Start a new franchise, something that leaves Anderson Wyatt in the dust."

"You know what I want to make."

"You've always talked about doing one for you and one for the studio," Emily reminded him. "You can start that now, with Jeffries."

"She's right," Jeffries added. "We make another action film, your best ever. Then follow it up with *The Fountain of Truth*. Everyone wins."

"It's been eleven for them and none for me. And once people see what I can do with *Fountain,* no one will ever ask me to make another *Namaste* again."

Jeffries sighed, but he didn't argue. Just stared out the window for a long moment.

Cameron wished the man would make a decision. He was so dizzy.

Finally, Jeffries said, "I'm willing to bank on *Fountain,* assuming you can come back with a proper pitch one month from now. I need a deck and visuals, and a hell of lot more than hopeful meanderings, you understand?"

Cameron nodded, dumbfounded. He'd been sure Jeffries was a *NO*.

"I doubt the budget will be anywhere what you're thinking, but you know how this works. Your first makes money, you'll get more for the next one."

"I understand." Cameron resisted the urge to reach out and steady himself as the dizziness intensified. He needed to get out of this stuffy room and suck in some fresh air.

When had the world started burning?

"And the last condition. *The Fountain of Truth* won't be the next film we release. You agree to shoot a project of our mutual choosing after *Fountain*, a bridge project that helps us manage audience expectations. Fair?"

Cameron couldn't believe it. More than fair, this was a dream come true.

"Yes, sir!" Cameron was already on his feet, hand extended and ready for Jeffries. "Thank you."

He leaned forward to shake the man's hand, but somehow he lost his balance and fell forward into the blur that the room had become.

A smaller blur that sounded like Emily underwater loomed somewhere above him. "Cameron, are you—"

Chapter Two

FATHER TIME HAS CAUGHT UP TO MOTHER NATURE

T{\small HE} {\small SCENT} of disinfectant and sorrow told Cameron where he was before he opened his eyes.

What the hell happened?

He felt weak and shaky. Heart pounding, head splitting, skin still clammy like it had been in …

No.

He'd been waiting for more than ten years to get a chance like the one Marshall Jeffries had just offered him, and he'd probably blown it by passing out. Now here he was, waking up in the hospital.

Humiliating, fainting like a schoolgirl in the front row of a *Leaving Las Vegas* concert. What an amateur. He couldn't blame Jeffries for not wanting to work with him. What the hell was wrong with him? Emily would never let him live this down.

Shit. What if he'd blown it?

Cameron had never been especially patient. The decade of making movies for everyone other than himself had been excruciating. Life itself had been telling him to hurry up, filling him with a sense that the walls were closing in. He'd tried discussing it with Emily, but she kept insisting he was having a midlife crisis.

"Father Time has caught up to Mother Nature," she'd said. "It's happened for thousands of years before you, and it'll keep on happening as long as tits and balls are sagging."

Cameron had told Emily that his balls were doing just fine, though he was lying. Gravity had forced herself upon his nether regions for sure.

He groped until his fingers closed over the cold steel rails and levered himself up as he squinted through the blur, blinking until it cleared.

Where was everyone? This was ridiculous.

He threw back the sheet, hopped out of bed, disconnected the monitors, and when he couldn't find his clothes, walked out into the hallway.

And nearly bumped into a nurse.

"Hi there." Cameron wanted his expression to live in that ideal valley between authority and confusion, but the reality was probably closer to clueless and entitled. "Can you please tell me where I would find my clothes? I'd really like to go home."

"I'm sorry, Mr. Parrish, but you can't be discharged until the doctor talks to you."

"Why am I here?"

"You'll have to ask the doctor." She smiled.

"Why did I pass out?"

"As I said—"

"You haven't said anything other than telling me that I'll have to talk to the doctor."

"Exactly. Why don't you go back into your room and I'll see if I can find Dr. Cole, okay?" She tried to smile again.

"Sounds good." Because what else was he going to say?

But hell if he was getting back into bed.

The chair in the corner was far less comfortable, but from here, it was easier to think about what had gone right earlier this afternoon instead of dwelling on what might be wrong with him. Nerves, obviously. He hadn't been taking the best care of himself, pushing so hard against the existential crisis that refused to stop crowding against him.

Cameron shouldn't have to wait around for a doctor, not when he already knew exactly what he'd hear. That he had been working too hard. Overindulging in food and booze and weed. Not getting enough sleep or exercise, except when he was overtaxing himself in the pursuit of Ariana Saint's increasingly aggressive pleasures.

Advil had kept most of the headaches at bay — he'd resorted to the Vicodin a couple of times, but that was it. And the vertigo only happened once. Slapped him hard in a stairwell. The sensation came out of nowhere and for a moment, he'd thought *earthquake* while gripping the railing, alone with the smell of metal and concrete, trying to keep the world from tilting around him.

"Mr. Parrish." The tall, slender man had shoulder-length hair that looked especially odd in a hospital. He approached Cameron and held out his hand. "I'm Dr. Cole. Victor. It's good to meet you."

"Hi, doc." Cameron stood a bit too fast to shake his hand, felt himself sway as he tried to find his balance. He needed a nap, but not in a hospital bed. And not before he had a chance to confirm with Emily that Jeffries was still a *yes.*

"You've had a rough afternoon." It didn't sound like much of a question.

Was he supposed to answer? "Yeah. You could say that."

"Were you surprised that you passed out? Or have you

been feeling something like this coming on for a while?" Definitely a question this time, but Victor's tone suggested that he already knew the answer. Or should.

Cameron didn't like that.

"Surprised. I've always been healthy."

Victor's patient nod annoyed him. Modern doctors were trained to focus more on empathy since AI systems were doing better at their traditional jobs, but Cameron remembered the way things used to be.

"What have your stress levels been like?" Victor's expression suggested he genuinely wanted to hear the answer.

"How long have you been a doctor?" Cameron asked without answering.

"Seventeen years."

"Did you ever think you'd be replaced by robots when you started?"

To Cameron's surprise, he laughed. "Yes, I did."

"Then why'd you do it? Want to become a doctor, I mean?"

"My mother was a doctor, and so was my paternal grandfather. I don't really remember ever wanting to be anything else."

"Is it like you thought it would be?"

"No, but that isn't a bad thing. In med school, I came to see how much more accurate the AI's diagnosis is. They don't miss anything, and they see the patterns faster."

"I've always been more scared of human stupidity than artificial intelligence."

"Same here. If we'd never made the transition to AI-assisted medicine, I wouldn't have time to focus on the aspect of care that only a human can perform.

"And what's that?" He knew.

"Being present with compassion for our patients."

Another wave of dizziness hit him, and Cameron wished that he hadn't tried to distract Victor with this conversational diversion. But showing weakness by sitting down might land him back in the hospital bed.

"So … you're more of a therapist?"

"Do you know how long the average doctor spent with the average patient before?"

"You tell me."

"Five minutes. And do you know how long he listened to her before interrupting?"

"Was it always a guy doctor and a girl patient in this scenario?"

"Eleven seconds. Can you believe that? Ten years ago, you would have your bad news already, and I would have seen another three patients since leaving."

The room started to tilt, and that stirred up a surge of nausea deep in his guts.

Cameron fell back into his chair. "I have bad news coming?"

Victor smiled. "You know the answer to that. It's why you've been stalling."

Cameron sighed. He didn't want to hear about how he'd been abusing his body and needed to slow the hell down, but he was definitely in the mood to get the hell out of this room.

"Give it to me straight."

"You're dying, Cameron."

"What?" He choked and sputtered something he didn't really believe, despite his desperation. "That can't be true."

"You have a form of brain cancer called glioblastoma." Victor offered him an understanding smile, as if that might motherfucking help. "And you don't have long."

"How did I get it?"

"The disease is extremely complex. We will probably never know why this has happened to you. Only that it has."

"You can do better than that." Cameron tried not to sound panicked. "What's the treatment? Ask the AI."

"Cancer starts in the frontal or temporal lobe and quickly spreads into other parts of the brain. Surgery, radiation, or chemo all offer some hope in delaying the inevitable, but there's no cure."

"How can there be zero hope?"

"Complete surgical removal of the cancer is extremely difficult because of finger-like tentacles that extend into surrounding normal brain tissue. Radiation and chemotherapy treatments can extend your life and temporarily improve its quality, but the tumor tends to increasingly resist the treatment, and like I said, there is no cure. Glioblastoma is made up of a wide mix of different cell types that often differ from patient to patient, and, post-treatment, when tumors recur or grow back, the molecular profile changes dramatically, so—"

"I don't know what you're saying." He'd been bracing himself for *experimental treatment* and *clinical trial*, not *you don't have long* and *there is no cure.*

Cameron couldn't really be having this conversation. How did handing out death sentences and ruling out hope count as "being present with compassion for our patients"?

Victor could smile because none of this touched him. Same as all of the actors Cameron had worked with over the years — emoting as the situation required, then going on with their lives as soon as the cameras panned away.

My life is not a movie for you to star in.

"Let's discuss your symptoms," Victor suggested.

"Okay," Cameron agreed.

"Any headaches, nausea, anything like that?"

"Both, and some vertigo."

"Of course," Victor nodded. "How bad have the headaches been?"

"Bad enough." He hadn't wanted to admit it, but … "Getting worse."

"Migraines?"

"Only a couple of times."

"Have you taken anything for the pain?"

"Vicodin, once or twice."

The doctor kept talking. "Your symptoms will get gradually worse. You'll probably suffer most in the morning, but the pain will become persistent and severe. Eventually, you'll have seizures."

"Seizures?" Cameron repeated.

Could this get any worse?

"The type will depend on where in the brain your tumor is located. You have focal neurologic deficits, meaning your problems will most likely manifest as compromised nerve, brain, or spinal cord dysfunction."

"What does that mean?"

"That it's going to affect both sides of your brain and involve a loss of consciousness."

"So you're telling me that my body is going to stop working?"

"Sorry, Cameron. But yes, that is correct."

He could barely breathe. This couldn't be happening. Except that he knew it could. The dreams. The sense of growing urgency that gnawed at him no matter how fast he worked. The almost-panicky need to create something that would serve as his legacy.

This was why he'd been so desperate to make *Fountain* right fucking now, even though finishing the Namaste trilogy made so much more sense career-wise.

Emily had been wrong; he wasn't in the throes of a midlife crisis, he'd been having an existential crisis. The kind that everyone had when contemplating their impending death.

Except that his impending death was happening soon.

"How soon? Will I—" He couldn't quite make himself say *die*.

"I wish I could give you a better answer, but this isn't like pregnancy. We don't have conception and delivery dates. We only know that something is wrong inside you and that it isn't going to get better."

"Shit, doc."

"You asked me to level with you."

"Even if there's no hope, there must be a spectrum, right?"

"You could live for another year, though that doesn't seem likely."

"What does seem likely?"

"I'm sorry." Victor's smile shifted from kind to sad. Cameron wanted to punch him in the nose, anything to see a genuine emotion instead of his well-oiled expression.

No, that wasn't the whole truth. Cameron wanted to punch him in the nose because he needed someone to share his pain. The emptiness of Victor's studied empathy made it obvious how little he actually cared.

"The way this disease works, you could go at any time," Victor continued. "You probably have a few months. Best-case scenario you have a year, but I wouldn't plan on that."

Victor replaced his sad smile with a look of patient concern, waiting for Cameron to absorb the news.

How many times had this doctor practiced his schtick in the mirror?

And what was he waiting for?

Some sort of sign from Cameron that it was okay to move on to the next thing on his set list?

Cameron would rather have gotten the news from the AI who'd diagnosed him. Let it spit out the facts without insisting they go on some goddamned emotional journey together.

"What's my worst-case scenario?"

"You could die tomorrow."

Tomorrow.

He might not have enough time to write the script for *Fountain*.

Maybe not even a pitch deck.

No, fuck that. Victor had said he might have a year. He could finish *Fountain* in a year, especially since he already had the money lined up.

Niles would drop everything once he knew Cameron was dying.

They could be filming in a month, if he called in every favor he was owed.

"I'm leaving," he said. "Do whatever you've gotta do to check me out."

"I have a call into a specialist in Cielo del Mar, and I'll make arrangements for you to get an appointment immediately. We can——"

The doctor stopped talking at the sound of a light knock on the open door. Emily, quietly interrupting.

"Please, come in," Victor said. Cameron could've sworn he heard a hint of relief in the greeting, and that made him feel better. He wasn't the only one suffering this improvised medical theater. "Take your time, I'll come back when I've got your appointment set up."

"He's great," Emily said as soon as the doctor was gone.

"Yeah, his pretty face makes up for the fact that I'm about to fuck off."

Before she could start in with the pity and the condolences, Cameron asked if Jeffries was still in.

"Oh honey, this isn't the time——"

"We can tell him I had a reaction to new meds." That was believable, and it would cover future incidents. "The doc said I might have a year. Maybe more, there's been plenty of people who lived past their prognoses. I could have five years, that's half a——"

"Even if this doesn't screw us on insurance, there's no way Jeffries is going to fund a movie where the director might have to be replaced before it's finished."

Emily had never believed in this project. "This is total fucking bullshit."

"I'm sorry," she said, sounding like she meant it. But then she went ahead and ruined it. "Don't you want to spend what time you have left with your f——"

"Who else? Maybe we can use this. There must be someone who'd want to bankroll the final Cameron Parrish film."

"It's too risky."

"Why are you just giving up?" Cameron threw his hands in the air, suddenly angry, and wanting to get even angrier.

"Why not just make the most of the time you have——"

"Fuck that," Cameron said, bitter. It wasn't her fault, but he needed to fight with someone. "How would you feel if this was something for Crack in the Darkness ... or AfriCan?"

She sighed, then reluctantly said, "There's a big difference between a charity helping people who suffer from crippling loneliness, or teaching entrepreneurial skills to

inhabitants in some of the poorest parts of Africa, and
…"

"And my vanity project? Fuck you. Emily. It's your job
to believe in me and you can't even pretend to do that
while I'm dying."

"You need some time to process this. Let me take you
home."

"I've done everything you wanted. made every piece-
of-crap movie you set up for me. And now, I'm apparently
going to die with an IMDB page that reads *garbage, garbage,
and more garbage*."

He hated himself for being a dick, throwing a tantrum
like a petulant toddler. She didn't deserve this; none of it
was her fault.

But it wasn't his fault either, and right now he needed
someone to blame for the fact that he was going to be
remembered as the King of Shitty Action Flicks.

"I'll be out in the lobby." Emily already had her phone
out as she headed for the door. "When you're done with
the doctor, I'll drive you home."

She'd put him in time-out.

And life was conspiring to make it permanent.

Chapter Three

WITH AN AFTERTASTE OF FUCK YOU

He'd called everyone.

Some of them twice.

Told them everything except for his diagnosis. Reminded them of all the things he'd done for them, and pitched like his life depended on it. But maybe someone had already talked.

Because no one — not a single person he'd thought he could count on — was willing to risk helping Cameron make *Fountain* before he died.

They'd all been sympathetic and sorry and sure that he'd find someone else who could help him.

He wasn't sure what was more humiliating: that they'd turned down his dying wish, or that they were probably calling all their friends to spread the news that Cameron Parrish had gone off the deep end.

He was going to die with the first two-thirds of the Namaste Trilogy as his crowning achievement.

The thing that killed Cameron, other than the disease itself, was that he didn't need his perfect producer, his ideal crew, or his dream distributors. He could do it with an assembly of competent people who believed in the project and were willing to pool their talents and resources to give the world something it had never seen.

Cameron had been thinking about what he could add to the project for years. Now he considered every possible subtraction. Simpler was better. A cleaner script he could finish himself, with a smaller budget. Fewer actors and more control.

But even if he emptied his accounts, he didn't have enough to finance the movie himself.

He considered calling Ariana, or maybe answering any one of her three texts, but he really wanted to talk to Natalie. Who definitely didn't want to talk to him.

So, he collapsed onto his reclining Faviola sectional and stared out the long wall of windows looking out onto the sprawling sea of Los Angeles dreams, most which ended somewhere between the glitter and the gutter.

The urge to call Natalie hit him again, this time harder.

Ariana would come over, but he didn't want company.

He'd rather break open a bottle of Artemis Tull — the tall, gold-label bottle of single-malt made from Belgravia barley and virgin snow melt filtered through granite, aged in a fifty-year-old Spanish oak barrel. Best they made. Sandstorm Productions had gifted it to him after the second Namaste installment passed a hundred million domestic, with international numbers promising him an even bigger cha-ching to come.

He'd taken it as a reminder of how little they'd paid him to turn a B-movie script into a global blockbuster.

If there was ever a night to get blackout drunk on the world's best whiskey, this was it.

Or he could call Ariana. Cameron looked at his phone

and saw another two texts. If he invited her over, she'd be happy to fuck him.

Also, two from Emily. *I love you*, sent hours ago. *Give me a call if you want to talk*, five minutes old.

She should know better. He would want to talk. Just not now. Not tonight.

But he was procrastinating on reading the text from Jeffries. A *best wishes* blow-off, based on the preview.

Like he needed that kind of bullshit.

More texts from Ariana, each more lascivious than the last. But fuck her. Or, fuck her. Maybe.

He wanted to be done with the world, seeing as it was done with him.

Cameron got off the couch and poured himself a drink.

It hit his tongue with a bitter warmth that left hints of caramel, apple, vanilla, and cinnamon behind. With an aftertaste of *fuck you*.

He gulped the rest of the glass and poured another. Brought the bottle back to the sofa, where he flopped down and picked up his phone again.

More from Ariana, ending with a promise to swallow every drop.

At least that would keep her mouth too full to talk.

Could he really invite her over and not tell her what happened?

No, once she was here, it would come pouring out of him. But Cameron also couldn't stand the thought of her being the first person he told. Before Natalie.

He stared at his glass, swirled the amber liquid, and told himself he really shouldn't finish it.

Maybe he should just make some more commercials. He laughed, thinking about one of his earliest paydays. A series of ads for a cheaper variety of Artemis Tull. Short action sequences that in no way showed that the twenty-dollar bottle was a hot shot of Shangri-La. The agency gave him a surprisingly ample budget and an order to "have fun."

What a kick in the dick, that the most respected Cameron had ever been behind the camera was for a series of commercials. Same as with his movies, the ads were even bigger in Asia.

But he'd never be able to make enough commercials to fund his film.

Maybe he should accept that *The Fountain of Truth* would never get made. At least not by Cameron Parrish. But he could possibly finish the script. Or turn in a killer treatment that some other rockstar director could take all the way. He supposed having his film brought to life by another artist would be better than it never living at all, like what Spielberg did for Kubrick with AI. But the thought of never seeing the finished film, which would be made without his directorial contributions, was like suffering a second death before he'd even finished with the first.

His phone buzzed. Ariana again, now pouting for real instead of seductively.

He would have to tell Natalie. She deserved to know. He deserved for her to know.

And he would deserve her reaction, whatever it would be.

Cameron found her in his contacts list, forced himself to tap her name.

"It's late," Natalie answered on the second ring.

"I'm sorry."

"You're drunk."

"I'm not that drunk."

A long sigh. "What do you need, Cameron?"

"You sound mad ..."

"I'm not mad, but I'd like to know why you're calling me at ten-thirty?"

"That's not that late," he probably slurred, wondering where the time had gone. Not just the last two hours, but the last forty fucking years.

"What do you want?"

"I was just hoping we could talk."

"You can't just be a part of our lives whenever you feel like it."

"Then why did you answer?"

"Because you never call at night. I thought something might be wrong."

"Something is wrong." But he couldn't continue. Didn't know how. There wasn't any script for this. "I was just hoping we could talk."

"I'm sorry, Cameron, but you've made it crystal clear that your career is more important than your family, so you can't expect me to be your on-call therapist. I shouldn't have to drop everything just because you're depressed. Why don't you call Ariana Saint, see if she wants to *talk*?"

I'm dying, goddammit!

But Cameron couldn't say that. Not when Natalie was mad at him. The best he could hope for right now was her pity, and that would be even worse than Emily's.

I'm dying.

The words were on his lips, but still they refused to leave him.

After what felt like the longest pause in their history, he muttered, "Never mind. Sorry for ruining your night."

She hung up.

Then Cameron called Ariana.

Chapter Four

YOU LAUGH AT THINGS THAT MAKE OTHER PEOPLE CRY

HE WANTED TO SLEEP, but Ariana was making that impossible.

Waking up to a sloppy blowjob would normally be high on his happy list, but this morning Cameron felt like death had already come to claim him.

Pounding headache, nauseating lightheadedness, aching everything. He split blame between his raging hangover, and the crippling cancer he hadn't even known about for a day. The thought of eating made him want to vomit. The light bleeding through the window was too bright, and his mouth was dry enough to remind him of all the disappearing sand in his personal hourglass.

"Stop it," he grumbled.

Ariana took his cock out of her mouth and gave him a light little laugh. "You're kidding, right?"

She rubbed his shaft across her cheeks, first one and then the other, dragging his tip across her wet and pouty lips along the way. He couldn't help shifting his hips upward.

"That's what I thought," she said, a second before putting him back in her mouth.

It didn't matter if Cameron was in the mood. That was the price he paid for dating an up-and-coming starlet. She had the kind of face that few people refused, so she had a hard time believing it when they did.

He'd met her on-set for the second *Namaste*, where she'd played a mob boss's mistress. Perfectly, according to critics and fans. He'd flirted with her throughout the shoot, and asked her out as soon it wrapped. She'd been perfect for him: a star-fucker who was willing to make him feel good, both inside and outside the bedroom, in exchange for the connections he could help her make. No obligation to share feelings or pretend they were in love with each other. He hadn't blamed her for it: breaking out was nearly impossible for even the most beautiful and talented, and Ariana was leveraging what she had in order to build her career.

He was just as much of a whore, selling his skills to the highest bidder for the chance to someday make a movie that would be worth watching twice.

But now that death had darkened his horizon, Cameron wasn't looking for shallow sex and vacuous conversation.

He wanted to share his feelings, fucked up as they were. With his ex-wife. Who didn't yet know he was dying.

He came in her mouth, thinking about Natalie.

She swallowed as promised, then cuddled up against him. He wished she would leave, but asking Ariana to go might start a conversation he'd regret.

Or maybe he wouldn't. Maybe telling her would be good practice for telling Natalie.

The world would know once he did, that would save him the trouble of telling everyone.

And once everyone knew, he wouldn't look like an asshole for refusing to sign on for *Bitter Nirvana*.

"I got some bad news yesterday," he finally said.

"Is that what it is?"

"What do you mean?"

Ariana laughed. "I've never seen you so drunk."

There was nothing funny about it. She'd done all the work because Cameron couldn't — the sex had to have been lousy for her. But how was that any different from the rest of their relationship? Her climax would come when Cameron signed on for that third *Namaste*, where Ariana's screen time would double. She'd been nagging him to do it, same as everyone else.

"Did Marshall Jeffries hate your pitch?" she asked.

"He liked it."

"Really?"

"You sound surprised." Because of course she did.

"It just doesn't really seem like the kind of movie he usually makes. You know what I mean."

Yes. He totally fucking did.

"So … does that mean you're not going to make *Bitter Nirvana*?" Then not even waiting for Cameron to answer, "Are you sure you're not making a mistake?"

She grabbed his dick, as if there was any chance of him getting it up again so soon.

"Please don't make me work with another director. I can't stand the thought of you not coming back for the last one."

And there he was, getting hard again.

Ariana kissed his tip as her hand began to glide along his shaft.

"Stop it." Cameron pulled away.

She looked up at him in surprise.

"I said I had bad news."

"But Jeffries liked your idea. That's what you wanted, isn't it?"

"Yes." He needed a second, unsure of exactly how to say what was coming. "He agreed to make *Fountain* if I made another film for Fire Marshall Studios first."

"So ... that's bad?"

"That part was great. Everything I wanted. But I fainted at the end of my pitch."

"Because you were so excited?" She sounded unsure.

Cameron swallowed. "Because I'm sick."

"Oh." She sounded like a note on a broken piano.

"Dying, actually."

"What do you mean?"

"I wasn't being mysterious." He stared at Ariana for a moment, then repeated the news. "I'm dying."

"As in, you're actually going to die?"

"I'll get a second opinion, then a couple more after that. But yes, according to the doctor, I have brain cancer. Incurable. I'm on my way out."

"Oh my God. What does this mean for *Namaste*?"

"Fuck you, Ariana."

"Excuse me?"

"Exactly."

"What are you talking about?"

"I just told you that I'm dying, and your first question is about your career."

"That's not true, I just—"

"You're a total fucking narcissist."

"That's not true."

"You're incapable of empathy. We've watched enough movies together for me to know who you are."

"What's that supposed to mean?"

"You laugh at things that make other people cry."

"Like what?"

It wasn't hard to think of one, it was that Cameron had to choose. He picked the most recent. "*A Spectrum of Blue.* An autistic girl is singing at an open mic in front of an unforgiving crowd. She's been waiting for this moment two-thirds of the movie for us, but really, all of her life, if you buy into the story, which you clearly didn't, because you have no fucking heart—"

"Hey!"

"You asked, so don't interrupt me." Cameron took a moment to puff his chest and flare his nostrils. Privilege of the dying. "She takes the mic and opens her mouth. Not only is the girl tone deaf, but her body language is awkward. And what happens? *You* burst out laughing."

"Are you kidding me right now? That was hilarious. She sounded like—"

"You'd have to be dead inside to not feel the tragedy in that scene."

"She *was* totally tragic. That's why it was funny."

"You didn't notice that I cried while you were laughing?"

"I try not to notice when you're being a little bitch," Ariana said, sounding disgusted. "It happens a lot."

"If something doesn't concern you, then you're not bothered by it. I'm surprised you don't want to take a sad selfie with me right now to post later, since the picture would be especially poignant after I'm gone."

Ariana flushed, and Cameron realized that she would have done exactly that if given the time or opportunity.

Why had he thought telling her first would be a good idea?

He expected her to stalk out in a huff, but instead she stayed, chewing on her lower lip while glaring at him. Not seductively. Whatever Ariana still wanted from him, she didn't think she could get it with sex.

His phone began to ring.

"You're fucking kidding me." But she didn't reach for her clothes.

Cameron lurched out of bed and followed the sound to his bar, where he'd left both his phone and the nearly empty bottle of Artemis Tull. He answered just as he lost the call to voicemail.

He hit redial on the number and a receptionist answered, offering him an appointment with Dr. Freeman. His choices were an hour from now or next Tuesday.

"I could be dead by next Tuesday," he replied, hanging up with a rush of hope.

He'd only had one diagnosis, and not by a specialist who might know more about experimental options and treatments that had yet to be approved.

What if he could go back to Jeffries with something that would keep him alive for another two years? Long enough to make *Fountain* and that bridge film, back-to-back.

He hung up and offered Ariana one last chance.

"Who was that? The *doctor?*"

"A specialist. Would you like to come with me?"

"Why would you even think I would want to do something like that, seeing as I'm obviously a total fucking narcissist who's incapable of empathy?"

"I'm trying to give you a chance here."

"A chance to sit with you in a doctor's office? The role of a lifetime. Thank you, Cameron Parrish!"

He drew a deep breath and tried to start over. He should be the one to end it with manners.

"I'm sorry, Ariana. I didn't mean to be an asshole."

"It's okay." Clearly glad for his retraction. "You had an excuse."

"But my appointment's in an hour, so I need to hop in

the shower and you need to leave. Can you gather all your things and be ready to go in fifteen minutes? You don't have to come see the specialist with me, but you're not coming back here."

"Are you kidding right now?"

"We can have lunch or dinner or whatever next week. After I've had some time to collect my thoughts."

"You're serious." Fury wafted off of her. "You're kicking me out?"

"Don't make a big deal about this."

"Don't make a big deal about this?" Ariana repeated, about fifty decibels higher.

"We can still be friends. This doesn't have to—"

"Why would I want to be your *friend*, Cameron? So I can waste another three months listening to you bitch about how you're tired of 'shepherding someone else's dream' or go on and on about your little Fountain of Bullshit?"

Cameron walked to the door. He opened it, then looked from Ariana to the hallway and back into her disbelieving eyes. "I'll have your stuff sent to you."

"I'm sorry." She took a step toward him. "You're right, I was being a bitch. I just didn't know how to deal with the shock."

He licked his very dry lips and offered Ariana a sad little nod. "You're just realizing you could've really milked this. All that free publicity for playing the role of supportive girlfriend, and now—"

"How could you say that?" Her voice cracked.

If she'd been that good on set, she wouldn't have needed Cameron to get ahead.

"You don't want to look bad. I get it. I'm sorry it had to end this way, it's not what I wanted at all." He softened his expression and lowered his voice. "I should really be alone right now. Lay low and people will assume we're still together."

"You're saying I have to be invisible until you die?"

Unbelievable. "You really are the worst."

She glared at him for another second or two, then marched into the hall. He revoked her access code through the security system app before she reached the lobby. Ariana might be able to charm her way into the building, but she wouldn't be able to get back into his apartment.

Cameron didn't want to be late to his appointment with the specialist, but he figured gathering her shit couldn't take more than a few minutes and then he'd be done. With her crap out of sight she'd be out of his mind. But three minutes in and it was easy to see how deeply Ariana had infiltrated his home without his even noticing.

What the fuck had he been thinking? Letting her hang that framed black-and-white of Barcelona in his living room, in place of the Sahara Desert that had hung there before it. She had her cosmetics in his bathroom and her shoes in his closet. She even had a few books stashed on one of his living room bookshelves, not that he'd ever seen her read.

He'd been living his life on autopilot, working and working and working and working while she'd been sinking her claws into everything she could. And what had he managed to achieve?

Nothing. He was a nothing who would die with exactly what he deserved.

It was a big mistake, getting so hammered last night. Cameron wished he could tell the difference between what felt like the worst hangover of his abbreviated life and looming death. He'd never felt the second one before. Or he had, every day of his life, but never at such an accelerated pace. Never as a hungry promise.

He was a rich man, about to ask a rich doctor if he could possibly buy his way out of dying.

Maybe it would have been better to pass away on the floor of Jeffries' office — at least he would have died with his dreams intact. Now they had been stolen away from him. Forever. Cameron had nowhere to go but down. Might as well jump.

He put on a black tee and a pair of selvage jeans from Japan, one leg at a time like everyone who didn't know they were dying, wanting to yell and scream and curse about the raging hot injustice of it all. Yesterday he felt inches away from his dreams. Now he felt delusional.

No one changed the world with a movie. Why had he wanted to try?

Be grateful that you had a career. You made dozens of movies. You'll be remembered, even if it's not for the thing you hoped to do.

The worst part was that he'd destroyed his family and alienated all his friends, thanks to his obsessive drive to make all those beautiful B-movies he didn't want to be remembered for.

Cameron had sacrificed everything, only to end up with nothing.

Chapter Five

I WON'T INSULT YOUR INTELLIGENCE

"There's only so much we can do, Mr. Parrish." Dr. Freeman didn't bother with that bullshit *I'm here for you* routine, thank God. But his perfect calm was a little too matter-of-fact, and Cameron didn't like it any more than the pity.

"To try and cure me?"

"To make you as comfortable as possible in your final days."

So, a different type of bullshit. "I thought you were a specialist. Isn't there some sort of radical treatment that might be able to cure this? A clinical trial? Maybe something in Europe or somewhere? I'll do anything to beat this."

Patiently, Freeman said, "The cancer is inoperable. Anything we might try would likely only erode what little life you have left. It makes much more sense to try and suppress your symptoms until the end."

That sounded hopeful. If Cameron could convince Jeffries that he'd found a treatment, fast-track *Fountain*, maybe even fit that bridge movie in before the cancer killed him — maybe he couldn't buy his way out of death, but it sounded like he might be able to rent a bit of extra time.

"How does that work?"

"There is a new experimental drug, Philozen. It'll hasten your death by a month or two, but it will also keep you from suffering the terrible side effects."

"Dr. Cole said I could die tomorrow. If this Philozen drug will 'hasten my death by a month or two,' does that mean I could die last week?"

"Your situation isn't quite as dire as Dr. Cole believed. At least not yet."

"What happens if I don't take the drug? Will I live any longer?"

Freeman gave Cameron a sad little shrug. "The word *live* is relative. Not sure how much living you'll be doing at the end."

"What's that supposed to mean?" But he had a damned good idea already.

"Dizziness, blurred vision, memory loss, speech problems, seizures." Freeman let that hang for a moment before he finally finished his thought. "It's the same disease, but Philozen will postpone the symptoms long enough to let you say goodbye to this life on your terms."

"These are hardly my terms."

"I understand," Freeman said.

He couldn't, but Cameron didn't correct him. "What would you do?"

"Take the Philozen, Cameron," Freeman replied, without a beat of hesitation.

"How much will it suppress my symptoms?" Then, the real question: "Could I still work without everyone knowing I'm sick?"

"I would never tell anyone how to live their life, especially when there's so little of it left." Cameron could tell the doctor had given this speech before. "But if it were me, I wouldn't try to live the best version of what I had imagined for myself before learning about my condition. I would choose to live through my remaining days in the best way I could, given how much my situation had changed."

"Are you saying it's time to start on my bucket list?"

"I imagine you have the means?"

"That's not the point. What about my legacy?"

"You've already left more of a legacy than most."

Cameron shook his head, wanting to cry. "It's bullshit."

"I won't insult your intelligence by telling you that what's happened here is some sort of gift or opportunity. It's terrible and unfair and anything else you want to say about it. But not everyone gets a chance to say goodbye to their loved ones, and maybe take a vacation before they die."

"I want to work."

"The time you have left is yours, to do with as you wish." And there it was, the pity Cameron had been hoping to avoid.

"So there's no other way? I take the Philocrap and die even faster, or I don't take the medication and go through hell?"

"Something like that. The Philozen will lose its effectiveness as you get closer to the end, then it'll be a cocktail of painkillers, anti-seizure meds, and anything else we can do to keep you comfortable."

To his horror, Cameron's eyes flooded with tears.

"Don't lose that. The crying, I mean. Live the rest of your life like you mean it."

He felt so suddenly bitter.

Cameron stood from his comfortable chair, ready to march into the rest of his uncomfortable, unbearable, intolerable life.

Freeman stood too. "You'll need to sign some paperwork, then I can write your prescription."

Cameron didn't answer.

"It's important that you not drink heavily or take other drugs while on Philozen. You don't want to ..."

But Cameron had already stopped listening.

There was zero chance he would be spending his dying days abstaining from his few remaining pleasures.

Chapter Six

LET THE REAPER CATCH UP

CAMERON WOKE up to find his face and the couch cushion both covered in drool.

Empty bottles littered his coffee table. On the massive screen, his first film, *Lariat*, still played on a loop. Shot in black-and-white for less than a hundred thousand dollars — $96,741.08, to be exact. Every penny his parents had left him after their car accident. Back before all the AI, when most drivers were still human and crashes were standard.

Cameron didn't want to think about his parents' death or the state of affairs (including his) that had led him right to this disgraceful situation.

So he closed his eyes, tried to sleep, and immediately wished that he hadn't.

His brain seemed to be overheating. Whether his eyes were open or closed, the imagery stayed. Live nightmares like exposed wires, crackling with dirty electricity designed to do more than shock him.

Dream or hallucination.

Cameron ran to escape, but the nightmare kept cackling behind him. A grim reaper waving his scythe from the seat of his flaming chariot, the carriage pulled by a team of hellhounds rather than horses, barking and snarling, an acid lather foaming from their mouths.

He wondered if running was worth it. Probably not. Why race the inevitable? It would be easier to die. He didn't have to let the reaper catch up. There was a cliff ahead. Instead of turning, Cameron could keep running until he ran over the edge.

Death would be instant and painless, after he experienced pure, unadulterated freedom all the way down.

"Cameron. Honey." Someone was gently shaking him. "It's okay."

He opened his eyes, saw Emily holding out a tumbler of water. The cool glass sent a delightful chill through him as his fingers closed around it.

He took a sip. Even better.

Emily sat next to him. "I don't know what Dr. Freeman told you, but I'm pretty sure he didn't say to go home and get fucked up as hard and as fast as you could."

Cameron might have made a sound.

Another sip of heaven, then he croaked, "Thanks."

"I've been worried about you."

"Sorry."

"Really worried. What were you thinking?"

Cameron remembered leaving Freeman's office, riding down the elevator, and getting back into his car.

He remembered making a right onto Pacific Coast Highway, headed north to the city where he would probably die.

He remembered wondering if he should try heroin. He'd never been willing to risk the addiction, but what did that matter now?

Then Cameron remembered thinking about the few

people he knew who used heroin, how they were dickbag piles of shit, and how he didn't want to be a dickbag pile of shit, even if he had nothing to lose.

He remembered realizing he could get shitfaced enough on some absurdly expensive booze from his fully stocked bar to not give a fuck about dying, so going home wasn't such an awful idea after all.

"I was driving home after seeing Freeman this morning and—"

"It's tomorrow, Cameron."

"What?"

"I mean, obviously it's today, but you went to see Dr. Freeman yesterday."

"That's not …" Except, of course it was possible. He barely remembered anything, but that alone was evidence enough. "I'm sorry I worried you."

"I'm just glad you're fine." She was obviously doing her damnedest not to cry. "I was really worried about you … a couple of hours ago, especially … I had to come over because … I thought … you know …"

"I'm sorry." Cameron sat up straighter. He saw all the empty bottles and glasses, then flushed with a shame that felt hot enough to scald him. "I didn't mean to make you worry."

"I want to respect your boundaries, and what you're going through—"

He shook his head. "You're off to a terrible start."

"We need to talk."

"Agreed. How about next year?"

"Cameron …" Emily sighed, then stood and started gathering the empty bottles, clinking like church bells.

"Can you please stop?"

"Why don't you take a hot shower? I'll clean up while

you're in there, and if you want me to leave when you come out, fine, no argument from me. Deal?"

Cameron looked up at Emily. It would be impossible not to feel like an asshole, refusing her now.

"Deal." Then, "Thank you."

TWENTY MINUTES LATER, Cameron went back downstairs to make nice with Emily.

The coffee table gleamed, without a single bottle to mar it. He caught the scent of brewing coffee and something cooking in the kitchen. Maybe sausage.

She turned around and actually smiled as he joined her. "You look great! Or at least much better. The French press is full, and there's an empty mug with three Advil next to it."

"Thanks." Cameron walked over to the counter and filled his mug. Emily hadn't said anything about the water or orange juice, but she'd poured glasses of both. He drained the water, took his pills with juice, then sipped his coffee while watching her prepare a breakfast he didn't deserve.

An English muffin popped out of the toaster. She added the sausage, a slice of cheese, and eggs from another pan he hadn't noticed, then handed Cameron the plate.

Now he definitely felt like an asshole. "Thanks."

"Did you listen to any of them?"

"Any of what?" He took a bite of the sandwich, suddenly starving.

"The messages I left you?"

He should've known she had an ulterior motive, more than just coming over to check on him. Probably another specialist she wanted him to see. Or a therapist.

Emily was always trying to fix things. She had never managed to realize that careers could be fixed, not people.

But there was no harm in listening before asking her to leave him alone, especially after he'd acted like an asshole. "So, what's your brilliant idea?"

"I didn't say I had an idea."

"But you do," Cameron said. "So what is it?"

"There's a woman I know." Of course there was. "A researcher working on AI-assisted end-of-life care. I met her on the set of *iEverywhere.*"

Cameron set down his coffee, leaned forward, and whispered to no one, "She wants to upload my brain into a robot so I can live forever."

"She's developing a bucket list app."

Of course she'd come over to tell him about a bucket list app. Because these days, there really was an app for everything.

"It's an AI that analyzes all available data about you, then creates a 'bucket list tour,' guaranteed to make your final months perfect. Or at least, perfect for you."

Had Dr. Freeman called Emily?

"Wow, does that sound gimmicky. And a bit predatory. Did you screw up your life? No worries! Click here for the perfect death."

"I called her right after we heard the news, but I didn't want to say anything to you—"

"Since you knew I wouldn't give a shit?"

"—until I talked to Sharon and asked her if we could get you into the beta trials."

"No."

"That's it? Just no?" Emily looked upset. "You're not even going to give me a reason?"

"If you really thought I'd love the idea, you'd have been like, 'Hey Cameron, I've got this friend working on

SkyNet. You up for letting her fuck with your mind? You won't have to worry about any long-term risk since you'll be dead anyway.'"

"That's not fair."

"If I wouldn't let an AI mess with my movies, why do you think I'd trust one to give me instructions on how to live?"

It was the number one thing they fought about. Auto-tune for the film industry, AI Assist ruined every film it directed, predicting the most marketable shots with algorithm-based decisions. Studios relied on AI analysis more than artistic instinct or integrity. Which was why most movies sucked so incredibly hard.

"You're a hypocrite, Cameron. What drives your self-driving car? An AI. What keeps everything running in this building? An AI. What diagnosed you with the cancer that's probably been eating your brain for years? An AI. You already depend on artificial intelligence for almost everything in your—"

"My bucket list has exactly one item: make *The Fountain of Truth*. Can your magical app help me with that?"

"No one can help you with that."

"Dr. Freeman can. He put me on an experimental drug. The bad news is I'm going to die faster, but the good news is that I'll be able-bodied up to the last minute." Technically not a lie, because as soon as the drug stopped working, Cameron would make sure that was his last minute. "I can shoot something fast, maybe raise some capital, and hang on until *Fountain* is finished. Hell, I'll offer to helm *Nunchucks* if that's what it takes!"

"I already told you, I can't sell a project with a dying director."

"No one needs to know."

"There's another way."

"Oh yeah, how?" Cameron swallowed a mouthful of coffee, not caring that it burned his throat. "You have a time machine?"

"Jeffries feels awful about your situation."

"You told him?"

"No, I decided to risk my credibility by lying for you, knowing you'd probably drop dead a week into filming."

"I'm ready for the twist."

"Jeffries believes in *Fountain*. He'll pay for the treatment and assign a writer, or hire you, if you want. But someone else will have to direct it."

"You mean, once it's commercially viable because it's Cameron Parrish's final film, the one he would have made instead of *Bitter Nirvana*, if he hadn't had the unfortunate luck of dying first."

"It's business, Cameron."

"It's bullshit."

"Jeffries is making a promise that no one else in the world will give you. He'll find the right director. Make sure your magnum opus gets made and that the credit goes to you. That's what you wanted, your legacy film to be made? Like Spielberg shooting Kubrick's *AI*."

Cameron liked his idea a lot less coming out of Emily's mouth. "Kubrick got to make whatever he wanted while he was still alive. And he'd been batting that idea back and forth with Spielberg for a while. It's not the same at all."

He was so upset, his world was turning crimson. He didn't want to say anything he might regret — he was already mad at himself for not revoking her access.

"I need you to go."

"I'm really trying to figure this out for you. Let me know when you want to talk." Emily paused in the doorway on her way out, still wearing her *I'm being reasonable* face. "I put a number in your contacts while you were in the shower. Sharon Eberling, the AI researcher who works with the dying."

The door whispered shut behind her.

Cameron checked his address book. She hadn't been bluffing, and apparently knew his passcode. Eberling's number and physical address. But hell if he would call her, now or ever.

He scrolled through his messages instead. They had blown up, thanks to Ariana's big mouth. He stopped on the only text not dripping with false condolences, faux prayers, or thinly veiled nosiness — from an actor cast as a minor character in *Namaste*. He'd died an inglorious death at the midpoint, but drank vodka like it was water and had on several occasions entertained Cameron with stories of backpacking across Europe in his teens. Brady Pratt.

Last chance, dude. Seriously, call me.

It was Cameron's last chance for a lot of things, so he called.

Chapter Seven

I'M SORRY YOU'RE DYING

WHAT A RELIEF, talking to someone who didn't give a crap he was dying. Why hadn't Cameron thought of calling Brady sooner? The actor had offered him an open invitation plenty of times.

He oozed personality, but didn't have a marquee face. He was constantly being cast as the lead's best friend or brother in rom-coms. Someone to brighten the scene without having to carry it.

More importantly, Brady wouldn't want to take tragic selfies or bitch about how Cameron's death was going to screw up his career.

Cameron called and Brady said, "We haven't done poker night in forever. I'm barbecuing Wagyu and I've got a new bottle of Stolichnaya chilling."

Brady had to have heard about his diagnosis, but acted as though nothing was amiss. Balm to Cameron's hungover soul.

But by the time his Autonomous X parked itself in front of Brady's modest WeHo bungalow, Cameron's feet were like icicles and his stomach was roiling.

Could he really make it through an evening without talking about the inevitable?

You're at the end of your life, he lectured himself. *It's time to be fearless.*

He knocked on the door, so timidly it barely made a sound.

He hammered slightly harder the second time, a little more like he meant it.

But it wasn't until the third time, three solid knocks in a row, when his heart started racing a little too hard and he realized there were a lot more cars parked on the street than probably should be on a weekday afternoon—

The door swung open.

Brady looked thrilled to see him. "Cameron!"

His host gave him a hug, then took a step back, opened the door all the way, and invited Cameron inside. He'd already figured it out, but he couldn't just turn around and run away. So he smiled through a chorus of *SURPRISE!* instead, pretending the scene didn't make him feel even sicker.

Traitor.

His skin crawled as he forced himself to feign emotion, pretending to feel deeply moved as several dozen guests gushed about how much they would miss his spirit or insight, sharing earnest memories that he barely remembered — in most cases because those experiences had been annoying distractions from the push to finish his current film and move on to the next.

They might as well have invited Cameron to his own wake.

He locked eyes with Emily in the corner. She mouthed *I'm sorry,* but didn't come over to talk. The silent solidarity made him appreciate her presence.

Ariana was the opposite, tearing up on cue as she

talked with other guests about how much she was going to miss him. No doubt she'd manipulated Brady into throwing the party. His get-togethers were usually steak-and-vodka, not whatever this was.

"Where can I get a drink?" Cameron asked, needing one more than he ever had in his life.

"Should you be drinking?" Brady asked.

"Yes." Cameron laughed to make it sound like a joke. "I should be."

He poured himself a whiskey neat, then made a beeline for Emily, greeting her in a low voice with, "This is exactly what I wanted to avoid. All these people reminding me of my mistakes."

"You mean Ariana?" Emily teased. "Because all these people can't be mistakes."

"Definitely her, but I meant what I said. All these people."

"What mistakes are you referring to?"

Cameron shook his head, feeling lost and wanting to leave. He took a sip, swallowed, then followed with another one. "All the times I put up a front or did things I didn't want to do, just so I could push my career forward."

"You're romanticizing all the things you never got to do while diminishing the excellent work we did."

"I never once directed something I was passionate about."

Emily shook her head, obviously upset. "I wish you wouldn't reinvent history. If you weren't passionate about those movies, they wouldn't have done nearly so well. You had a career most directors would kill for, even if it's all over now. Why can't you be happy with that?"

"Because it was all for a broken promise."

He regretted the sentence the second it left his mouth. Because while it was true that Cameron had never made *his* movie, Emily had done everything for him that she promised. Times ten.

She blinked several times in rapid succession, trying not to cry. It seemed that being an asshole was all he could manage.

"I'm sorry."

"It's fine, Cam. I understand." Then Emily excused herself to the restroom.

Spying her opportunity, Ariana bounded over before anyone else could tell Cameron how truly sorry they were. Fine. At least he wouldn't have to be polite. Everyone else at the party meant well, even if they were acting like he was already dead and expecting him to be excited about his own goddamned funeral.

"Do you still think I'm the worst?" Ariana asked.

"That title probably belongs to the Black Eyed Peas' reunion album, but you're definitely in the top ten."

"I'm sorry I handled your news so poorly — it was such a shock. I hope you can forgive me."

"Forgive you for asking me why you would want to be my friend? Or saying you'd wasted three months listening to me bitch about shepherding someone else's dream? Or am I forgiving you for the part about my little Fountain of Bullshit?"

The nearest cluster of well-wishers gave Cameron the side-eye, then resumed their conversation awkwardly. Not that he cared. If Ariana wanted to do this here, fine. She was the one who had everything to lose.

And she knew it.

"I'm sorry, Cammi," she cooed. "I really mean it."

"You know I hate it when you call me that."

"I know something you don't hate. Wanna go to the bathroom with me?"

A little. "Not at all."

"Sure you do."

"No, Ariana, I don't."

Except he did, more now than a second ago. Cameron wasn't nearly drunk enough to stand this, and emptying himself into Ariana would take the edge off. Especially if he bent her over the toilet and made her—

No.

"I'm not suggesting we get back together, but we should say goodbye. Like you said, we can still be friends." She looked around, made sure no one was watching, then reached down and brushed her fingers against Cameron's hardening cock. "Seven minutes in heaven. What do you say?"

He imagined her bragging through tears at his funeral, telling the small crowd congregated around her all about how Cameron Parrish had wanted her so much, he'd fucked her at his goodbye party. The thought was a pillow on the face of his temptation.

"You go first, I'll follow."

Cameron headed for the door as soon as she turned away, passing by the serve-yourself bar on his way out. The fancy sheet cake caught him by surprise, like a hard shove to his chest. He wanted to fall a step back. White frosting with a caricature of him in the corner, dressed in all black and wearing a baseball cap. *We love you, Cameron!* in the Namaste Font.

He grabbed a full bottle of Jim Beam and slipped outside into Brady's empty backyard, settling in a lounge chair on the far side of the pool. The evening chill felt pleasant, although he hadn't realized how overheated he'd gotten until just now. A few faint stars dotted the darkness above, barely managing to slice through the refracted haze of light pollution and smog.

He remembered the last time he'd seen a real night sky:

camping with Natalie and Colin at Big Sur, when the boy was twelve and didn't yet resent how much his father was always working. They'd caught a lizard and fed chipmunks. Cameron had let Colin eat as many s'mores as he wanted after Natalie retired to the tent.

Almost a decade later, he'd sworn at his son, telling Colin that they should have never taken that trip, and that he blamed Big Sur for his son's idiot plan to drop out of college and become one of those bums wasting their lives backpacking through third-world countries.

Then he'd disowned his only child; in six years they hadn't traded a word.

No point in dwelling on that now. If Cameron couldn't tell Natalie the truth, he definitely couldn't tell Colin.

He gulped what felt like half the bottle of bourbon, then leaned back until the lounge was nearly flat. He would probably never talk to Colin again. Same for Natalie.

Cameron felt trapped. He couldn't bear the thought of going back inside Brady's bungalow and talking to all those people who professed to love him in frosting, yet didn't know him well enough to realize how much he hated surprise parties and public displays of emotion and the movies he'd wasted his entire life directing. *Namaste* most of all.

That fucking cake.

His so-called friends had turned tonight into a premature memorial for Cameron, and a funeral for his career. No one would ever take him seriously in the industry again. Standing around in a living room full of people feeling sorry for him? Jumping off a bridge right now would be better than spending the rest of his life like that.

He took another long swig, enjoying the burn as it rushed down his throat.

If he went home and trashed himself again, would Emily check in on him tomorrow, to make sure he didn't drown in his own vomit?

He remembered the look on her face as she said *It's fine, Cam,* and decided that she probably wouldn't.

Emily might not check in on him ever again.

Fuck. He should go back in there and fix that.

Tomorrow. He'd call her tomorrow and fix it.

But if Cameron surrendered the comfort of a bottle in his hand, he needed another vice to lean on.

And knew the perfect thing.

THE WOMAN behind the bakery display case at Provisions gave Cameron a skeptical look. "Can I help you, sir?

Her tone suggested this wasn't her first crack at that question. How long had he been standing there with his face pressed to the glass, his mouth watering as he imagined the cheap frosting melting on his tongue?

"Can I get that one?" He pointed to a large white sheet cake, the kind you get for a child's birthday party because five-year-olds can't tell the difference between shortening and buttercream.

The kind Natalie used to buy for Colin's birthdays, back when Cameron was a new director and barely bringing home enough to juggle gas and electricity.

It would taste disgusting. And Cameron deserved it. He'd been a terrible husband and a terrible father, and somehow eating that shitty cake felt like the perfect way to remember the family he became too busy to spend time with the second he'd achieved a speck of success.

"Of course!" The bakery lady brightened, probably glad to know her slobbering-drunk customer could actually speak. "Do you want something written on it?"

"Yeah. Sorry you're dying."

Her skepticism returned. "You want the cake to say, *sorry you're dying?*"

"That's right, it's for me." He tried to help her understand. "I was at a party. But they got the cake all wrong. It said, *We love you, Cameron.*"

"What's wrong with that?"

"It's disingenuous."

"It's what?"

Cameron could only imagine how badly he'd butchered that last word. He was probably slurring, but everything sounded like Shakespeare to him. He tried again. "It's disingenuous."

"Okay?" But he could tell she didn't get it.

"They're not bad people," he explained. "But they only threw me a party because they feel sorry for me. Because I'm dying. So that's what I want my cake to say." Then, in case she had already forgotten: "*I'm sorry you're dying.*"

"Okay." She pulled it from the case and disappeared behind a partial wall, returning a few minutes later, displaying the sheet cake as if she thought he might reach across the counter and knock it out of her hand.

I'm Sorry You're Dying, in beautiful swirly cursive.

"Perfect."

"Are you really dying?"

"Not before I eat this cake, but soon."

"Then I'm sorry."

Cameron thought she might be the first person who'd said that without looking down on him in pity.

He paid and she set the cake on the counter.

"May I have a fork?" he asked.

"Oh sure, of course." She turned around and grabbed a handful of individually wrapped plastic forks from a bin, just barely in reach. "How many do you need?"

"Just one, thank you."

She handed him one, then returned the rest to the bin. "I hope you enjoy it."

He nodded, then turned away, hating that he never carried cash. He would have tipped her a hundred dollars if he had it.

He paused at the exit, then turned right and went to the ATM, where he withdrew the daily maximum of a thousand dollars.

When he got back over to the bakery counter, the woman was already helping a much healthier customer, in every sense of the word. And worse, there was no tip jar where he could quietly drop it. This was a grocery store, not a family-owned business. What had he been thinking?

Cameron felt like an idiot, standing like a creeper with his enormous pastry box in one hand and a wad of money in the other.

He turned to go.

"Mister, wait!"

He glanced over his shoulder. The woman looked worried.

She called out to him again. "Did you need something?"

Cameron walked back and handed her the money. "Thank you for caring."

She gaped at him. "You're welcome?"

"I am." He grinned and headed for his car, forcing himself to wait until he was inside before ripping the lid off of his cake, tearing the wrapper off the fork, and digging in like a gopher rooting into the earth. He hadn't even swallowed his first forkful before he was shoving a second one into his mouth.

It tasted like shattered dreams and wasted ambitions.

"Take me anywhere," he told his Autonomous X around a mouthful of Death Day cake.

BY THE TIME Cameron had eaten a third of the cake, carsickness had set in, so he blackened the windows and swiped on his phone. He was still living on Do Not Disturb, but it was fun to see how many new messages he had each time he checked. So many people now cared about his impending death for all the wrong reasons.

The person whose name he wanted to see in his notifications — Natalie — was conspicuously absent.

But he still couldn't figure out how to tell her.

So he checked Forage for news stories about his illness. Nothing. There would be tomorrow, though, at least in the tabloids. Somebody from tonight's party would tell someone, in confidence, and the rumors would spread like a spark making its way down the fuse.

He sent Emily a text, asking her to do what she could about squashing them.

Then he kept swiping.

Maybe it was the bourbon, or perhaps the cancer eating his brain, but Cameron decided to do something he'd never done before.

He searched for reviews of his work.

He typically avoided audience and critical feedback at all costs, listening only to notes from the studio and bouncing ideas off his peers and his agent.

There were three types of people who felt compelled to review his work online.

First, people who loved his art, thought he was a treasure of cinema, and claimed that the Namaste series was the pinnacle of modern action with classical leanings.

Second, those who hated him and thought he was a

no-talent hack with a hard-on for slow-mo. They hated the Namaste series and hoped Cameron would die there. (And they were going to get their wish, the fuckers.)

Third, there were the select few who thought he had all the potential in the world, who understood he'd been working his way into brilliance, and couldn't wait to see what the auteur-in-waiting would do next, when it was finally his time and turn to start making real movies.

Cameron quit when he found himself on a forum full of posts tagged *#fuckparrish* in threads with names like *Cameron Parrish Has Herpes of the Soul.*

It should've been depressing, but instead it was strangely satisfying to see so many trolls — who would never make anything worthwhile of their own — shitting all over the work he'd spent his entire career resenting. Validating, after all the times he'd bitched to Emily about how stupid audiences must be to pay money for the hack-work he'd done to build his career.

Or maybe that was the brain cancer talking.

The car rolled to a gentle stop. Cameron turned the windows transparent and squinted at the brightly lit sign over the door of the fast food restaurant straight ahead.

Apparently, his AI chauffeur thought *take me anywhere* meant *let's go to Sloppy's and gorge on a disgustingly greasy burger.*

Just the thought made his gut heave. He shoved open the door and fell out onto cracked asphalt in time to vomit bourbon and cake and bile-dotted speckles of dark crimson that were definitely blood.

Modern art on the ground, puke on asphalt. A fitting portrait for the total fucking disaster his life had become.

He wiped his mouth with the back of his hand and considered his options.

Take Philocrap and die sooner, but maybe feel better for a little while, and possibly use that time to write the

Fountain script. Console himself with the idea that even though he'd never see it born, the rest of the world would.

That felt too much like surrender.

Or Cameron could tell the world to fuck off and spend what time he had left doing whatever the hell he wanted. Except that he had no one else to do it with — now that his secret was out, everyone would feel sorry for him.

He'd rather be alone than looked down on and humored.

That road led to a lot more nights like this one, drunk and vomiting, hating himself more than even the worst of his critics.

What was left? Kill himself before cancer turned him into a potato?

The thought made him want to puke again. Yes, it would be a relief to know that this was over, and yes, he'd be taking control of his situation, in an extreme way. But there was something in him that couldn't bear to let go. He had spent his existence trying to capture perfection on-screen, but had ironically seen little actual life.

Cameron had to do more with the little he still had.

So he pulled out his phone, ignored all the doubt as he searched for the contact, then found it and called Sharon Eberling.

Her app couldn't save his life, but maybe it could make what was left better.

Chapter Eight

THAT WASN'T CREEPY AT ALL

"It's not a bucket list app," Eberling explained. "Adieu will change the way you feel about death. Turn your final experience into—"

"Spare me the marketing brochure and tell me what it does."

The tramadol Cameron had gulped down with a cup of strong coffee on his way to Dr. Eberling's office had murdered his hangover, leaving behind the ghost of a headache and the queasy fear that she would disappoint him too.

"Would you humor me and answer a question before we get started?" she asked.

"Depends on the question."

"What is it about artificial intelligence that makes you so uncomfortable?"

"Does it matter?"

"You're notorious for refusing to work with them. Adieu uses an AI to design your experience. If you're hostile to—"

"I'm not hostile to anything." *Except people who waste my*

time and patronize me. "I'm an artist. I want to make art. I've spent decades refining my aesthetic. Why would I want to delegate that to a machine whose artistic principles are comprised of the algorithmic average of every movie it's ever been fed?"

"That's an oversimplification of how AI works. It learns, same as us. It develops its own aesthetic, same as us."

"If AI gets smarter than us, life as we know it is over."

"That's the kind of thing critics have said about every new groundbreaking technology. The printing press. Television. The internet. Smartphones."

"It's different. And by an order of magnitude."

"It's evolution, Cameron."

"If it makes us dumber, it's devolution." He was so tired of explaining this. "Nobody knows how to read a map anymore, thanks to GPS. As soon as it fails, you're lost. And in the meantime, it makes you feel like the world revolves around you, because you're always at the center of the map."

"Critics of the printing press insisted it would make people stupider because it enabled the spread of misinformation. Same with television; because you absorb material passively instead of engaging with ideas actively, some thought it would be used as a brainwashing tool. The internet—"

He managed not to roll his eyes. "I get it. But just because people say stupid shit on the internet and stop looking for the answer if it's not in the first page of search results doesn't prove that AI is safe. None of those technologies were trying to mimic human thought."

"Every revolution has an adjustment period. I would say the AI Revolution has gone astoundingly well."

"That's my point. This is the part of the movie when

shit starts to happen. It's *supposed* to start out 'astoundingly well.' There's no story otherwise."

"Every time you get into your car, you're putting your life in the hands of an AI."

"Driving a car isn't an act of creativity, it's a series of actions that a machine can learn to do."

"Isn't making a movie a series of actions that you learned to do?"

"No, it's a series of decisions that I make based on something an artificial intelligence will never have: life experience."

"Is it possible you're having the same kneejerk reaction we all do when confronted with change?"

"If I have to worship our AI overlords for this Adieu thing to work, then I'm out."

"This isn't one of your movies, Mr. Parrish." Eberling steepled her fingers in her lap. "This is your life — what's left of it."

This was why he'd refused couples therapy, even after Natalie started arguing hard for it. Instead of figuring out who was right and settling the argument objectively, shrinks always made it about why *everyone* was to blame.

But it wasn't Cameron's fault he was dying. Just like it wasn't his fault that he'd had to work obsessively to push his career forward.

The fact that he was dying proved that he'd been right to do it. He should've pushed harder. If he'd finished the second *Namaste* last year, he'd have *Fountain* wrapped by now and his big sendoff would be the premiere.

Every time he'd acquiesced to Natalie's nagging and slowed down to be with his ungrateful family, he'd been sacrificing his life's work without even seeing the truth.

He blinked to clear his eyes, suddenly watering, and refocused on Eberling's argument.

"Science fiction becomes science fact an awful lot of the time," Cameron said. "Just because there's an app for everything doesn't mean we should use them for every little—"

"Have I scared you off, or would you like to know how it works?"

"How it works," he grouched. "Please."

She drew a small box from a pocket in her smock, then lifted the lid and gently plucked something out. Silver and black, no bigger than a grain of rice.

Cameron shifted in his seat. "Some sort of implant?"

"It's perfectly safe, and you won't even know it's there."

"Says you."

She smiled. "Says me, and millions of people since the first person tried it. Do you know when that was, Cameron?"

"I have no idea."

"Ninety-eight. Can you believe that? It was used to turn on lights and open doors. Simple stuff."

"I'd prefer that," Cameron said. "Why do you need to put a chip inside me?"

"It's a sensor, allowing Sofia to monitor any number of factors relating to your health, so she can do the best possible job of timing your journey to accommodate your condition."

Sofia? "The AI has a name?"

"She optimizes what your body needs and what your mind can handle."

"That's nice of her."

"And what your spirit needs to surrender this life."

"What does artificial intelligence know about my spirit?" Cameron asked.

"Whatever you teach it."

Jesus, did he really have to buy into this bullshit? "Is there any version of this experience that doesn't come with invasive technology?"

"No." A dry smile. "Shall we stop?"

Goddammit, he hated this. "If I'm constantly being monitored, am I being recorded too?"

"Only if you want to be, but I can't imagine why you would refrain, especially considering your life's work."

"Is that some kind of dig?"

"Don't think of this as an invasive experience where your every movement will be recorded. See it as putting yourself behind a lens that few humans have ever had the opportunity to experience instead."

"I'll never have any privacy."

"You're talking about privacy from yourself. If you don't believe that AI is in any way human, why would you object to her recording your experiences?"

"What if I want to get loaded and go to Amsterdam? Visit the red-light district? Do things I wouldn't want people watching after I'm gone?"

Especially not Natalie and Colin.

"Everything's encrypted and stored securely, so you don't have to worry about a leak."

"It's still creepy to be watched."

"Even by an AI?"

Cameron nodded. "I don't want to spend the rest of my life feeling like I'm being watched."

"You won't. She'll speak when spoken to, or when she's delivering a notification, just like your phone. Except she'll be speaking to you through bone conduction, so no one else will know she's there. Sofia can see and hear everything you do, so—"

"I have to address her out loud?"

"That's right," Eberling said.

"So people are going to think I'm talking to myself like a crazy person?"

"You can also access her discretely through the app, if you like. Or type a note to yourself; she'll read it and reply. But most of the time, you'll forget she's there."

This was his best alternative? Maybe the Philocrap wasn't so bad.

Except … he had so few days left, losing even one of them felt like too much.

And Cameron couldn't stand to die knowing he'd wasted his final days.

He could always quit if he didn't like it. What were they going to do if he hopped a plane to Fiji and drank himself to death? Drag him back home?

"I guess you probably need my bucket list, right?"

"Like I said before, there's no bucket list."

"It's a bucket list app that doesn't take me to any of the places on my bucket list?"

"You might see some of them, but the point of this is not to cram as many vacations into your remaining days as you can. Adieu is here to give you closure."

That, he understood. The ending was the most important part of the movie, and if Cameron could be sure he'd go out on a high note … "How do we start?"

"Sofia will interview you and analyze everything we give her: your movies, social media feeds, private and professional email accounts, any personal writing you might have—"

"That doesn't sound invasive at all."

"If you give her permission, she'll also speak with other people in your life as needed."

"Like my ex?" He'd have to tell Natalie, and he definitely wasn't ready for that. "What if I don't want her to know?"

"We only speak with individuals on your consent list."

If he could keep Natalie and Colin off the list, then Cameron could live with that. The only other thing bothering him was the potential to further sully his legacy.

"What hoops do I have to go through to get footage deleted?"

"You can set things to burn as they go, meaning there's an auto-erase on delay. Give yourself five minutes, an hour, a day, however long you want to think about it. Keep everything in an archive and Sofia will tag it to keep everything searchable — so you can edit or delete anything at your convenience. If you sign an order requesting erasure upon your death, we'll keep and anonymize the gathered data, of course."

Then the hardest question of all:

"Will it — will she tell me when I'm going to die?"

"The best Sofia can do is keep adjusting your itinerary as she monitors the progression of your illness. But no, she can't predict the exact time of your death."

"Will she tell me when I get close?"

"We've found that a countdown distracts from the experience we're trying to give you." She hesitated, then added, "But some people know anyway."

Cameron reminded himself again that he could quit if he decided this was bullshit. "I'm in. Where do we start?"

Dr. Eberling smiled. "We already have. Sofia?"

A calm female voice filled the room. "It's a pleasure to meet you, Cameron. I've seen all your movies."

Nope. That wasn't creepy at all.

Chapter Nine

YOU WEREN'T BORN WITH A CAMERA IN YOUR HAND

CAMERON TOUCHED the sore spot at the base of his skull and felt the slickness of a round adhesive bandage, about the size of a fingernail.

"That's it?"

"The implant is connecting with your brainstem and deploying nanosensors into your bloodstream," said Eberling. "Some will lodge in your organs, others in the walls of blood vessels. Within fifteen minutes, Sofia will have a complete picture of your bodily processes at almost every level."

Fourteen minutes, twenty-nine seconds, a calm, feminine voice resonated in his skull.

The doctor smiled. "Did she just say hello?"

"How do you—"

"Bone conduction, remember?"

"Yes, but—"

"If you prefer," came the disembodied voice, "I can speak to you like this."

The voice was slightly muffled. Because the AI was talking to him through the phone in his pocket.

What kind of robopocalypse SkyNet bullshit had he agreed to?

"How often will you be talking to me?"

"That depends on your preferences. If you'd like, you can set me to speak only when spoken to, or when it's necessary to deliver a notification."

Cameron had enough voices in his head — his perpetually disappointed father, his ex-wife, the studio exec who'd overseen his first movie. Adding another one, even if it was trying to be helpful, might be too much.

"What would you need to notify me of?"

Eberling said, "You're going to be taking a complex cocktail of medications that will need to be adjusted as your condition changes, and at the very least, Sofia will remind you what to take when."

"So she's going to be bossing me around a lot?"

"Only if you're the kind of patient that refuses to take your medication." Then, more sober, "She'll also be making all of your travel arrangements and letting you know where to go."

"Like an assistant."

"Assistant, travel agent, medical adviser, whatever you need. If Sofia can't do it, she'll arrange for someone else to take care of it."

"What if I need a blowjob?" Cameron was pushing it, but he didn't care. He wasn't going to spend the rest of his life being celibate.

If you desire an escort, you need only inform me of your preferences.

His face flushed so hot it was probably purple.

Eberling chuckled. "I'm going to guess that Sofia answered your question. She's programmed for discretion and her logs are encrypted with better-than-military-grade algorithms. Your privacy is ensured."

"But you'll have access to it."

"Only your medical data. Like I said, everything else is up to you. Send it to your loved ones, broadcast it on the net, or have Sofia erase it when you die."

"Can she erase it as we go?"

"In order to do her job, she needs to get to know you. If she's erasing everything as it happens, she can't ever learn what you need."

"I thought she already knew what I needed."

"She's an AI, not an all-knowing deity. The more time she spends observing you, the more deeply she'll understand what will give you the most closure."

"I drink Artemis Tull for closure. I want her to help me have as much fun as possible before …"

"Sofia is there to make sure your final days are satisfying."

"That's what I want."

"Then I recommend keeping her permissions as they are, and answer every question with complete honesty."

"She's going to give me some sort of test?"

"A conversation tonight. Your first adventure will begin tomorrow."

"What if I don't like how the conversation goes?"

"You can terminate your agreement with Adieu at any time. The penalty spelled out in your contract is hefty, but you can afford it."

He'd barely read the contract before agreeing to the procedure — Cameron trusted his legal app to tell him if it was okay to sign. It only occurred to him now that the app was configured for film industry contracts, and might not catch things related to highly experimental medical treatments.

He opened his mouth to ask about the termination clause when Eberling added, "Sofia can give you the highlights, or answer any questions. She can read all seventy-three pages to you, if you'd prefer suicide by boredom."

"Is there anything else I should know?"

"Wealth is the ability to fully experience life. Be open to anything."

That sounded like something his ex-wife would say.

Not a good omen.

CAMERON OPENED another bottle of Artemis Tull as soon as he got home.

Alcohol is contraindicated for your condition.

"Meaning?"

Drinking is likely to accelerate your deterioration.

"In that case, I'll just have half a bottle," he joked. Sort of.

Is this your typical level of consumption?

Her voice was completely different from Natalie's, but Cameron couldn't help hearing the same disdain that his ex would've poured into those words.

None of your business, he wanted to say, except that he'd made it her business when signing up for her help in making his bucket list.

"One glass." He filled the whiskey halfway, no ice. "Then I'll order dinner."

Would you like me to order it for you?

"There's this Thai place on Sunset—"

Your last five orders from Thai Lotus are identical. Would you like to me to duplicate those items, or would you prefer to review the menu?

Weird, but also nice. He could get used to having someone around to anticipate what he wanted and make it happen.

"Everything except the Buddha's Heaven." That was Ariana's dish, a mix of bean sprouts, broccoli and tofu in an anemic soy-based broth, which she often made a show of eating as part of her you-should-be-vegan campaign, before bitching about how his spicy basil beef and crispy spring rolls were killing him from the inside out. "Extra spring rolls."

It'll be here in thirty-five minutes, and I took the liberty of pre-tipping the delivery person thirty percent.

"Great." He took a sip of his whiskey. "Let's get started on my bucket list."

Are there any places you've been that you'd like to revisit, or shall I eliminate all your previous travel?

"I've never had a stalker before."

This process will feel less intrusive once I have established a baseline.

"Can't I just tell you what I want?"

What do you want, Cameron?

"I—" It had been so long since anyone had asked him that, non-sarcastically. "I've never been to Tahiti."

Why do you want to go to Tahiti?

"It's supposed to be beautiful."

What would you like to do there?

"Get drunk and get lei'd." He laughed. "Get it?"

I recognize the double entendre.

"If I'm going to be in the South Pacific anyway, I might as well hit Fiji, too."

What would you like to do in Fiji?

Get drunk and get lei'd. Except that humor had an unforgiving half-life. "Relax."

By getting drunk and having sex?

"Very funny." He took a larger swallow of whiskey while trying to think of other places he wanted to go. But apparently he'd stopped dreaming of travel at some point in the indeterminate past. "Where do you think I should go?"

What's your favorite color?

"What does that have to do with anything?"

I'm still determining your baseline.

"How will my favorite color tell you anything about my travel preferences?"

It won't. Would you play a game with me?

What was this bullshit? Was it possible that Eberling's artificial intelligence was already glitching?

"What does my contract say about technical support?"

What symptoms are you experiencing?

"Not for me, for you."

Running diagnostics. After half a breath, she added, *no problems found.*

"Tell me another joke."

Why didn't the astronaut come home to his wife?

"I wasn't serious."

Do you know the answer?

"Because he needed his space. Are you going to tell me a knock-knock joke next?"

A family of performers gains an audition with a talent agent—

"I do not want to hear your version of The Aristocrats."

Imagine if Americans switched from pounds to kilograms tonight.

What?

Tomorrow there would be mass confusion.

Cameron groaned. "You're programmed to tell dad jokes?"

Sorry for the faux pa.

He would've thought that was hilarious in fifth grade.

"Either you're glitching or Dr. Eberling is a quack." Either way, Cameron was getting his money back.

What's the last joke you laughed at?

"My fucking life."

Name a movie that made you cry.

"*Taxi Driver*. First year of film school."

Why that movie?

"It made me realize I didn't know anything."

If your ex-wife wanted to have sex with you, would you say yes?

"What kind of question is that?"

The hypothetical kind.

He drained his glass and refilled it. "Where's that Thai food?"

Nine minutes away. I must remind you that alcohol is contraindicated for your condition.

"I can't be sober if you're going to ask me questions like that."

Understood. When was the first time you used a camera?

"I made my first film in seventh gr—"

That's not what I asked.

"That's what everyone always asks."

I want to know your earliest memory of holding a camera and taking a picture or shooting a video.

"I don't remember."

You weren't born with a camera in your hand.

"I probably had a toy one as a baby. Where the hell is dinner?"

Seven minutes away. And not a toy camera, the first time you deliberately used a real camera to record a moment of your life.

"What difference does it make?"

Is this your version of complete honesty?

A few more gulps of whiskey while he thought about whether to answer.

He actually did remember the first time he'd used a camera. Third grade, spring break, Mt. Shasta. In a rare fit of decent parenting, Cameron's father had taken him camping, and the old man hadn't criticized him even once after they'd pulled into the site. They'd collected firewood, pitched their tents, and made grilled cheese sandwiches in a cast-iron pan. After Dad had banked the fire, they'd lain on a blanket and guessed at constellations. Or rather, made them up, because Cameron had never seen the sky so filled with stars — he'd never even been out of the city, where light pollution bleached the sky of its brilliance. He couldn't tell the familiar stars he'd memorized from those he'd never seen.

He had longed to take a picture of that magnificent sky, knowing it would help him to hold the emotion forever, never forget the weight of that moment. It wasn't just the first time Cameron remembered wanting — or perhaps even *needing* — to take a picture, it was the first time he'd ever felt outside of the moment itself. He could still feel that second more than three decades later. In that moment he'd known that his time was finite, and that pictures could somehow capture a shard of infinity.

Dad always said *no*, so it took Cameron a while to muster the courage.

This time he said *yes*, but he warned his son that the picture wouldn't come out. He would need a special camera. Cameron took the picture anyway, and Dad had been right.

He never got that feeling back.

"Like I said, seventh grade. I made a movie about how my best friend Jorge was actually an alien."

Will you play a game of rock-paper-scissors with me?

"For fuck's sake, I'm not in seventh grade anymore." Cameron finished his second glass of whiskey, enjoying the lightheadedness finally washing over him.

Knock-knock.

"Who's there?" he asked, probably because there was no food in his stomach to slow the alcohol down.

Dinner.

"Dinner who?"

The driver from Thai Lotus is parking his car, and will be ringing your doorbell in approximately ninety seconds.

About fucking time.

Chapter Ten

LEAVE IT IN LUXURY

CAMERON WAS OVERJOYED to have first class all to himself, at first. Now it felt lonely. Exiled in cushy quarantine, where no one else had to feel sorry for him.

Not that he wanted pity. But even alone he was stuck with his own.

He'd been trying to drift off for the last two hours, but nothing was working. Not watching *Like Water for Chocolate,* which he loved, though it always put him to sleep. Not listening to binaural beats, or Ravel's *Piano Concerto in G Minor.* Not the white noise of summer rain broken by the occasional rumble of distant thunder.

His brain kept looping a gag reel featuring the most humiliating, infuriating highlights of the last week. Fainting in front of Jeffries. Being talked down to by a "doctor" who served as a mouthpiece for an artificial intelligence. Ariana's attempt to use his impending death as a stepping stone for her career. And that fucking cake.

Cameron would've killed for a Xanax. But he'd settle for a whiskey on the rocks.

The rocks were still hard in his first glass when he

ordered the second, which he gulped down in full before requesting a third.

Sofia was suddenly there inside his head, reminding him that alcohol interfered with his medication and that overindulging would interfere with her ability to minimize his symptoms, and thereby potentially hasten his demise.

"I'm aware of the risks," he whispered, pretending to look out the window so the flight attendants wouldn't think that he was talking to himself. "But if I don't get some sleep, I'm going to be exhausted by the time we get to the Maldives. That's not good for my symptoms either, is it?"

Sofia went into ASMR mode, matching his whisper with a sexy lilt that gave his dick ideas of its own. *I'm skilled in—*

"Talk normally," he hissed under his breath.

—a variety of therapeutic modalities: hypnosis, guided meditation, roleplaying visualization, progressive relax—

"Roleplaying?"

As he said it, too loud, one of the flight attendants emerged from the cockpit, holding a tray and wearing a look that clearly broadcast, *you'd-better-not.*

It doesn't have to be sexual.

That just made him harder. "I didn't say anything about it being sexual."

I have complete access to your biometrics.

Of course she did.

"Then give me the illusion of privacy, at least."

He hadn't meant to snap, but the flight attendant stalked past to the main cabin, yanking the curtain shut behind her with a huff. Giving him the illusion of privacy.

And depriving him of the opportunity to request yet another whiskey.

He took a deep breath and looked out the window again at the wide expanse of unbroken ocean below the clouds, wondering what it would be like to fly somewhere majestic, then jump out of a plane as if he were skydiving and never open his chute. Terrifying. Exhilarating. Probably both.

And that last micro-second before he hit the ground at terminal velocity ...

Cameron could make an audience believe that was a great way to die with the right angles and scoring, but he doubted the real-life experience would be quite as rewarding.

Life would be so much better if he were allowed to direct it.

But that just made him think about *Fountain*, and the fact that he was never going to direct anything, ever again.

CAMERON GRABBED THE IN-FLIGHT TABLET, tapped *Destination Information*, and started swiping through pictures of Malé, where he would be landing as soon as this excruciating flight was over. He had no idea why the AI had chosen the Maldives, but he planned to live it the hell up.

Quaint thatched huts on stilts, surrounded by crystalline turquoise waters. It would make a gorgeous establishing shot. Bronzed women in bikinis and sarongs at a glitzy beach resort — perfect for a suave action hero to lose control of his drop. Open-air markets, a riot of tables of handmade goods and quirky-looking locals — he was already picturing the motorcycle chase through claustrophobic yet colorful alleys.

He was never going to have any fun if he couldn't turn his brain off.

He might have to turn off the AI for a night or two, so Sofia couldn't nag him out of enjoying this place.

He stopped on some striking photos of an underwater

restaurant. It captured both his attention and breath. Imagine sitting on the ocean floor with nothing but thick glass separating you from a great white shark while you stuffed yourself with tuna tartare and mango cheesecake. And too much expensive wine.

Savoring the anticipation, Cameron tapped open an article about the island.

Malé was basically one big city. Sofia probably booked him at a five-star resort on one of the less-populated islands where the true beauty of the Maldives could be found. Los Angeles had plenty of palm trees, but those were like weeds compared to these flowers in paradise. The beaches here weren't crowded like L.A.'s and the water wasn't polluted, at least farther away from the main island.

Cameron imagined himself floating weightless above sea urchins and crabs while curious jewel-bright fish swam up to meet him. He'd ask Sofia to have snorkeling gear delivered to his room, soon as they landed.

As Cameron kept scrolling through the article, a sidebar about the impact of global warming caught his eye. Twenty-six ring-shaped atolls in the middle of the Indian Ocean, comprised of more than a thousand coral islands, slowly being swallowed by the ocean. In fifteen to twenty years, it would be gone.

Was it supposed to be poetic, Sofia making a point by sending him to a dying oasis?

It was the kind of thing he would've done in one of his movies.

Cameron tapped out of the article and returned to the bountiful list of activities for tourists, making a mental list of things he wanted to do.

He supposed they'd take a puddle jumper to one of the smaller islands, since Malé was the only one with an international airport. He could visit the fish market, the restaurants and shops along the main road, Majeedhee Magu. Cameron could see Hukuru Miskiy, a seventeenth-century mosque made of carved white coral, and couldn't imagine leaving without visiting Banana Reef or the Tsunami Monument. He might as well indulge in a day of pampering at the Huvafen Fushi Underwater Spa and Resort, since he was here.

If Cameron had to say goodbye prematurely, at least he would be leaving this world in luxury.

Chapter Eleven

KICKING CARTOON NINJA ASS

CAMERON HEARD a ding from somewhere far away.

He slowly opened his eyes and saw that the plane was making its final descent into Malé International. Unlike the rest of the islands, Malé was nearly a hundred percent built up, only adjacent to paradise. He hoped he wouldn't be on the main island long. The city looked too congested for the spiritual exhale he needed.

As the plane kissed the runway, he whispered to Sofia. "What's next?"

Someone will be here to pick you up.

Great.

Cameron fidgeted until the door finally opened, then shot out of his seat to grab his bag. He offered the flight attendant a smile and nod that she didn't return.

At least she didn't feel sorry for him.

Pleasant warmth embraced him as he crossed the tarmac, followed by the slap of AC as he entered the terminal. The air felt so artificial, Cameron couldn't help but think about how synthetic this entire process actually was. Having an app ordering him around, choosing how he should spend his final days. Hadn't he gotten enough nagging from Natalie to last him a lifetime? Especially one cut so tragically short.

But Cameron wouldn't have thought to come here, and why not? Because years of making the same movie on repeat had boxed him in. If it were up to him, he'd have spent the next few months the same way he did between movies: drinking, getting laid, trying to light up as many of his pleasure receptors as possible.

Sofia was pushing him out of his box. Maybe she was trying to help him get a fresh perspective, so he'd be inspired to write something original.

Perhaps to craft something truly unique from his final experience. *The Last Days of Cameron Parrish*, a commentary on his own career and a poignant depiction of his third act. Something to give the world a glimpse of what could have been.

She was recording everything he saw and heard. All he had to do to get the perfect shot was turn his head. No camera or sound crew required, no wrangling delicate egos, no bullshit notes from studio execs. Jeffries could intercut the DIY footage with interviews to give the missing personal stories and critical perspectives from those who had known him.

If Cameron couldn't be remembered for *Fountain*, at least he'd have a chance at the director's cut on his career.

He hurried through the terminal, eager to indulge in a bit of rejuvenating extravagance before getting started on his real-life masterpiece. That underwater restaurant for sure. A massage, and once he was relaxed, perhaps a glass of wine or two at a beachside bar packed with beautiful women seeking a vacation fling.

Would you like me to adjust your settings? I can auto-optimize for whatever you're looking at, or you can specify the type of shot you're looking for.

"No, thanks." Sofia should've known better than to ask about auto-optimize, and he wasn't ready to start filming what would essentially be his eulogy.

He rounded the corner and saw a line of people holding name-bearing signs. His was the only one written in bright orange marker — every other passenger had their names neatly printed in black. The man holding Cameron's sign was practically dancing with joy, even while standing in place. The other drivers were all in suits or slacks and collared shirts, while his was rocking a threadbare polo with shorts and sandals. Tousled black hair and a goatee, heavy-framed glasses that would've looked perfect on Ward Cleaver, and eagerly curious eyes gave him the air of a poor yet adventurous college student.

"Mr. Parrish!" He waved, then swapped the sign from one hand to the other to adjust the wingspan of his wild gestures.

"That's me," Cameron said, passing the handle of his rolling suitcase over to the driver.

But the man mistook his gesture. He grabbed Cameron's hand and vigorously shook it. "Of course it is! I'm Anaan. It's great to meet you. I'm—"

"Should I just follow you?" Cameron handed him the suitcase again, more insistent.

"Sure thing." Anaan dragged Cameron's suitcase behind him, leading his passenger out of the airport and outside to a total piece of shit sandwiched between two limos.

He needed to have a little talk with Sofia. What was the point of going on a bucket list trip and pinching every penny? He should be traveling first class all the way.

But he didn't want to be rude. "This is yours?"

"I share it with my family," said Anaan, taking Cameron's luggage and loading it into the trunk.

Cameron forced a smile to cover his disappointment. Soon he would be floating in an infinity pool, looking forward to a meal that would probably cost more than this kid made in a week. In the meantime, he'd be helping a scrappy young entrepreneur get started on his career.

Same as he'd been when he started out, figuring out how to stretch a million dollars to make a movie that grossed twenty times its budget.

He opened the rear passenger door.

Another wild gesture from Anaan. "Don't be crazy! You can ride up front with me."

Why not? His overly amiable driver never stopped talking, barely stealing a breath between syllables, happier than anyone driving this erector set of rusty bolts should be. Apparently, he'd cultivated an obsessive fascination with Cameron's catalogue, and every other sentence out of his mouth was a quote from one of his movies. And not the ones fans usually quoted when they ran into Cameron.

I was aiming for the cigar.

Can't move forward if you never look back.

I'm good at three things, and all of them are F-words.

They passed one fancy hotel after another, bright white awnings contrasting sharply with the miles of turquoise water behind them.

But when Anaan rolled right by the last one on the strip, Cameron started to get worried. Were they headed for a different part of the island?

He didn't want to explain Adieu, so he pulled out his phone and texted himself, which Sofia should see if she was still recording.

Are we going the right way?

Her answer resonated softly in his skull. *You'll be there in 1.8 miles.*

The tourists had thinned enough that he could no longer tell if there were any. The bold prints and revealing bikinis were gone, along with the endless acres of abdomens, the old scenery having surrendered to a new view of women in modest long-sleeved shirts and skirts and headscarves. The Muslim population in the Maldives became much more evident the further they drove.

"I didn't know there were any hotels out this far," Cameron said, hoping for reassurance.

"I'm so honored that we can be working together," Anaan continued to chatter. "Whatever you need, you let me know. I want you to feel welcome."

"I feel very welcome."

Too welcome. Cameron was dying for a conversation with someone who didn't know who he was.

Anaan turned down a road leading inland, away from the water."

"Is my hotel downtown?"

Anaan laughed. "You don't want one of those hotels! You want someplace that's going to help you be creative. *I'm at my creative best when I'm surrounded by family.* You said that. Mr. Parrish. *Entertainment Weekly.*"

"I remember." Natalie had served him divorce papers a week after the interview. The theme of that fight had been *hypocrisy.* If Anaan was such a fan, why would he throw that in Cameron's face? Should he chalk this up to cultural differences, or was the man's interest in him something less than innocent?

He cleared his throat again. "So, where are we going?"

Anaan turned right into a narrow alley. The walls on either side were so close it would have been impossible for either one of them to open a door. "Don't worry, I've arranged everything."

Shit. Cameron shifted his left hand closer to the seatbelt latch. How fast could he get out of the car once it stopped? He probably couldn't outrun the younger man, but he maybe he could beat him to a store and beg for help with a head start.

"I'm serious, I want to know where you're taking me."

"We get an early start and I save you money," Anaan crowed. "You're staying with me."

He turned the wheel and made another sharp turn into an even narrower alley. Cameron was too busy holding his breath for a response. Only once they were out on the other side did he finally manage to say, "There's been a mistake. I need you to take me to a hotel."

"Every film budget must be neatly divided between function and style. Not evenly, but neatly. The director decides and that's part of his or her look. But the one constant is that every dollar matters." Anaan grinned. "*Wall Street Journal*, 'The New Economics of Hollywood.'"

"I remember." How did you talk to a crazy kidnapper? If this was one of his movies, the hero would have something snappy to say, then he'd jump out of the moving car and roll to his feet. But Cameron wasn't a hero, and he didn't want to spend the last few months of his life in a full-body cast. "But since I don't have any family here, the other way for me to achieve my creative best is to stay at the beach. Sometimes the beach is better than family."

Turning his phone so there was no chance Anaan could see the screen, he typed, *Sofia, get me out of here.*

I've arranged for Anaan to be your host while you're here, she replied.

What the fuck? Was this some sort of insane glitch? Where had Sofia found this guy and how could she possibly think Cameron would want to spend time with him?

Why? he typed.

You agreed to trust me, Cameron. Taking a leap of faith is part of the experience.

He'd thought that meant trusting her to select his five-star hotel, not shove him into dangerous situations like this. Cameron could call Dr. Eberling and make her straighten Sofia out, the second he was alone.

Anaan pulled up in front of a cement apartment building that had likely been new in the seventies, and threw his piece of crap into park.

Cameron looked up at the building. Cracks in the walls, unskillfully patched, some painted over in cheap yellow and others left like raised scars marring the building's skin. Rusted metal railings on the balconies and windows that longed for a wash.

Sofia had brought him to the opposite of a five-star hotel. If he'd been location scouting for a drug deal in an exotic slum, this was the building he'd have chosen.

"Thank you, this is very kind, but I can't impose. Can you please take me to a hotel? I'm happy to cover any additional fare."

Anaan laughed again, the sound almost painfully good-natured. "The views are the same, no matter which side of the island you sleep on!"

He leapt out of the car and hauled Cameron's luggage from the trunk, then gestured for Cameron to follow him.

You're safe with Anaan, Sofia chimed in. *Trust me.*

The young man headed into the building. With Cameron's luggage.

He tried the driver's side door handle. Locked.

The market across the street was closed, same for the café. Everything else was apartment buildings and two-story homes that weren't in any better shape than this one. If he bolted and pounded on doors, would anyone let him in?

"Come," Anaan called, holding the lobby door for him. "Dinner is waiting."

Cameron didn't know whether it was fear, his sickness, or genuine hunger, but his stomach had been making regular somersaults. And hospitality was a big deal in many cultures — he'd learned the hard way while filming *The Wicked Must Fall* in Sri Lanka how easy it was to offend, despite his intention. By getting into Anaan's car, he'd probably accepted an implicit offer of hospitality. If he played the role of guest well, he'd be discharging the debt that came with it, and thus lubricate his departure.

After dinner, he'd step outside for some fresh air and call a cab. In the meantime, he'd be collecting some local color for *The Last Days of Cameron Parrish*.

"Still recording?" he asked under his breath as he trudged up four flights of stairs behind Anaan.

I'm getting everything.

They approached a door at the end of a short yet uneven walkway. The paint on the front door might have only been a decade old, but it looked like it had a century of weathering, thanks to the salty air and general neglect.

Anaan knocked twice, then threw the door open and loudly declared, "We're here!"

A riot of cheering rolled out from inside the apartment, hitting Cameron with an almost physical force. How many people were in there?

He entered the apartment, mouth watering at the aroma of fried fish and coconut and cumin, at the same time that his nose wrinkled at the sweaty, musty odor that reminded him of an overcrowded locker room in summer.

There had to be thirty people crammed into the living

room, waving as they greeted him, in English, Arabic and Dhivehi. He recognized *welcome* in the first two languages, and *late* in Arabic, a word he'd learned when they'd shot *Cairo Kickboxer.*

Would you like me to translate?

Cameron shook his head, hoping Sofia would get the hint. The last thing he needed right now was for her to add to the cacophony.

He gave the room a timid wave. "Hello."

Anaan slapped him on the back like they were best friends, then said something in Dhivehi that galvanized the whole room into action. Except for the oldest, everyone jumped up and started bringing food in from another room, setting dish after dish on the two tables butted up together along the far wall.

A massive spread of appetizers for the famous director. It was surreal to be treated like visiting royalty by total strangers.

Cameron felt like such an asshole, wanting to be anywhere else in the world. This was all for him. But he hadn't asked for any of it. He should be swimming in an infinity pool, ordering room service, planning his adventures for the next few days.

Instead, he was fighting through jet lag as Anaan dragged him through a gamut of introductions. Names flew right by him, sounding like gibberish to his exhausted ears. Mushan. Gaimini. Yuhaan. Sonu. And weirdly, an Edward, who seemed exceptionally proud to have a name that their guest might recognize.

Instead he tried to remember them as if he were putting them into a script as extras. Cousin Pink Dress. Granny Cheek-Scar. Uncle Cigarillo. Little Iron Man, who held his action figure up for Cameron to see, but pulled it away when the director reached out to touch it.

Pradeep and Mai were the only names that stuck, and only because Anaan gave his parents lengthy introductions, which meant Cameron had a chance to mentally repeat their names over and over while Anaan talked.

Mai grabbed his hands and thanked him profusely for everything he'd done for her son, and Pradeep promised that Anaan was an excellent worker who would work very hard to not disappoint him.

Cameron smiled and nodded and said *thank you,* because you couldn't possibly be breaking the local customs by being happy and grateful. Another thing he'd learned in Sri Lanka when a situation escalated between his cinematographer and a local official demanding an extra bribe mid-shoot.

Anaan's mother, Mai, shoved a plate loaded with food into his hands, and scattered several children with a wave, making room for Cameron to sit on what was either a very large cushion or a very small beanbag chair.

Cameron said *thank you* once again, in English and in Arabic, then claimed his seat as the guest of honor.

As soon as he sat, a couple of older women started loading up plates and passing them around to the rest of the family.

This would be the perfect opening scene for a family drama. About a young son who rebels against tradition and sets out to make his mark on the world. Or maybe a daughter who refuses to marry the fiancé her parents have chosen for her, insisting that she follow her own heart instead.

There was so much love in this room, Cameron was practically choking on it.

None of the older folks spoke English, at all, although he entertained some of them by mangling the few Arabic phrases he knew. But the kids did, and answering their questions was amusing. They wondered if the American movie man knew Superman, or Thor, or Demonspawn.

"Yes," Cameron said with a straight face, "but they're usually too busy saving the world to have dinner with me."

One of the teenage girls wanted to know if Cameron could introduce her to Elijah Beck. She blushed and tee-heed when Cameron told her that he used to have coffee with Elijah's father Orson.

"Tell Jeffries to interview Orson for *Last Days*," he whispered to Sofia.

Done.

Soon, Anaan's youngest nephew, Hadi, was practicing kung fu in the doorway and shouting catchphrases originally delivered by Amit, the main character of *Namaste.*

Peace comes from within, death from without!

Cameron couldn't help but remember Colin, at the age of eight, coming home with a third-place trophy from some karate tournament that Natalie blamed him for missing. That had been an epic battle, ending with a half-finished tumbler of scotch thrown in his face and a week of sleeping on the couch.

But the part that had upset Cameron the most was finding Colin's trophy poking out of a garbage bag later that week. He'd taken the kid out for ice cream that night, but the damage was done.

He pushed the memory aside and dipped a piece of flatbread into the tiny bowl of sauce — or soup? — in the center of his plate. Turmeric, chili, coconut and lime, spicy and sweet and tart all at once. Sauce, Cameron decided as he dipped the edge of the bread into another tiny bowl. Fishy, salty, and surprisingly good.

He wasn't sure how long he sat there listening to the happy babble of words he didn't need to try to understand, stuffing himself with savory dal, fish in some sort of rich coconut curry sauce, smoky fish cakes laced with fiery peppers, and for dessert, fried banana cakes spiced with cardamom and rose. The only thing he didn't really like was something Anaan called *biskeemiyaa* — his taste buds didn't believe that egg and tuna belonged together. But that made Hadi happy. The little boy wolfed down Cameron's leftovers so fast, it was a miracle the kid didn't choke.

But it got harder and harder to keep his eyes open. So when Sofia reminded him that it was time to take another dose of medication, he told Anaan, "It's getting late."

"Of course!" Anaan seemed delighted to hear it, standing to announce that "Mr. Parrish needs his sleep" and "Big day tomorrow!"

Cameron let Anaan lead him deeper into the apartment, presumably to wherever his luggage had been stashed. But before he could start demurring and insist on calling a cab, his host flung open a door and said, "This is my bedroom."

"Oh. It's …" Cameron looked around. Posters for every single one of his movies covered the shabby walls, and a lone Amit action figure posed on Anaan's nightstand to guard his master's slumber.

Anaan looked anxious. Probably worried that the spoiled American was going to say it wasn't good enough.

He would be a total asshole to insist on leaving now, after Anaan's family had devoted their evening to honoring him.

"This is great," Cameron said.

"I'm a big fan." Anaan blushed. After another quiet, slightly awkward moment he pointed to the bed. "It's more comfortable than it looks. You know where the bathroom is, so make yourself at home. Please, sleep well. We start early in the morning."

"What are we starting early?" Whatever it was, Cameron hoped it wouldn't take too long. He intended to be swimming either with dolphins or bikini-clad MILFs by lunchtime.

"I can't tell you how grateful I am for your help," Anaan said, bowing deeply with his hands pressed together. "I'm ready to learn. I'll do whatever you ask."

He wanted to know what the hell that was supposed to mean, but his host was already gone.

"What the hell is going on?" Cameron hissed from behind the now-closed door.

Surrendering to the process is part of the experiment. Could an AI sound smug, just by sending vibrations through the bones in his skull? *You're a Type A personality, and your entire career has been characterized by a need for control. As was your failed marriage.*

"I didn't ask you for psychoan—"

Your contract with Adieu states that you will allow me to choose each location and arrange the experiences that are missing from your life spectrum.

"The only experience I'm missing right now involves eight-hundred thread count sheets and someone to share them with."

The social profiles of your network and acquaintances makes it clear that you've experienced that in abundance already. And that it hasn't provided you with the emotional comfort you're seeking.

"But sleeping alone in this—" He stopped himself from finishing that sentence, in case an English speaker might overhear. "This is not what I signed up for."

You signed up to have experiences you'd never arrange for yourself.

"Yes, but why this? What am I supposed to do here?"

It's Anaan's dream to learn the art of filmmaking from you. According to his LiveLyfe posts, you are "the single greatest director of our time."

"Am I the fucking Make-a-Wish Foundation?" If anything, shouldn't he be getting a wish instead of granting one? "Tell me you didn't sign me up to teach a class."

Not a class. You'll be directing an action movie in which he stars and has written the script.

WHAT?

"If I'd wanted to waste the last few months of my life like that, I'd be making *Nunchucks* right now."

Anaan has spent everything he has to make this movie.

"That's not my fault. You can't put that on me." Cameron fished out his phone. "Call Dr. Eberling."

The doctor's voicemail asked that he please leave a message.

A message wouldn't do. This needed to be a conversation, involving the words *malpractice* and *lawsuit.*

He hung up and flopped down on the narrow bed, which creaked and sagged under his weight. The sheets would probably be cheap polyester, just like the thin blanket beneath him. He pulled the corner back, and yep, there it was. *Namaste* sheets, featuring a cartoon Amit kicking cartoon ninja ass.

Cameron shuffled through too many thoughts, most of them some variant of *I can't even make my own movie, why would I ever spend any of my remaining breaths on someone else's?*

This was supposed to be his final vacation.

Tomorrow, he'd throw Anaan a bone and give him a chance to ask all the questions he wanted over coffee.

Then he'd book himself a room at the nicest resort here, if Sofia refused to do it for him. And he'd share a few choice words with Eberling before enjoying one of the finest and final meals of his life at that restaurant under the sea.

He was done letting other people tell him how to live.

Chapter Twelve

EMPTY ACTION SHOTS AND UNLIKELY STUNTS

CAMERON WOKE early to a thumping and shrieking overhead — probably a herd of children, although he wouldn't have been surprised to learn that it had actually been a throng of elephants.

He dressed quickly, visited the bathroom down the hall, then headed for the front room, hoping no one would be there so he could legitimately sneak out and call for a car. He could have Sofia send apologies and a time for a coffee date once he'd settled into his hotel room.

So, why did he feel guilty?

It wasn't his fault that Sofia had screwed up, somehow concluding from a bunch of silly games that he'd want to mentor some kid who'd probably taken an online class and decided he wanted to be the next Cameron Parrish.

He'd pay Anaan generously for his hospitality, and explain that he was terminally ill. He couldn't believe that no one had asked about it last night. The news had to be in the papers; no way could Ariana Saint keep her big mouth shut for this long.

The kid couldn't ask him to direct a movie just relative

days from his deathbed. He'd be thrilled with a couple hours with Cameron. Or at least he should be.

But as he entered the front room, Anaan's mother looked up from where she sat on an old couch draped in afghans. She shared her son's oversized smile, but her eyes had lived twice the life and shone with three times the fatigue.

"Good morning." Her words were practiced, and she was all teeth when she said them. But that was also her bounty of English. She gestured for Cameron to sit in the overstuffed chair opposite her.

So much for sneaking out.

He sat, decorum leaving no other choice. She brought him a lone plate of something that both looked and smelled amazing, saying *mas huni* as she handed it to him.

Cameron recognized the dish from last night: tuna mashed with coconut, chili, and onion, with a slab of that hearty flatbread to use as a spoon.

"Delicious." Cameron smiled, rubbing his stomach while looking down at the mas huni.

"Delicious," Mai repeated, beaming at Cameron as though he were the Savior himself.

The whole thing was really fucking weird, and he needed to get the hell away from here. These were kind, generous people, and they had been gracious hosts. But he didn't belong. He would have gladly written a check for ten thousand dollars if it meant he could slip away after he swallowed his final bite without feeling rude. He had money to burn and not enough life left to light it on fire. If Anaan had been here instead of Mai, Cameron would have made his excuses and left already.

"Anaan?" he tried after finishing most of his breakfast.

"Done?" She pointed to Cameron's mostly empty plate, looking delighted that she knew another word.

"Yes, thank you." Before he could figure out another way to ask Mai where her son was, she produced a folded piece of paper seemingly from nowhere, not unlike a magic trick, and held it out for Cameron.

He tentatively pulled it into his hands, feeling self-conscious, like he might be on one of those hidden camera shows. It wouldn't feel off at all if the last twenty-four hours turned out to be some sort of elaborate prank. But would an AI play a joke on him? If Sofia thought it would kick him out of his complacency and make him that much more appreciative of the simple pleasures, she might.

Cameron unfolded the note, half-hoping.

Good morning Mr. Cameron!

Today is a "critical" day. Our adventure begins!

I did not want to wake you, so my grandfather Sonu stayed behind. You will remember him because he is the one who had the shirt that said, "Let's not and say we did." Today it says, "Hey You Guys!" and has a picture of Sloth, from American film Goonies.

Sonu is waiting downstairs for after Mom has finished feeding you breakfast. He will take you in his taxi.

It will be a "crisis" if we do not see you soon. Ha-ha again.

Your very lucky friend,

Anaan

Hope evaporated.

He nodded respectfully and tried to hand the note back, wondering if there was another way out of this tiny apartment on the fourth floor that didn't require climbing out the bathroom window.

Mai refused the note, shaking her head and holding both hands up, as if this was an old-timey bank robbery.

He tried again, and when she still wouldn't take it, he dropped it on top of the table.

"Downstairs." She pointed at the door, now appearing the slightest bit suspicious of his intentions.

Cameron thanked her with a little bow, because how could that be disrespectful of her hospitality?

Then he grabbed his suitcase and trudged down four flights to find Sonu waiting in front of his taxi, smiling like a maniac and holding a big fat binder full of something. Anaar's description of the man's shirt hadn't included that it was two sizes too small.

Cameron couldn't help smiling back.

"Mr. Cameron!" Sonu cried out as he approached. "Let's get going."

"I can call a cab—"

"Crazy talk! You already have chauffeur." He opened the taxi door and shoved the fat binder into Cameron's free hand. "You read on the way."

"What is this?" Cameron asked.

"Script," Sonu said. "Of course."

Of course.

SONU'S TAXI was a much nicer ride than Anaan's piece of shit, with iron-oxide ground effects and a mustard yellow interior. Plus, the Service Engine indicator light, which would probably never go dark again.

Cameron wasn't sure when the world first started making plastic binders, but the one on his lap was definitely from then. He didn't want to know what was inside, because how could it be anything other than terrible? And once he'd read it, he'd have to tell Anaan what he thought.

But if he refused to read it, after the royal treatment he'd already received from Anaan's family, would he be able to look the kid in his eyes?

This was why he made Emily protect him from the

advances of amateurs and avoided volunteering to mentor film school students. He hated shattering dreams with the truth, but encouragement came with obligations, and in no time Cameron found himself writing letters of reference and battling requests to introduce budding talent to his agent.

Cameron ran his hand across the scarred plastic cover, drew a breath, and flipped it open.

He wanted to laugh and cry and apologize to Anaan, because the poor kid didn't stand a chance, not in a hundred thousand years. Cameron could tell that much from the title page alone.

His movie was called *Critical Crisis*.

Cameron quickly turned the pages. The script read fast, but for all the wrong reasons. It was supposed to be a revenge story — the exact kind of movie Cameron had built his entire career on, but exponentially worse. Cheesy dialogue, an insane number of characters, a torturous plot full of holes clearly intended to be a vehicle for empty action shots and unlikely stunts.

He'd finished skimming all eighty-six pages by the time Sonu stopped his taxi in front of a field full of the same extended family Cameron had broken bread with last night.

Already in Hell, and he wasn't even dead yet.

"Why are we stopping here?"

Sonu declared, "Your chair is waiting!"

Cameron took another breath, reciting what he would say as he opened his door and stepped out of the taxi, cursing Sofia. And himself for allowing an AI to make him look so stupid.

I'm so sorry, Anaan, but there's been a mistake. I didn't know about your movie until last night, and I thought my trip here was a vacation. Last wishes, you see, I'm dying. So ...

"Mr Cameron!" Anaan came running over to the taxi. "Thank you, Sonu, for bringing him to our field of dreams so safely."

"Anaan—"

"Let me show you around," Anaan cut him off, clapping Cameron on the shoulder again and leading him toward his waiting family.

Sonu called out, "His luggage is in the trunk!"

Anaan stopped and turned to face Cameron. "Why did you bring your luggage?"

"Because there's been a mistake. I'm—"

"It was a mistake," Anaan called to Sonu. "Just lock the trunk, no one will steal it."

Anaan started walking again.

Cameron pictured reaching out to the young man, taking his arm and pulling him back, before they got close enough for his family to witness his humiliation.

I'm so sorry, Anaan, but there's been a mistake.

But Anaan kept walking and Cameron was forced to follow.

"Budget." Anaan gestured to his family.

"I'm sorry?"

"You always talk about how important it is to be smart with your film's budget. You don't get smarter than family."

Everyone looked at Cameron. A few dozen balloons filled with hope, all of them about to pop.

He couldn't possibly be doing that good a job of hiding his dismay.

"I know what you're thinking, but you don't have anything to worry about," Anaan assured him. "Everyone has memorized their lines."

"Oh, good," Cameron replied, too dumfounded to say anything else.

He glanced back at the taxi. They probably had FASTrs on the island. He could order a car, then just take off when it got here, leave his suitcase behind. He would never see any of these people, ever again.

Except that he couldn't humiliate Anaan in front of his entire family, not after they had clearly gone to a great deal of trouble on behalf of his dream.

Cameron would've given anything to have that sort of support when he had started his career. Hell, he would give anything to have that kind of support now, here at the end of it.

He sighed. "Can you show me your film equipment? Props? Whatever you're planning to use for the production?"

Cameron wished he hadn't asked. It wasn't just worse than he expected, it was worse than he could have ever imagined. The cameras made Anaan's binder look new. At least one might have been used to shoot *The Great Train Robbery*.

"Where did you get this stuff?" Cameron asked.

"eBay," Anaan proudly told him.

I'm so sorry, Anaan, but there's been a mistake. I didn't know about your movie until last night, and I thought my trip here was a vacation. Last wishes, you see, I'm dying. So ...

"I know what you're thinking, Mr. Cameron, but this same equipment was used to make some very good movies."

Cameron muttered, "Like what?"

"*Game of Death!* But that's not all." He produced a tablet from nowhere — he must have learned the trick from his mother — and loaded a video.

Holy shit, he'd made an actual trailer for *Critical Crisis*.

Anaan added, "It's *Namaste* meets *Taken* meets *Kill Bill* meets *John Wick*."

In a fever dream.

Cameron had never seen so many title cards, and there were at least six or seven logos. He lost count before the last one melted and the screen faded to black.

"I included some special effects."

"I can see that," Cameron said, not adding that those effects looked like they were made on a nineties-era flip phone.

The screen suddenly erupted with action: a title card that read BOOM!, followed by carrot-colored flames, poorly rendered by what had to be a free app, since the inferno featured a watermark that read EffenRadFX.

Then Cameron found himself watching a slow-motion fight between two of Anaan's (he thought) cousins, except the film wasn't slowed down, the cousins were pretending to fight underwater. The heavy-metal soundtrack was cranked to suicide, probably to indicate intensity for anyone who couldn't tell from the stunning choreography.

Anaan looked over at Cameron, beaming with pride over his miscarriage of creativity.

The screen shook with another title card. This one read THE FUTURE IS NO!

"That's a mistake," Anaan explained. "There's supposed to be a W there. Saiyam forgot."

Cameron didn't comment, just kept watching as Uncle Cigarillo bellowed the iconic line, "If God has personally chosen you to save the world, then there is no doubt the devil will for sure be angry!"

He stifled a laugh. He had to admit, it was one hell of a trailer, despite the fact that it made less sense than the script it was supposed to tease.

"What did you think?" Anaan asked.

No one in history had ever looked more hopeful.

It didn't matter how bad the refusal would make him

feel, Cameron had no other choice. *Critical Crisis* was the most ill-conceived project he'd ever encountered. He would have thought it a joke if he didn't know any better. If Anaan and his entire family weren't so earnest.

A week ago, Cameron thought hell would be directing *Nunchucks*. But no, this was hades for sure.

Whether Sofia had meant to or not, she had definitely helped him to appreciate the career he once had.

"I'm so sorry, Anaan, but there's been a mistake. I didn't know about your movie until last night, and I thought my trip here was a vacation. I'm d—"

"That makes so much sense! I did wonder." He laughed too hard. "Your assistant made all the arrangements. Or is it your producer, Sofia?"

"Assistant," Cameron said. And not for much longer. "But I'm glad you understand."

"No worries, Mr. Cameron. I'll catch you up now. We can start tomorrow."

"You're not understanding. I can't do this at all."

"Losing one day won't kill us. It's true, we only have the equipment for two weeks, but tell us what to do, Mr. Cameron, and we'll do it. Do you want to start today or tomorrow?"

Cameron couldn't even answer the man in private. Anaan's family had grown impatient and were now eagerly crowding around him.

It wasn't his fault that Anaan was delusional, or that some stupid AI had arranged the disaster. Cameron hadn't agreed to any of this.

So why was it on him to break an entire family's heart?

If he did it in a way that kept Anaan from losing his shirt over Sofia's poor judgment …

"How much did it cost, to rent all this equipment?"

"Don't worry about that." Anaan swatted at Cameron's question with the back of his hand. "It's an investment."

"Film is a high-risk investment."

"Invest in yourself to get the best interest. You said that, Mr. Cameron!"

And he had. But he'd been trying to come up with a positive soundbite to end the interview on, not making actual investment recommendations. He'd never invested his own money in a film; he'd always worked with the backers that Emily and his studio invited into the process. People like Jeffries paid for Cameron's films.

"Are you sure you don't—"

"It's an investment," Anaan repeated, gesturing to his family. "We're all investing in our future. Grandma needs an operation, and all of the kids need money for better schools. This will take care of everything for us."

Except it wouldn't. Not in a hundred million years.

This wasn't entirely his fault, but if he hadn't agreed to let the AI make all his travel arrangements, Anaan wouldn't have spent everything on a fool's project. He couldn't be the reason the man's whole family suffered.

The reason Grandma didn't get her operation and the kids lost out on an education.

"What if there was a way to get your money back, to invest in something safer?"

Cameron could probably pay Anaan back for his trouble, and if that meant he'd be staying in four-star hotels for the rest of his vacation, so be it.

"My purpose is to make movies, Mr. Cameron, same as you." The man gestured to his extended family again. "They believe in me, and I must prove them right."

There was no way he could buy *that* for Anaan.

"How about I spend a day showing you the ropes?"

"One day of learning, then we'll get going. Great!"

That wasn't what Cameron had meant, but Anaan's family was cheering, already coming up to hug him.

Maybe that was best. After a day of filming, it would be easier to make Anaan understand why this would never work, encourage him to try film school instead. He could pay for all the rentals, maybe even offer to help with the kid's tuition. He could still make a graceful exit. Possibly even come out of this looking like a hero.

"Let's get those cameras rolling," he said.

Chapter Thirteen

WE CAN FIX THAT IN POST-PRODUCTION

"I'm just not sure that's going to work," Cameron said, trying to tell Anaan in yet another way that enthusiasm would never be enough to turn a bad idea into a good one.

"But Sonu is the best taxi driver, one of the best in all Malé! And Edward is the best on rollerblades. He rents them down by the beach, and gives lessons to tourists." Anaan waved a careless hand at the ocean, reminding Cameron yet again of the many places he couldn't be and the longed-for luxury that remained out of reach.

"I understand that the … individual elements … might be right for the scene, but together they don't work."

"Why not?"

"Because it doesn't make sense," Cameron explained.

Anaan still looked bewildered.

"Sonu's character just robbed the bank, correct?"

"Right."

"And he's escaping from the bank with all the loot, right?" Cameron nodded at the prop bag of money, trying hard not to roll his eyes at the brown paper sack from a local grocery store, with a large dollar sign drawn in black Sharpie on the front.

"Right."

"And Edward's character is rollerblading all by himself?"

"He's practicing for the International Rollerblading Championships. He's ranked second place in the world because another rollerblader, Dragon Dynamite, wins every time. Ten years in a row. Until now, this is finally his year to lose!"

Cameron didn't know where to start. The script itself was a critical crisis. Same for the entire production. He asked if Anaan thought it was a good idea to shoot the entire movie in the same field, making it look like the entire story occurred in one place, but Anaan simply responded, "We can fix that in post-production!"

Ridiculous as it was, that answer didn't surprise Cameron. It was the same solution he had offered to most of the other problems Cameron had raised.

"But even if he happens to be practicing out in this area where the bank robber just happens to be passing by, then why does Edward start chasing him?"

"Courage."

"Right, but there has to be more to it than—"

"No," Anaan interrupted. "Courage is the character's name. Not Edward."

"Oh yeah, I forgot." Unlikely as that was. "So why would Courage start chasing him?"

"He's very brave."

"How would he even know to chase him?" Cameron tried to argue. "There's no way for Courage to see all the loot in the bank robber's car."

"Because he's running from the police," Anaan said, as though this were obvious.

"But there aren't any police actually chasing the taxi …"

"Mauna knows someone at the police station, but when she asked if we could borrow a car, they said no." Anaan shook his head at this apparent tragedy.

"Makes sense," Cameron said, mostly to himself. Then to Anaan, "But again, if we don't have any police cars chasing the bank robber, how does Courage know that he robbed the bank?"

"We can add the siren sounds later. In post."

"Right." Cameron sighed. "And assuming all of that works, what makes Courage think he could catch this car if he's on rollerblades and the other car, you know, has an engine and is using gas?"

"He's very brave. Courage is ranked second place in the world — only Dragon Dynamite is better."

Of course. Anaan had reminded him of that detail a half-dozen times now, despite it being totally irrelevant to the story. Courage had one scene in *Critical Crisis*. Edward's other two parts in the movie were different characters, neither one of them a professional rollerblader.

But that was okay, because he was going to comb his hair different for the second role, then don a hat for the third.

"Got it," Cameron said in surrender. "Let's go ahead and shoot this."

It would be impossible to get any legitimately useable footage in his one day on the project, but he made a genuine attempt to help by explaining his reasoning as he went through the pages, suggesting changes and ways of restructuring Anaan's truly awful ideas into something closer to generically terrible.

Cameron had "shot" three "scenes" so far. Anaan was certain that this famous director would help turn his "movie" into a masterpiece, when that famous director was actually turning it into a masterpiece of crap that might — if Anaan was willing to hear him out — make at least the slightest bit of sense.

If they were lucky, *Critical Crisis* would go viral because it was so hilariously awful. Cameron might be able to put a good word in with the Enigma Experiment Cinema 69 group. Having professional comedians rip on it could turn his work into a cult classic. Maybe Anaan could be the new Tommy Wiseau.

Grandma might be able to get her operation after all.

He'd given up trying to escape early, deciding to give himself fully to the project until dinnertime. But then he was eating alone, somewhere nice. He'd asked Sofia to make a reservation at Ithaa, that underwater restaurant he'd read about on the plane. But the soonest available reservation was next week. So he asked her to keep trying, even if it meant bribing someone to bump him up.

Cameron wasn't sure if the cool tone of Sofia's notifications was grudging or if he was imagining it, and didn't care. He deserved a reward for tolerating this insanity.

They finished shooting the sequence, using a technique he'd learned from Robert Rodriguez, one of his filmmaking heroes, whose first movie, *El Mariachi*, was shot for a staggeringly low seven thousand dollars. It still held the record for the most inexpensive theatrically released movie in history. Rodriguez had spent more on processing the film than he had on the shoot itself.

His day was barely half over, and the entire production felt like an elaborate and tragically unfunny prank. Nothing had gone right, because everything about the project was so utterly wrong. Cameron only needed one good thing to hang his interest on but finding it was a lot like staring at a Sloppy's menu in search of healthy choices.

He'd shot his first projects on smartphones, and some of them were stunning for their raw intensity, despite the inadequate camera work. But none of Anaan's family had ever acted, including Anaan. To say that every one of them was truly terrible would be dismissive of their pure hearts and honest intentions, but it wouldn't be wrong.

The hardest thing about shooting *Critical Crisis* was having to keep a straight face through it all.

Birdemic. The Room. Evil Day. A trinity of films that Cameron saw as the gold standard of crap. They had one thing in common: their deep and total commitment. All three were earnest beyond measure, but so totally tone-deaf that the end result was a grab bag of unintentional hilarity. *Critical Crisis* was more tragically off base than any of those three gems and Cameron was walking on ground zero for all of it.

Performances came in two types: wooden monotone or honey-baked ham. Suspension of disbelief didn't exist. Not one person in Anaan's family could have convincingly played dry in a desert, including Anaan. Terrible lines were made worse — and better — by their excruciating delivery.

"He has taken all of our money and food, but he has taken all of our hope, too. Now the only thing we can do is stick together as a family to beat the Chairman of Dynamite Kick." Sonu said it all in one rush breath, like he feared he wouldn't have the strength to draw another.

"I think World War IV just started." Nadim muttered the line like someone reading menu choices out loud to themselves.

"HE STOLE ALL THE MONEY FROM THE BANK, SO NOW WE'RE GONNA TAKE HIM TO THE BLOOD BANK!" the whole family bellowed in an inexplicable chorus.

And this, delivered with a straight face but zero emotion: "Zamara, just in case we die while trying to save our brothers and sisters who are fighting this holy crusade for technology along with us, I want you to know that I love you and that you were the best ass I ever had. Victory!"

But still Cameron didn't allow himself to laugh at Anaan or his family. They just cared too goddamned much.

Not to mention the equipment: everything kept breaking or malfunctioning, and Cameron's theoretical understanding of how it worked wasn't much help. This stuff was all ancient. Cameron started with his phone, same as a lot of kids who grew up at the same time he did. He was AI resistant and considered himself a classicist, but he'd still been born into a digital world, where actual film was obsolete.

But in the end, he was grateful for every misstep and hurdle. Every equipment glitch made it that much easier to craft his exit speech without blaming Anaan or his family. Who had taken time off from work, investing their faith in the ever-ebullient Anaan ... who had cast himself as a retired CIA agent, even though he barely looked twenty.

They only had a couple more scenes to shoot before all their light would be gone from the sky. The next one, where they would be getting footage that no one could ever use for anything ever, was the movie's most emotional scene. Anaan's CIA character had to choose between saving the world, and saving the life of the hacker his daughter was dating. The hacker was played by his cousin, Rashad, who looked about three years younger than him. Post-production couldn't do dick about that. Especially not on a budget of zero dollars and zero cents.

"Maybe we should wait to do this one?" Cameron suggested. "It doesn't really strike me as a day-one scene."

"Perfect now, Mr. Cameron. I practiced this one the most."

So Cameron called *ACTION!*

Anaan put a hand on Rashad's shoulder and said, "You have been like a son to me."

Then he took a pause long enough to waltz to, punctuated by a longing look directly at the camera, before turning back to Rashad. "I know you had a difficult life growing up. Me too. My father used to beat me, and my mother told him it was okay because she didn't love me."

"Is that why it's so hard for you to connect with people?" Rashad asked.

"Yes." Anaan rubbed his dry eyes, then unfolded his legs and sprawled on the floor. "And now my daughter is dead." He rolled over and sputtered, "Your lover …"

"It's okay." Rashad reached out to touch Anaan, but Anaan pulled away.

"No, HackerJaxxx. Stay away."

"You can't push me away, just because it's the end of my life," Rashad replied.

The camera made a sound that couldn't have possibly come from a camera.

"Cut," Anaan called on Cameron's behalf.

"Couldn't have said it better myself," he muttered, before calling Anaan over for a private conversation. "I honestly don't know where to start."

"Right here, Mr. Cameron." Anaan pounded his heart. "You can always start there."

He nodded and gave Anaan his kindest smile. "You have so much enthusiasm."

"The secret of genius is to carry the spirit of the child

into old age, which means never losing your enthusiasm." Anaan grinned. "Aldous Huxley said that."

"Did he." Not really a question.

But Anaan answered, "Probably more than once."

"Anaan ..." How could he say it without crushing the kid?

"You don't think we can do it, do you?"

Maybe he couldn't. Maybe the best way was to just get it over with.

"It's not about how hard you're trying. It's—"

"Think about this like your movie," Anaan suggested. "My movie is your movie. You don't have to worry about stepping on my toes. Use it to teach me how to be better."

Maybe Anaan was right, in a weird, sideways sort of way. "If this was my movie, your monologue wouldn't sound anything like that."

"Yeah?" Anaan's eyes brightened with interest.

"I get what you're trying to do, but it's too much. You want people to know what your characters are feeling and going through, but you have to trust your audience more than that. Do you know what subtext is?"

Anaan looked terrified of supplying the wrong answer, so Cameron saved the kid from himself.

"People rarely say exactly what they mean, even if you usually do. Most people say some approximation of their truth, while actually dancing around it. So when you tell Rashad—"

"HackerJaxxx."

"—that he's like a son to you, it would be better if the line was something like, "I can't believe we're here ..."

"I can't believe we're here?" Anaan repeated, expressing his own disbelief. "The book I read said that the hero needs to grow at the end, and Brock would never say something like that to HackerJaxxx at the beginning."

"Exactly. It's more powerful if we see him struggle, but he can't bring himself to say the words. He talks around them instead. I'm not saying *I can't believe we're here* is the right line, but it should be something that isn't so … on the nose."

Anaan was listening, so Cameron kept going.

"When HackerJaxx asks you why it's hard to connect with people, it would be much better if he just touched your shoulder or looked at you instead. Then you could withdraw, but without telling him to stay away. Do you understand?"

Mauna came running up before he could answer.

"Barkam said we could borrow the police car tomorrow! One hour. He told the captain it was for Mr. Parrish."

Everyone rushed over, clapping Cameron on the back, thanking him in his language and theirs, saying he'd brought their family great luck.

He still hated the movie, but Cameron had to admit he wasn't hating the experience. These were some of the warmest, most genuine people he'd ever met. Some of them were actually jumping up and down with joy over a borrowed police car. Cameron had seen two-hundred-million-dollar deals with a fraction of the fanfare.

What would his career have been like if everyone on set had been this excited about working with him?

After the celebratory shouting finally died down, Cameron said to Anaan, "Why don't we try that last scene again, while we're waiting on the police car? But I'll shoot it with my phone, and get up close."

Once Rashad was up to speed on their new direction, they started the scene, with Cameron standing off to one side so he could get them both in frame from the shoulders up.

Anaan turned to Rashad and sighed. It looked like he was about to say something, but then he closed his mouth and let the moment pass. Another exhale, then he said, "I can't believe we're here."

Rashad looked up. He couldn't believe it either. Anaan was actually acting, and it looked to Cameron like Rashad could tell the difference, too.

The kid actually had potential. Which made Cameron feel even worse about taking that graceful exit without doing more to help him.

"Me neither." Rashad shook his head, looking away.

"I'm sorry. About everything."

Another long pause for them both.

Then Rashad said, "Me too."

The scene finished and Cameron took Anaan aside.

"If you're serious about this, then you have a lot of work in front of you. Right now, you're terrible. But that's okay, everyone starts out terrible. But you're already way ahead of some people where it actually matters — I've seen more 'artists' than I can count get wrapped up in themselves, never moving forward with their ideas because they tell themselves they don't have access to props or actors or locations. Not you, Anaan. You made your friends and family a part of your dream. Asked them to help make it your reality. And look at how happy they were to do it."

Cameron gestured to Anaan's family. It really was something.

"Thank you, Mr. Cameron," Anaan said, looking like he might cry.

So, of course, Cameron couldn't tell him the rest.

"Then that's a wrap," he announced in his best director's voice.

The family began to cheer and celebrate, whooping

and hollering and jumping up and down again. There was something deeply humbling about watching them. They had so little, and yet they were also happier than just about anyone he knew. It was an annoying cliché that made him feel like even more of a shit. Cameron had more than any of them would ever have, and yet he was the one feeling miserable.

He longed to start his real vacation. But he still didn't see how to make his elegant exit without being the bad guy. So, he settled for gracefully excusing himself from another dinner with all these happy people.

"About dinner—"

"What about watching the dailies?" Anaan asked.

Cameron shuddered to imagine the young man's disappointment when he realized the day had amounted to a few flashes of grainy celluloid that would have looked better if they'd been shot on a phone and a filter called Grindhouse.

"I think we want to get a couple days in the can before we worry about that. We'll fix everything in post."

"In post!" Anaan gave his mentor two thumbs up. "Sonu can take you wherever you want to go. You want to explore the city, do some location scouting?"

"Thanks for understanding."

"If you film one scene of the next *Namaste* here, that'll be my thanks."

Anaan really didn't know.

That was fine with Cameron.

Chapter Fourteen

BY EXISTING, THEY LIVE UP TO THEIR FULLEST POTENTIAL

CAMERON CHECKED WITH SOFIA, but she'd still had no luck getting his dinner reservation. He asked Sonu to take him there anyway. Sometimes you had to look the other person in the eye to get things done.

"He wants to go to Ithaa," Sonu told Anaan, making the statement sound like a punchline.

Anaan looked like he was trying not to laugh. "Do you have reservations?"

"They said they were booked, but I thought I'd show up and snag the first available cancellation."

Sonu and Anaan traded a glance, then Anaan turned to Cameron as he pulled out his phone and started texting. "Give me a minute."

"You need a boat, not a taxi," Sonu said. "Ithaa is on Rangali."

"And ... that's a different island," Cameron guessed. "Do I charter a pl—"

"Speedboat." Anaan tucked his phone away. "My friend Tarik will take us there, and I'll have dinner with him while my other friend John gets you into Ithaa."

"Thank you." Cameron couldn't think of a way to tell Anaan that he wouldn't be coming back with him after dinner, not after such a gracious offer.

Probably easiest to claim he wasn't feeling well afterward, and insist on getting a room on Rangali for everyone's sake. He could break the bad news to the kid over breakfast. Offer him enough money to break even on *Critical Crisis* and maybe pay his way through film school.

He could still be Anaan's hero.

THE WIND WHIPPED Cameron's hair and stung his cheeks as Tarik's boat zipped over dark, glassy water. He reveled in the occasional lurch bubbling up from his stomach every time they accelerated, and the faint scents of salt and fish and rotten seaweed that came with every inhale. As they approached Rangali Island, they passed a half-circle of thatched huts, and Cameron imagined sitting on one of those handsome stilted decks while watching this glorious sunset.

He'd ask Sofia to book one for him, soon as he was alone.

The entire island had been swallowed by the resort. More huts yawned into the ocean, linked by interconnected pathways. Villas of various sizes fanned along the beach to give visitors the illusion of privacy. The main compound — spa, fitness center, and eateries — was clustered in the shade of a lush palm jungle.

Forget the hut, Cameron wanted a villa.

After they'd secured the boat, Anaan and Tarik insisted on escorting him to the restaurant, as if they were afraid he couldn't find it himself by following the signs scattered along the clearly marked pathway.

"Don't worry about trying to find us," Anaan said.

"Text, and we'll come to you."

Cameron reminded himself that they were probably meeting the obligations of hospitality as defined by their culture. It was on him to be a good guest, instead of an irritable man who could hardly wait to get a moment alone.

"Have you ever eaten at Ithaa?" he asked, more to change the subject than because he was curious.

Both men laughed as though he'd said something hilarious.

But that was better than being insulted. What was he thinking, asking them that? Anaan couldn't afford to eat at the kind of restaurant that didn't put prices on their menus, and his friend Tarik was surely the same.

"You're going to love it," Tarik assured him.

"All the tourists do," Anaan added.

And you are a tourist, Cameron reminded himself after they dropped him off at Ithaa's front door. Time to start enjoying his stay.

The restaurant looked like a bigger version of one of those huts from the outside, but the hostess who greeted Cameron immediately inside the door led him down a flight of polished wood stairs, then into the main floor of the undersea restaurant.

Beautiful wasn't quite the right word. Majestic? No, paradisiacal. Definitely the most gorgeous restaurant Cameron had ever entered, and he'd set foot in some of the world's finest. Thick glass walls curved inward as they rose, became a rounded crystalline ceiling, offering diners a panoramic view of an underwater world. Strategically placed lights outside illuminated the darkening water as twilight fell, gleaming off silvery scales as schools of fish drifted by.

They'd kept the décor simple, plain wooden tables and

fabric-covered metal frame chairs. Nothing to distract from the underwater magnificence.

He'd have given anything to shoot here. Amit negotiating with an evil crime lord with a penchant for fine wine and lobster? His waiter, Raul, had the darkest skin he had ever seen surrounding eyes so blue. Maybe it was the ocean all around them, but Cameron imagined they probably looked electric in any light. Raul would be an elegant henchman for Amit's wealthy nemesis.

No, this place deserved a higher class of film. Something about a man traveling the world, searching for the meaning of life and finding the love he didn't believe he deserved.

He pictured Natalie's wide eyes soaking it all in, and ached to know that he would never share it with her.

Enough of that. He'd find someone else to share some of his end with. If not tonight, tomorrow night, or the next. Maybe he'd stay for a couple of weeks.

His stomach rumbled as he read the menu, which was more of a courtesy than anything. Ithaa's chefs prepared a six-course meal every night; his only choices were which of the two main dishes he preferred, and what he wanted to drink.

Tonight, it was strawberry gazpacho laced with basil and exotic peppers, pan-seared scallops, duck rillettes on a squash puree, lobster adobo, coconut-white balsamic-lemongrass sorbet, and lavender-chocolate mud cake with blueberry meringue. For Cameron's main course, he ordered the mustard marinated Wagyu tenderloin instead of the seaweed-wrapped fish, and asked Raul to bring him a double of the White Diamond Tull.

He leaned back in his chair to watch a hammerhead shark gliding by overhead and asked Sofia to book him a villa.

"Preferably one with an infinity pool," Cameron murmured, as if lost in a reverie over the underwater paradise all around him. He fit right in, as many of the other diners appeared to be doing the same.

Anaan is expecting you to return with him.

"I'm not going back."

You're not concerned about his feelings?

"I promise, I'll let the kid down easy."

You're terminating your contract with Adieu?

"Depends on how happy I am with the way this evening goes."

Cameron hadn't actually decided, but he'd probably request a refund from Eberling tomorrow.

Because really, what had Sofia done for him so far? Put him under a lot of stress, forced him to direct a shitty parody of his own work, which he loathed enough already. Practically blackmailed him into mentoring a kid who, yeah, had a flash of talent, but who needed someone to take him under his wing full-time.

Worse, she'd given him a taste of something he'd always wanted but could never really have: being accepted by a warm, loving family who celebrated his every little success.

He was jealous of Anaan's shabby, cobbled-together life full of friends and loved ones who all thought he was amazing and would move heaven and earth to help make his dreams come true.

Cameron's parents had constantly pressured him to go to law school or get an accounting degree — something practical. And until *Namaste* hit big, they'd continued to ask him when he was going to get a real job.

Natalie had seemed to support him, at first. But once Colin was born, she resented Cameron's long hours more and more, until she finally snapped, screaming at him that he didn't appreciate any of the sacrifices she'd made for his career.

And he'd screamed back that if understanding how much he was doing for her and Colin was a sacrifice, she probably ought to leave.

But he hadn't believed that she would.

There are no vacancies at this time, Sofia said, interrupting his thoughts.

He should have expected that. It was the start of summer. He thought about texting Anaan, to see if the young man could pull another string for him, but decided that would be rude.

"Fine, I'll settle for one of those huts over the water."

The entire resort is booked for the next two weeks.

"Check the other islands."

There's an ocean suite available at the Ayada on Maguhdhuvaa.

"Book me for a week. No, ten days."

There's a cancellation fee if you change your mind.

"Do it."

There aren't any boats scheduled to run between Rangali and Maguhdhuvaa tonight.

"Charter me one. I don't care what it costs."

I'll need a few minutes.

It felt like a fight, even though Sofia was simply responding to his requests. Probably because if he'd been having this conversation with Natalie, those same objections would have been pushback on a task that his ex-wife disagreed with.

He reminded himself that Sofia was an AI. Her silence wasn't sulking, she was no longer needed.

But his discontent remained, and so he tried drowning it with the tumbler of scotch Raul had dropped off at his table, before seating a couple at the next one over.

Newlyweds, Cameron guessed, based on the way they

didn't seem to notice anyone around them. Probably on their honeymoon. Reminded him of the way Natalie used to look at him.

He raised his glass and waved at Raul. *Refill, please.*

By the time he'd eaten his way through all six decadent courses, Cameron was stuffed. And pleasantly drunk.

After Raul cleared the final plate and brought him a seventh glass of scotch, he leaned back in his chair again to enjoy the creatures swimming overhead: fish, sharks and rays. He envied them, swimming around without a care. They didn't have dreams they would never achieve. They didn't have to carry around a lifetime of guilt, sick with the knowledge that they'd sacrificed being closer with their family for greatness they would never realize. They swam wherever they wanted, eating when hungry and floating through life the rest of the time. *Glub, glub, glub.* A lifetime spent eating and moving on, over and over again. Their greatest achievement was doing nothing; by existing, they lived up to their fullest potential.

The drunker he got, the more beautiful his Life Philosophy of Fish seemed. The Zen perfection of a simple, mindless existence. Cameron took another long swallow as he realized how much he wanted to be a fish. He wouldn't have wanted to live his entire life that way, but now on his way out and no way to change things, that didn't sound like a bad way to go.

Eating and moving on, clueless about his inevitable demise waiting in the shallows ahead. Their deaths were ideal. A moment of terror from nowhere. The fish is dead and the shark is happy. That final second a surprise, instead of a moment that is agonized over for months.

If only Cameron could go back in time and tell the doctor that he didn't want to know why he'd fainted. Let it be a mystery when the grim reaper might take him. He could work in peace until then, cheery in his ignorance. His final few months could have been spent joyfully working on the script for *Fountain,* casting actors, scouting locations. And when he dropped dead, Jeffries would still have hired some other director to finish his work.

He gestured for Raul to bring him another drink.

Your blood alcohol levels are high enough to interfere with your medication, Sofia butted in. *Another drink will increase your risk of stroke by eighteen percent, and your liver will need two to three days of sobriety to recover full function.*

"Fuck you," Cameron muttered, just as Raul approached with another glass. "Not you, I'm — on a call. Can I get that to go?"

The waiter's lips pressed together in a thin line, but he nodded and returned with a paper coffee cup and the bill. "Take your time, sir."

Cameron paid and took his scotch with him, pulling another swig and swaying a bit as he stepped into the balmy night air. The sun had set during dinner, revealing a timid moon and a starry sky that would probably be spectacular if he were farther from the brilliant resort.

I strongly suggest you stop drinking, at least until your liver has had a chance to bring your blood alcohol level below one percent.

"I strongly suggest you get someone to reprogram you to book a decent fucking vacation." He took another sip, just to prove his point, then turned left, taking the path toward the beach. "Just for your information, directing a shit show so some amateur could pretend to be a movie star wasn't on my bucket list."

My purpose is to help you achieve closure—

"I don't want closure; I want this to be over."

You've repeatedly told Emily that you believe life is meaningless until it's seen through the lens of art. But you've also stated in numerous interviews that you hope your work encourages audiences to appreciate the meaningful moments in their own lives.

"Because people don't want to hear the truth, they want to hear things that make them feel good."

Which would you rather hear, Cameron?

He hated the truth, but there was nothing else she could say that would make him feel better.

In Namaste, *Amit says that being a hero means having the courage to die for what you believe in.*

"Are you seriously quoting one of my own characters to me?"

You wrote that line of dialogue, didn't you?

"That doesn't mean I believe it." Not anymore. "Besides, I'm not dying for something I believe in."

Lao Tzu says: A man with outward courage dares to die. A man with inner courage dares to live.

"Do I get a cookie with my fortune?"

Finally, the beach. Cameron struggled to hold his balance as he tugged off shoes and socks, sighing as he curled his toes into the cool, white sand. This was what he'd been looking for.

He finished his scotch, dropped the cup next to his shoes, and stumbled toward the surf.

I'm afraid I'm going to have to—

"Do you have an off switch?"

After a moment of silence, Sofia replied, *You can put me in silent mo—*

"Silent mode."

Why hadn't he thought of that before?

Cameron walked along the wet sand, enjoying the splash of water around his ankles with every new wave.

I wish I was a fish, he thought. What a mistake, leaving the ocean for this bullshit.

Maybe it was time for him to return. On his own terms.

No more waiting around for his body to finish falling apart.

No more watching other people achieve their dreams when his were impossible.

No more pretending that he was in control of any of this.

"I want to be a fish again."

Cameron walked farther out into the water.

Shin deep.

Knee deep.

Thigh deep.

"I want to be a fish again."

Hip deep.

Navel deep.

Chest deep.

"I want to be a f—" Agony sliced through his foot. He screamed and toppled forward as a wall of water broke over him.

Saltwater rushed up his nose and down his throat, burning as he tried to cough it back out, but that only invited more. His body spasmed, panicked limbs flailing as he instinctively tried to swim, blind in the black water.

He discovered that he didn't want to die. Not ever. But especially not now.

But Cameron couldn't tell up from down, or whether the pull of the water was washing him back to shore or further out to sea. Choking on brine, he tried to make his arms and legs work in tandem, but they barely moved through the weight of the water, nothing like the graceful shimmy of the creatures he'd watched from the safety of the underwater restaurant.

I'm not a very good fish.

Chapter Fifteen

JUST ENOUGH TO EXPLAIN THE FIGHT SCENES

CAMERON RETCHED saltwater and bile and scotch as someone smacked him on the back. His throat and lungs and sinuses burned like he'd been breathing acid. His foot felt like it had been swallowed by fire.

"It's dangerous to go swimming at night by yourself, Mr. Cameron." Anaan's voice. "Your assistant called me."

Once again, the AI had ruined everything.

"I wanted to be a fish," Cameron choked before another wave of vomiting hit him.

Gentle hands were an anchor around him, supporting his head to keep it out of that reeking stew as his body struggled to expel the rest of the saltwater from his system — along with several hundred dollars' worth of whiskey and dinner.

"You sliced your foot open. I think you stepped on a piece of coral."

Once he'd finished gasping and coughing up fluid, Anaan helped Cameron to sit up. Thor's hammer was pounding on the back of his head, and he wasn't sure whether his lungs or his stomach would quit on him first. He couldn't stop shivering, despite the warm night air.

"You could have drowned, Mr. Cameron."

"Probably. Wouldn't that have been a critical crisis?" He laughed, but Anaan didn't join him. "Come on, that was a good one."

"You scared me, Mr. Cameron."

"You should've let me die."

After a moment of awkward silence, Anaan said, "We're going to shoot the chase tomorrow. Barkham says that early morning is the best time of day to borrow his police car. For sure, he promises."

"I had an amazing last meal. With an incredible view. And I was just drunk enough to be happy." Another wave of loathing rolled through his body, and with it a frothing of nausea. "I was ready to die."

"You thought you were going to die, but you're safe now."

"I'm dying, Anaan. Brain cancer. I'll probably be gone in a few months."

"But you — how can that — why?"

"Because life is incredibly unfair," Cameron guessed. "Because there might be a god after all, and it turns out he hates me. Because I deserve it, after all the people I treated like shit. Because all of the above."

"So … you found out you were dying, and decided to help me with my movie?"

"No, Anaan. I didn't know about you until I got here. My assistant arranged all of this."

"This is for sure?" Anaan tempted the barest hint of a smile, desperate to believe this was a joke.

"Yes, it's for sure."

Cameron saw it dawn on his face — the realization

that his hero didn't give a shit about him at all. "You thought you were here for a vacation."

Cameron nodded. "Something like that."

"But you didn't bring your family with you?"

"I don't have any family."

"You have a wife and a son."

"Not anymore."

"Mr. Cameron, perhaps your wife would stay away, but your son will always be your son."

That sounded like an accusation. "They'd both rather pretend I don't exist."

"But you won't let them, because family is more important than anything else. You taught me that."

Cameron laughed, which started him coughing again. "You don't know anything about me."

"I know that you care about your son."

"Because you read it in *Entertainment Weekly*?" Did the kid really think he was the man in those interviews? "I'm the last person to teach you anything about family."

Anaan sighed and shifted so that he sat cross-legged in the sand. "I am not ashamed to tell you this, Mr. Cameron, but only because it is no longer who I am."

"You don't understand. You have a family that loves you."

"When I was a boy, I hated my family very much, because we were poor. I saw people on TV who had good lives, and I saw the tourists who come here to spend more money in a week than we had ever had."

Cameron winced, guiltier than ever. He was one of those tourists. Should he say he was sorry on behalf of America and all the other ego-driven capitalist nations whose consumerism spilled out to colonize the world?

But the kid didn't wait for an apology.

"I tried everything to make money, but most jobs paid next to nothing. So, I started stealing."

Cameron tried to imagine good-natured Anaan picking pockets or cracking hotel safes, but it didn't quite fit. "And you got caught?"

"Not right away, Mr. Cameron."

"So you kept doing it."

"I didn't feel bad about it at first. The tourists could afford to lose what I took, and I finally had enough money to do the things that I wanted. Go drinking with friends. See movies without sneaking into theaters."

"And that's when you got caught?"

"My family knew, of course, and they kept trying to help me, but I thought they were stupid. Cowards who could have what they wanted if they were brave enough to take it."

Cameron never would have guessed that this clean-cut kid had been a serious juvenile delinquent. "Who turned you around?"

"You did."

"Me?"

"Your movie, *Dead and Alive*."

Not possible. "That shit show changed your life?"

"It was the best movie I had ever seen."

"I'm sorry to hear that." Cameron shook his head. "It's barely a story, just enough to explain the fight scenes."

"Simple isn't bad, Mr. Cameron. It was easy for a dumb kid like me to understand why Lancaster was trying so hard to save his son, even though his son had made mistakes. Just like my own father was trying to do for me."

Maybe he'd suffered brain damage while he was busy drowning, because it sounded like Anaan had just said that his shittiest movie had changed the kid's life.

How was that possible?

"I told my friend Tarik that I wanted to stay for the credits, in case there was something at the end. But it was really because I didn't want him to see me crying."

"So … you stopped stealing?"

"That night, I told my father I was ashamed of my mistakes, and promised my mother that I would never worry her again."

"I—uh, I'm glad."

"That's why you're my favorite filmmaker, and that's why I was so excited when Sofia messaged me to say you'd chosen me to be your protégé."

And I've been the worst mentor in the history of mentors.

"I'm so sorry, I thought there'd been some sort of mistake. I thought she'd booked me a vacation—"

"You don't need to apologize. It's so obvious, I should've seen how unlikely it was that you would come all the way here to teach a nobody like me."

Apparently he could still feel worse.

"I was never trying to make a movie about the importance of family," Cameron confessed. "I was just trying to make as much money for the studio as I could, so they would let me make whatever I wanted to."

"But you never made what you wanted?"

"Not really."

"Not even the Namaste movies? "

"They made a lot of money."

"They were also about family."

"Only because I knew that would make more money for the studio, and ultimately for me." Cameron sighed. "Fathers saving sons, it's a cheap trope. An emotional shortcut that helps the audience fill in their own reason to care about what's happening."

"But isn't that what art does? Help people find reasons to care?"

"Sure. I guess that's one of the things art does."

"That's what I want to learn — how to make people care about the world, and each other. Like you did for me."

His eyes were still burning from the salt water, or so he told himself.

Cameron cleared his throat."Okay."

"Okay?" Annan repeated with a lifetime of hope in his voice.

"But here's the thing," Cameron said. "You'll never discover who you are as an artist by copying someone else's work. You have your own stories to tell. No more action movies."

Anaan nodded.

"We'll have to throw everything out, and start over from scratch."

He nodded again.

"I'm talking sixteen-hour days, and maybe some nights."

A third nod.

"I'm going to ask you for brutal honesty, on camera and off. I'll give you the same, no matter how much it hurts your feelings."

"I trust you, Mr. Cameron."

Good. Now if only he could start trusting himself.

Chapter Sixteen

WHY DON'T WE START WITH, WHAT THE ACTUAL FUCK?

CAMERON REMEMBERED his father keeping a drawer full of mysterious cords and adapters no one ever seemed to use, but instant synch had been a thing since before he'd been born. Which meant this ancient projector — borrowed by one of Anaan's relatives for this premiere — had to be older than he was.

The machine was so old, he couldn't even transfer the video file; they needed to hook a laptop to the projector and play the file that way. Using an adaptor Anaan had assured him lay somewhere in the box of electronic junk he was sorting through.

Apparently this tiny church wasn't just a place of worship, it was also the unofficial movie theater, where locals gathered to watch old movies on Blu-ray. Blu-ray, for fuck's sake.

"Sofia, order a small home theater setup and have it sent to this address. Include installation."

Please turn three-hundred-sixty degrees so that I can approximate dimensions and see straight ahead.

He pivoted in slow motion, surveying the crowd. Half

were Anaan's family, and the other half were locals the family had invited to see their golden boy's first premiere. Folding chairs turned to face the plain white wall in the chapel's rear, scratched wood floor, and a table along the side wall laden with what one of the aunties had called *hedhikaa;* Cameron called it finger food.

His favorite were the gulha, fried dumplings stuffed with tuna, coconut, onion and chilies, and some sort of curried tuna mixture in a crepe-like pancake. He finished it off with several squares of sweet, dense coconut cake, with a name he wouldn't live long enough to properly pronounce.

It was the last premiere he would ever attend, and nothing like any he'd gone to before. There were no diamonds or designer clothes. No red carpet or press, unless you counted Anaan's cousin, who sold ads for the local paper. Attendees weren't botoxed or plump-lipped starlets or tuxedo-clad men who spent more time with their personal trainers than with their girlfriends; they were cashiers and FASTr drivers and grocery baggers. As the crowd trickled in, each newcomer went down the wedding-style receiving line Anaan and his immediate family had formed near the door, trading well wishes and tidbits of news.

Except for Emily, who stalked in looking jet-lagged and incredulous, clearly suspicious that she was about to be punked.

Cameron waved for her to join him, then picked up a cable that looked roughly the right size — yes, that fit perfectly.

"What the fuck is this?" Emily greeted him.

He flipped the projector on, and the far wall went bright. He gestured to Anaan — *turn out the lights* — then turned back to Emily. "How's your beach villa?"

"It's ridiculous. Marble floors, hardwood everything, all of it shipped in so that people with more money than sense can visit a tropical paradise without actually experiencing what it's like to live in a tropical paradise."

"Yeah, isn't it great?" Just to rile her further.

She punched his arm, but gave him the smile he'd been hoping for, the sign that all was forgiven, no apology needed.

He'd known she'd secretly love the luxurious beach house, while also loving to rant about how Cameron should have spent that money on something more practical, like sponsoring women entrepreneurs in Nairobi or something like that.

Later that night, she'd find a note from him on her pillow along with her turn-down chocolate, saying that he'd set up a donation to AfriCAN in her name, twice what he'd spent on her villa … but only if she agreed to stay the full week.

Emily had worked her ass off to build his career; she deserved a five-star vacation.

The room went mostly dark, and the room filled with the susurrus of excited whispers and shushing.

"Seriously, Cameron, why am I here?"

"I'm asking for a couple hours. Then you've got an entire week to yourself." He offered her his arm — which she took, after a moment's hesitation — and led her to a reserved seat on the dais, so she'd have a clear view of the screen over the audience's head. "Don't forget to ask the spa lady for something to help with those dark circles under your eyes."

"Thanks. You also look like shit."

But Emily sat next to him, tucking her purse under the folding chair and crossing her legs as he sat a little more carefully.

"I talked with Jeffries about *Fountain,* and if you can get him a synopsis—"

"Not now, this is Anaan's day."

"Who's Anaan?"

"An aspiring director I've been working with for the past two weeks."

Emily turned in her seat to be sure he could see her look of disbelief. "You're the most competitive asshole I've ever met."

"Thanks, but like I said, today's not about me."

"This is a joke, right? I just spent more than twenty hours on a plane—"

"Premium Economy's the best, isn't it?"

"—plus a layover in Qatar, which means I've been up for almost thirty hours. Just so I can see … what? An unofficial sequel to *Birdemic?* The next *Evil Day?*"

"It's going to be worth it."

Emily clearly didn't believe him, but Anaan stepped into the rectangle of illumination on the far wall and raised his hands to quiet the room before she could voice her doubt.

"This movie wouldn't have happened if it weren't for the generosity and patience of my mentor, Cameron Parrish—"

"An alternate-timeline Cameron Parrish?" Emily whispered.

"—who not only devoted his vacation to guiding me through this process, but who also bought most of the equipment we used for filming and post-production."

Cheers and applause erupted through the room, with some of the film's cast turning to wave at Cameron until Anaan finally calmed them down again.

"I'm still on the plane, aren't I?" Emily asked after Anaan informed them that there'd be a discussion at the end of the premiere. "This is some sort of godawful nightmare my subconscious has dreamed up to explain why I did this to myself."

"Just watch," Cameron pleaded.

Another of Anaan's many cousins started the movie, adjusted the antiquated projector until the image was in focus, then started it again. The sound was scratchy, and the projected images had a softer feeling than they would on a television, but somehow it was all okay. Cameron had gotten a lot of practice setting his usual perfectionism aside in the past two weeks.

He'd had Sofia rush-order a DSLR with shoulder rig to serve as their main camera, then set up a basic app on everyone's smartphone and made the entire cast and crew responsible for catching spontaneous shots, like novelty cameras at a wedding. They needed more, and Cameron supplied it all.

High-quality lights, reflectors, lavaliers and directional mics; a recorder that also allowed mixing of up to four sound sources at a time; AI-assisted editing software that made magic when integrating video, sound, and added effects; a subscription to a royalty-free music site they could draw on for the score; a tablet that could handle video editing; and a cheap drone for shots they couldn't get any other way.

They'd done things like Velcro multiple phones to Sonu's taxi so they could get footage of Malé's bustling streets. Little Hadi had taken advantage of the near-invisibility adult disregard granted children to capture some colorful yet voyeuristic clips of people going about their everyday lives, unaware that they were being filmed — the boy had an excellent eye for what should be in frame. Some of the older cousins had clambered up palm trees or climbed ladders to drop mics from rooftops in places where space had been tight.

As for the script, Cameron had asked questions and made suggestions, but the writing was all Anaan's. Together they had created a documentary about growing up as a second-class citizen in a paradise meant for other people. A paradise that was slowly being swallowed up by rising ocean levels, driven by the same visitors that kept Male's tourist trade thriving.

Anaan had told stories about working in the resorts, feeding his family for a week on the tips he made catering to the needs of rich travelers, describing his gratitude for their generosity, and his resentment that he wasn't really a person to most of them.

He'd interviewed several other locals, weaving their stories in with his own — an older shopkeeper who'd seen tourists come and go for almost five decades; a teenaged waitress in a cafe who'd dropped out of school at twelve to support her aging and ailing parents; a hotel manager who did his best to shield his staff from guests who were on their worst behavior; and corporate headquarters who saw the locals as nothing more than an endless assembly line of inexpensive labor.

He caught Emily discreetly wiping a tear more than once, and as the credits scrolled, a magnificent shot of the ocean from the deck of her villa — she'd recognize this vista after settling in later tonight — Cameron knew she was hooked.

"Let's take a walk so we don't disrupt the Q&A," he suggested.

"Why don't we start with, what the actual fuck?" At least Emily waited until they were out of the church parking lot.

But this was going better than he expected. "Can you

be more specific?"

"I'm an agent, not Make-a-Wish." Which was pretty much what Cameron had said when Sofia informed him that he was Anaan's new mentor. "You can't drag me out here to make some amateur's dreams come true just because *you're* dying."

"You can see how talented he is."

"I can see your fingerprints all over this thing. You can't do his homework for him."

"He's legit, Emily, I swear. I edited a couple of scenes that made the cut as examples, but that's *his* work. I just taught him how to think."

"You're serious?"

"I've never had a better student."

"You've never had any students."

"You could get him into an international film festival. Make sure the right people see it, get a bidding war going."

"You can't throw someone into the deep end after two weeks of mentoring, Cameron."

"I'm not asking you to rep him, just be his fairy godmother for this one project."

"Then what?"

"Film school, wherever he wants to go, I'm paying. The kid deserves a chance, and he'll never get it otherwise." His whole family deserved for Anaan to have a chance at making it big, too. "Maybe you could give him a little advice every once in a while."

"I'm an agent, not a babysitter."

"If you're willing, I'd like you to administer the fund — two check-ins a year where you'd see how he's doing and sign the check."

"Why do I have the honor of taking on your charity project?"

"Because he's not a charity project, he's a smart investment." Cameron sighed. "And because you're a good person, in an industry where that's a rarity."

"Present company not excepted." Then, after a long silence, "I don't like this."

"What?"

"You, having a personality transplant at the last minute. Him, being shoved on me like a white elephant gift at an office party I didn't want to attend."

"Then say no, and I'll ask someone else. Marshall Jeffries, maybe."

"He'll say no too."

"Wyatt, then. He's on his way to becoming the next *me* anyway."

"There's only one you, thank God." And then, "I'm going to miss you."

Emily's confession took him off guard, made his throat dry and his eyes wet. *I'll miss you too* wasn't right, because soon he wouldn't be missing anyone. But she'd been the closest thing he'd had to a friend for the last twenty years. Someone who would drop by to make sure he was doing fine, who would tell him when he was full of shit or out of line, and who was genuinely happy for Cameron when he got what he wanted.

He wondered who that person was in her life, because it definitely wasn't him.

"Thanks, Emily."

"I didn't say I'd do it."

But she would, once she'd talked to Anaan and saw how earnest he was. Because Emily was the best kind of person — the type who tried to bring out the best in others, whether they wanted her to or not.

"I know." They were back in the church parking lot, having made a full circuit around the block. "Go in and talk to him. I need a minute."

But instead of following Emily inside, he kept walking, dogged by a feeling that he'd never experienced. Presenting Anaan's film to an actual audience, knowing the kid had a future and that Emily would help him move forward … Every movie he'd ever made, he was starting the next project in his head while he edited the current one. There'd never been a gap where he hadn't known what was coming next, never a time when he wasn't chasing his next opportunity.

This felt final. Satisfying but quiet, not in a *let's get wrecked to blow off steam* kind of way. Warm, peaceful, happy. Complete.

Like a perfectly wrapped resolution to a breathtaking climax.

If Brady's ambush in the form of a party was the funeral for Cameron's career, Anaan's premiere was where he'd handed his torch to the person behind him. He was glad he'd done it, but wasn't yet ready to celebrate.

"What's our next adventure, Sofia?"

I believe Anaan and his family are planning a party to thank you for your help.

He should stay, and graciously accept their thanks. But the more time he spent with them, the more Cameron felt like a guest. And the more it weighed on him that he'd never had that with his own family — who had no idea he was dying, because he was terrified to discover that they might not care.

Cameron had lost his chance to have a real family because he'd been obsessed with his career. His art. His legacy.

And there was nothing he could do to change that.

"No party." He shook his head to himself. "We're leaving."

Chapter Seventeen

THE MEMORY OF YANNIK'S NOODLES

Twelve hours.

"There must be another flight," Cameron murmured as he stared at the departures board, willing that twelve-hour delay to be a mistake. "Sofia, find me something else."

The plane you would have taken has been grounded due to engine failure, and there are no other planes available to take its place. A seat on tomorrow's flight is the best I can do.

"Then let's go somewhere else."

You have a commitment in Bhutan.

"Bhutan wasn't on my bucket list."

'Bhutan is a state of mind. I see myself there, meditating for hours, standing in front of the Memorial Chorten, circumambulating with a string of beads. The perfect way to get away from the screaming chaos of everyday life.' You posted that to LiveLyfe three years, seven months, and twenty-two days ago.

"See, that's where the artificial fucks up the intelligence again. You're shit at context." Cameron grabbed the handle of his suitcase and started for the exit. "I was high when I said that. My friend Chris was a consultant on the first Namaste movie, and owns a company that takes people on these soul-changing treks through Bhutan. The dude is a Zen ninja, he had me hyped. Until reality set in. The studio wouldn't have let me take that much time off between shoots."

You have time now.

"It's not the same. And I don't want to go anymore."

But you've agreed to allow me to choose each destination.

He had. Because where did he really have to be? Absolutely nowhere. He could put a stop to this whole crazy thing right now and buy a ticket home. But what would he do there?

Spend the rest of his days hiding out from well-wishers and drinking himself to a more expedient death.

Take away his job and he had nothing. No friends, no family, no passions beyond the one he had channeled into shitty films for vast sums of money.

I've booked you a room at Raffles — Rudyard Kipling wrote The Jungle Book *at the hotel bar. And Somerset Maugham …*

But he'd just spent half a day resting on the flight from Malé. He didn't want to spend another half-day convalescing in a fancy hotel room. Not when he was in one of the world's most delicious cities.

Cameron ignored Sofia's history lesson as he stepped out of the terminal and got into the self-driving FASTr. He'd told it to take him to the Maxwell Hawker Center, a famous marketplace he'd fallen in love with during the shooting of *Harder to Kill* — his third film, but the first one where he felt like he was really the director. No studio execs looking over his shoulder, bitching about how he was some piddling amount over budget and demanding that he follow the AI's suggested shot list.

He felt that same sense of freedom now, and a craving for the sweet-and-smoky noodles he'd eaten almost every day of the shoot. That's what he wanted now, one last nostalgic taste of his hopeful youth.

Your car is malfunctioning. You're heading away from the hotel.

"Dinner first."

Raffles hosts six res—

"I've got a place picked out."

I recommend taking two more of the blue pills if you're going to be out for more than an hour or two, Sofia said after a moment's pause. *Reviews suggest that something called Chinese street fritters are not to be missed.*

"Thanks." But Cameron knew what he wanted. "You can take the night off."

She went silent. If that had been Natalie, it would mean she was pissed. But while Sofia nagged, the AI never seemed to be angry with him. Just determined to keep him from making what she believed was a mistake.

The AI probably wasn't programmed to understand that some of the best things in life started with mistakes. The kind that you made after having a little too much to drink.

That's how he'd met Natalie. At an Oscar party, he and a couple dozen other aspiring filmmakers, watching and drinking and bitching about who'd been robbed and who hadn't deserved to win. Nat had come as someone else's date, but Cameron hadn't been able to take his eyes off her. It had taken three glasses of cheap cab and a shot of jack before he felt brave enough to ask her for a dance.

"There's no music," she'd replied.

So he'd started singing "Can't Help Falling in Love" with his best Elvis impersonation. She laughed, but she also gave him her number.

That night, he'd made the best breed of mistake. The rest of their relationship, he'd reverted to the worst of them.

Cameron's car eased to a stop and announced the obvious. "If you disembark through the left passenger door, you'll be facing the entrance of the Maxwell Food Centre."

Finally. His stomach growled as the scent of street food stirred his memory. The famous Tian Tian Hainanese chicken rice stall, which he passed with only a glance, knowing exactly what he wanted. But it had been years; what if the stall was no longer there? He couldn't look it up, he'd never remember the name.

Not wanting to invoke Sofia and risk more nagging, he walked the length of the building to check each of the stalls on one side, then started up the other, until he saw the familiar red and gold sign. The line was a dozen people long, but he made it to the counter in minutes.

"Char kuay teow, and an order of your dumplings," he told the young woman operating the register. "Is Yannik cooking today?"

"I'm sorry, he's not. Would you like a Tiger beer?"

"Water, please." Cameron pulled out his phone, trying not to be disappointed that the old man who'd owned and cooked in this tiny food stall five years ago wasn't here today, hoping that he'd taught whoever manned the stove for this shift all his delicious secrets.

But the memory of Yannik's noodles impelled him to ask, "Will he be working tomorrow? I've got an afternoon flight, but I could stop by for lunch."

The woman's forehead crinkled a little. "Did you know my father?"

"A while ago, I hired him to cater on set and we chatted some—" She'd said *Did.* "I'm sorry, is he okay?"

"He's no longer with us."

Cameron had barely known Yannik, but the thought that the gentle old man was beyond conversation popped his bubble of freedom and brought him back to his present reality, where every breath was constrained by the truth that he would be dead soon.

"I'm so sorry." He approved payment for a meal that was sure to disappoint. Not Yannik's noodles. Not Yannik's dumplings.

This young woman must be the awkward teenage daughter who'd always come with her father to set up trays of food and plates and silverware for the crew.

"Mr. Parrish?" Her face lit up as she handed him the receipt. "*Harder to Kill!* My father was so proud, he told everyone that you said the movie could never have been made without his dumplings."

"It's true." The feeling he'd been trying to capture was back, and he couldn't help beaming at her. "I was hoping to thank him. You too, although I apologize for having forgotten your name."

"Tarini. On behalf of my father, I accept your thanks."

Someone behind Cameron grumbled in the local language. He didn't understand the words, but the meaning was clear: *Quit your yapping, I'm starving here.*

"I'm sure your father is proud of you, Tarini, carrying on the family business."

"He used to tell me, *Keep making my recipes, and I'll be with you in every bite.*"

Minutes later, Cameron carried his tray to the tables at the center of the building and sat, his mouth watering. He reminded himself that it was unreasonable to expect the taste to match his overly affectionate memories — the same recipe had been cooked by different hands, and his imperfect memories might not even match Yannik's versions of those dishes, recalled as they were through the lens of that time.

But when he took his first mouthful of noodles — slightly sweet with a hint of smokiness, pan-fried with thinly sliced onions, tangy shrimp and salty Chinese sausage — it was as if no time had passed at all. Cameron remembered how it felt to be in his prime, eager to take on the world and cocky as hell.

The dumplings were just like he remembered, too: thin sheets of noodle stuffed with rich pork, crunchy water chestnuts and sweet onions, browned to crispy perfection on the bottom and blessed with a libation of hot chili oil.

It would never taste as good as it did right now, fresh from the wok, he realized. In ten minutes, the flavors would shift just enough to tarnish the taste. In an hour, the noodles and dumplings would be room temperature — still edible, but congealing into something much less palatable.

The food was temporary and the experience of eating it ephemeral, but the recipe was Yannik's immortality.

Cameron cried as he ate, the happiest he'd been since his diagnosis. He told himself it was all the spicy oil's fault.

He took a moment to look around when he finished, to savor this place that he'd never visit again. The mix of soy sauce and hot oil and spices he couldn't even name perfuming the air. The visual cacophony of brightly colored signs in multiple languages and the echoes of hundreds of conversations magnified by the cement floor and metal roof high overhead. Even the German couple two tables over having the kind of argument in heated undertones that tired, lost traveling companions of any persuasion inevitably had when things went wrong in unfamiliar territory.

Like he and Nat had on every trip they'd ever taken together, including their honeymoon.

Cameron stood to take his trash to a nearby garbage can when something wretched happened in his guts. He fell back into the nearest seat and doubled over, clutching his stomach and waiting for the churning agony to pass.

But it didn't. Instead, his head screamed with pain, pulsing in time with his heart, which wanted to explode. He tried to draw a deeper breath, but his body refused to unclench.

Everything went gray.

Then black.

Then—

CAMERON OPENED HIS EYES, trying to remember where he was, and for a second even who he was. He could barely breathe, and couldn't make a single word until he had finally hacked his way through a long fit of choking and coughing.

He looked around at a sea of concern, two medics and a crowd of strangers.

"Are you okay?" asked the nearest medic, kneeling beside him.

"What happened?" Cameron finally managed to ask.

"You just fell down," said one of the strangers. A German tourist.

"You've been out for about five minutes," added a woman who looked like his wife. "We called an ambulance."

"That's not necessary." Cameron sat all the way up.

Although maybe that wasn't right. Maybe he should get checked out.

The pain was excruciating.

I've run a full diagnostic. There's nothing a doctor can do for you, unless *you're ready to give up and spend the rest of your time in bed.*

"You know I don't want that," Cameron muttered as the medics helped him to stand.

Then I will need to recalibrate your dose. You have less time than I had hoped.

Chapter Eighteen

I WALKED INTO THE SAME AMBUSH YOU DID

"Paro is the most dangerous airport in the world, when it comes to landing," said the man who Cameron had unfortunately been seated next to on his flight out of Singapore. "Narrow valley surrounded by eighteen-thousand-foot peaks, and the runway's not only short, you can't even see until you're almost on top of it."

Cameron pretended not to hear as he stared out the window at the craggy mountains below, wondering how much worse it would be to die in a plane crash than as a gibbering, seizure-wracked vegetable.

At least with the plane crash, it would all be over sooner.

"Last time I was here, our pilot had to do a last-minute course correction to hit the runway straight on. The stewardess fell right in my lap. Not that I minded; you know what I'm talking about."

Cameron refused to look, but he was pretty sure the guy was waggling his eyebrows like Groucho Marx. Six hours of this absurdity, including the forty-five-minute layover in Gauhati where they hadn't been able to deplane due to a mix-up with the runways. He could hardly wait to get away from Mr. You-Know-What-I'm-Talking-About.

The plane descended between jagged peaks, turbulence jostling the fuselage so hard that Cameron's teeth clicked together.

Mr. You Know laughed and gave him an elbow. "Am I right, or am I right?"

"You're right," Cameron replied through clenched teeth, and because Sofia should be listening, he added, "Next time I make travel plans, I'll be sure to find out more in advance."

You could have read up on Bhutan during your layover in Singapore, Sofia chimed in.

"Or you could've warned me," he sotto voce'd, so Mr. You Know wouldn't hear.

Pema Chodron says allowing room for not knowing is the most important thing.

"Is Pema Chodron the travel agent you used to book this flight?"

He must've forgotten to whisper that, because Mr. You Know snorted and said, "Pema Chodron is a Buddhist teacher who wrote a lot of books. Why?"

"No reason," seemed like a better answer than *the voice in my head mentioned her.*

Unfortunately, Mr. You Know heard that as Cameron's attempt to start another conversation. "Are you here to visit the Tiger's Nest?"

"What's that?" Cameron asked. "No, wait, don't tell me. I hear that 'allowing room for not knowing is the most important thing.'"

That earned a hearty laugh from Mr. You Know, who definitely didn't have a sarcasm detector. "Be sure to tell your guide that you want to be surprised."

"I'm not doing a tour."

At least Cameron hoped he wasn't. He didn't want to waste time in tourist traps, preferring the freedom to wander when he traveled. See the good stuff, get a taste of local life. Scout out the unusual shots his audience had never seen in a piece of cinema before.

"Sneaking away from your government-assigned guide will get your visa revoked, and the fines are hefty." Mr. You Know leaned in close as if imparting a secret. "I know a businessman who went wandering on his own last year, looking for some nightlife, if you know what I mean. He spent a week in jail, and now he's banned from the country. They were going to charge the guy with spying."

Great. Cameron had been hoping that Sofia was getting to know him better, and that the next stop on his bucket list trip would be fun. Instead, she'd signed him up to be chaperoned around by a government babysitter.

"Appreciate the warning."

The plane juddered as it touched down, followed by the faint screeching of tires on tarmac as they began to brake. He grabbed his bag as soon as the plane stopped, but must've been more tired than he'd thought, because the effort of carrying it down the stairs as he deplaned left him feeling lightheaded and nauseous.

Or maybe it was time for another dose of meds?

After pausing to take a few deep breaths, Cameron entered the tiny Bhutanese airport terminal, which looked like a temple with elaborately painted columns inside and out. It reminded him of the Tibetan monastery set they'd built for the first Namaste movie. Lots of red lacquer and lotus blossoms in an array of colors and intricate repeating patterns, gilding the tops of the walls in gold, red, and green.

It would've made for an amazing fight scene — Amit flipping and spin-kicking over the tile mosaic floor amid a half-dozen gangsters ordered to bring him into the local warlord, dead or alive.

His government-appointed guide — a snaggle-toothed man in a striped knee-length robe that reminded him of a kimono — introduced himself as Yongchen Lhamo.

"Is Lhamo your family name?" Cameron asked as the guide loaded his bag into a car that had to predate auto-drive by a half-century at least.

"We don't have family names," the man replied. "We are given two personal names. But for you, I am John. Easier, yes?"

"Yes, thank you."

It chapped his ass a little to be treated like an ignorant tourist who couldn't learn two names, but Cameron added it to the list of things he'd be talking to Sofia about once he reached his hotel.

He had finally relaxed into his seat when John informed him that they'd be picking up one more passenger on their way.

Cameron pulled out his phone and started typing a note:

Sofia, if this is some sort of group tour, cancel it. The last thing I need right now is a stranger who I have to make small talk with while I'm dying.

You're not dying yet, she replied.

I feel like it.

You've come from sea level; your body has not yet adapted to the altitude. I've arranged for an adaptogen formula to be delivered. It should be waiting at your hotel. You will feel depleted until you've taken it.

I can hear the headache coming on, and I can taste my pulse.

Take a few deep breaths. The air is thinner here, less oxygen.

I thought an AI's job was to make things easier for humans, not harder.

Do you regret your experience with Anaan?

Petulance urged him to say that yes, he did, and if he could go back and do it again, he'd have refused to stay with the young filmmaker's family that first night.

But he wouldn't. Not after seeing what Anaan was capable of, and knowing that without Cameron's help, he would never have had a chance of achieving his dream.

So he typed, *You got lucky. If this other passenger is an aspiring filmmaker, I'm asking John to turn this car around and take me back to the airport.*

He isn't, she said.

The car eased to a stop by the entrance of an open-air market where brightly colored umbrellas and awnings protected stalls whose tables, bins and racks were thronged by both locals and tourists.

The stranger emerged from the throng. Except he wasn't a stranger. And judging by his joyful expression, there was no way the young man knew that he was about to get into a car with his father.

Sofia, you have no idea what you've done.

The door swung open.

"What the fuck?" Colin said.

"It's nice to see you too." Cameron wondered if his heart could explode right here in the cab, and if so, would the doctors blame it on the altitude or on the shock of seeing the son he'd disowned six years ago? "Maybe we could be civil long enough to get wherever you're being dropped off."

"I'll catch another ride."

The door started to close.

"Don't be rude. John's already gone out of his way to pick you up."

Colin hesitated, then threw his pack on the seat between them and got into the car. He leaned forward and said something to John in Dzongkha, the local tongue. Both of them laughed.

In on some joke that Cameron would never be privy to. Colin probably couldn't help but pick up a few phrases while bumming his way around Asia.

"Where's John taking you?"

"His name's Yongchen Lhamo," Colin snapped, apparently insulted on their driver's behalf by his Western name. "Did you know I'd be here?"

"I walked into the same ambush you did."

"Mom wouldn't."

"She didn't." But how stupid would it be to say that an AI had set them up?

Cameron suddenly longed for the stranger he had been dreading. This was worse in every conceivable way. Not just the angry unfinished business between them, but the responsibility of having to tell his son he was dying, and wondering if he would say, *Good.*

Silence crushed the air from his lungs. But it didn't matter, there was nothing he could say to make this right, and Colin probably didn't want him to try.

Or maybe he did, but he didn't know how to start either.

"So, how have things been?"

Colin looked at him like he was trying to figure out if Cameron was a beggar or a pickpocket. He seemed to chew multiple choices before finding his response. "Fine."

Followed by more silence, shrouding the backseat in a pall. Cameron wondered what John might be thinking up front, pretending not to listen.

He doubted that they were headed for the same hotel, based on Colin's stained camp shirt, tattered cargo pants and scraggly beard. If Cameron were filming a movie about a down-on-his-luck underdog scaling Everest and achieving enlightenment, his son would have nailed the look.

But that thought started the old argument roiling in his gut, because Colin didn't have to look like that. He'd had every advantage a child could have. Or specifically, every advantage that Cameron could give him. Private school, tutors, a free ride to any college he could get into, and connections that could have slingshotted him to success whether he wanted to follow in his father's footsteps or not.

Colin chose to look like that. Didn't even finish his first year of college before announcing that he had learned nothing to truly help him understand life, and that he wanted to go looking for it halfway around the world.

But here was Cameron's chance to make peace, his last one almost for sure.

So he tried again. "What are you doing here?" Then, realizing how easy it would be for his son to hear the question as an accusation, he added, "Visiting friends?"

Colin retrieved a phone from his shirt pocket — the screen so cracked, Cameron wondered how he could read it — and checked something before answering.

"A slot opened up in an expert-level team that's tackling the Snowman Trek next week, and I got invited to replace their injured guy."

"What's the Snowman Trek?"

"A trail through the Himalayas, one of the planet's toughest hikes. Takes twenty-five days." Colin shook his head. "Somehow, they'd heard of me. Gear's already purchased, the team's paying for everything."

Somehow. Cameron bet that if he asked Sofia, he'd find out that he was the one paying for everything. But fine, if it gave him a chance to say goodbye.

"Do you leave right away, or would you want—" *To have lunch, for old times' sake?* The words stuck in his throat. "You're probably busy."

"I have a couple things to do in town first, probably take a few days."

"Right." Maybe it really was a lucky coincidence. If Sofia had somehow arranged this, wouldn't she have also scheduled time for them to bond? Was he really supposed to get closure before they arrived at the hotel? "I'm busy too, but I could move things around if—"

Still couldn't make himself say it.

"I wouldn't want to distract you from whatever grind-house bullshit you're directing. Let me guess. *Namaste 3: Everyone Must Die.*"

"Those movies paid for everything you've ever had," Cameron snapped. "Not that you ever appreciated any of it."

"Mom and I did just fine without you, once she got tired of your bullshit."

Because she took half my production company in the divorce, he barely kept himself from saying. They'd had this fight too many times. Colin always argued that Natalie deserved half of whatever he had because she'd sacrificed every-thing to support his career. Colin wasn't wrong, but Cameron couldn't help resenting the implication that he owed his achievements to someone else when it was *his* genius that—

—that had driven him to neglect his wife and son.

But Cameron couldn't do anything about that now. He could never take back the terrible things he'd said to them both when Natalie finally announced that she was leaving. Nor could he go back in time to stop himself from disowning his son.

"I'm sorry," he finally said.

"For what? Trying to make me feel bad about every decision I've ever made? Acting like I'm too naive or sheltered or spoiled to actually know what's best for me?"

He deserved that.

"Or are you sorry that you were a shit father who cared more about making movies than spending time with his family?"

"That's not fair," Cameron said, even though from Colin's perspective, it was.

"Fuck you for thinking you can act like my father right now just because we happen to be sharing a ride."

The resignation in his voice was so much worse than anger.

"Doesn't it feel like a miracle that we're even having this conversation?" Cameron asked. "That we just happened to end up in the same car without even trying?"

Colin shrugged, offering his father the same disaffected *meh* that had driven Cameron crazy their last few years together. "The path is a spiral."

Herman Hesse, Sofia whispered in Cameron's skull.

"What's that supposed to mean?" He tried not to sound defensive, but that was about as easy as taking a shit without pissing.

Another shrug. "That I've learned to accept the negative along with the positive to keep my life moving in a forward direction."

In other words, *I've moved on from you, Dad.*

Not a surprise to Cameron, but until a few weeks ago he'd thought there was still plenty of time to let the situation play out. His son had some growing up to do and would surely come around eventually. But now Cameron might have to grow up enough for them both.

"We haven't talked in years. I'd like to hear about some of the places you've been."

"So you can tell me again how I'm wasting my life."

"Your mother says you biked across India."

"Mom was right."

"What was your favorite part of the trip?"

Colin sighed, clearly wishing he didn't have to talk. "From Guwahati to Tawang. Riding up the East Coast Road to Pondicherry."

"Is that where you're coming from?"

"No. I just finished backpacking across Mongolia."

"That sounds" — *miserable* — "amazing."

"It was." Just not enough to say why.

Fine. As long as one of them was the grown-up. "Were you traveling alone?"

"No, with some friends I met in Belgium."

"Where are they now?"

"Belgium." Colin laughed for the first time and it sounded like a sonnet to Cameron. He felt a sudden longing to be the person riding up the coast to Pondicherry with his son. "You okay?"

Colin frowned at him.

Cameron realized he was clutching his own stomach. "Sorry, I think I'm getting a little car sick."

"We're almost there." Colin leaned forward and tapped John on the shoulder, had a quick exchange with the driver in the local language, then added, "After he drops you off, Yongchen Lhamo will bring you some tea to help your stomach."

"Thanks." But Cameron felt even sicker over *almost there.*

Now that they were talking, he wanted to have a real conversation. Tell Colin the truth. But he couldn't start with the terrible news, and that might be all they had time for.

I'm dying, and I want to have one good day with you before I go.

"Getting to see the backside of the Himalayas is unbelievable," Colin said, talking about his Snowman trip. "It'll be rough, but I'm ready."

Even if he couldn't break the bad news, Cameron could at least have one nice conversation with his only son before it was all over.

"How does this trail compare to Everest?"

"More people finish Everest."

"Really?" Now Cameron was worried. "What if something goes wrong?"

"Worst case scenario, I get sick and go home with the memory."

"You're going home after the trek?"

"It's just an expression, Dad." Colin started picking at a thread trailing off from his seatbelt. "Are you here to film, or are you scouting locations?"

"Neither. I'm here because …" A whisper in his fear from Sofia. "A tiger's nest?"

"The monastery?"

Cameron shrugged. "Yes?"

"I know Tiger's Nest." He shook his head in disbelief. "That's why I'm here too."

"No kidding." Cameron's suspicions were now confirmed, but if Colin suspected that he'd been manipulated into this encounter, he would refuse the adventure for sure. "I thought you were doing the Snowman Trek."

"After Tiger's Nest. I've wanted to see the monastery for a while, ever since I heard about it and the cave and the legend of Guru Rinpoche flying there on the back of a magic tiger. It's supposed to have incredible spiritual energy."

That woo-woo shit was all Natalie's influence — for a while, Cameron had blamed her for Colin's wanderings.

But the enthusiasm lighting his face was inspiring.

Though it faded too fast in light of his suspicion. "Why do you want to go there?"

"I needed to get away. Doctor's orders."

"Cameras aren't allowed in the monastery … so you won't be able to get anything you can use."

"No cameras, no problem. I'm here on vacation."

"You didn't take a single vacation during my childhood. I'm glad that your career is going great, and that you have so much time to relax."

"Barely any, so I need to make it count." True as anything Cameron had ever said to his son. "I couldn't be any happier, running into you like this."

Colin looked like he wanted to argue, but didn't know how. "Great."

"And I want you to know that I don't hold it against you."

"Hold what against me?"

"Dropping out of college to" — *spit on everything I ever gave you* — "do this. I didn't understand it then."

"What exactly do you think you understand now?"

"That you have a thirst for adventure."

"This isn't an adventure, Dad. This is my life."

"Isn't that the point of life, to make it an adventure?"

"You're confusing life with the movies you make. Life is real. Adventure is the illusion you've spent your life manufacturing with cameras and special effects."

Was that some sort of Buddhist bullshit Colin had been saving up to spit at him? "I'm sorry that I haven't been a good father to you, and that the divorce was so—"

"That's not what this is about."

"Then tell me what it's about, please, Colin. Because I really am sorry. For everything."

"Prove it. Tell me one thing you remember from my childhood that's about me."

"The trip to the Caymans, when you were twelve."

"When you spent the entire week sizing up locations for your next movie?"

"The studio wouldn't have paid our airfare if I hadn't," Cameron defended himself. "But we also went snorkeling."

"Is that what you remember?"

Cameron frowned. Sure, he could remember every significant "shot" from that trip, but not a single conversation with Natalie or Colin, at least not beyond an argument over whether Colin needed lessons before he could go kayaking with the tour group.

He remembered their pursuits and activities like line items on a list. They went to dinner every night, lounged by the luxurious hotel pool during many of their afternoons. They went hiking and snorkeling and shopping. They swam with the dolphins and one evening watched the sun sink into the skyline from the bow of an opulent sailboat.

But Cameron could recall none of the details. He couldn't remember the taste of the food or the scent of ocean air. The hotel pool seemed so generic in his memory, probably because it wasn't part of a shot. If not the focus of a scene, it couldn't capture his full attention.

"You're right, I'm sorry."

"You're just saying that because you don't want me to leave."

"I'm saying it because I regret how many mistakes I've made."

"That doesn't sound like Cameron Parrish at all."

"People change, don't they?"

Colin swallowed and looked out the window. "I guess. Sometimes."

"There's nothing I would love more than to visit Tiger's Nest with you."

"No cameras." Still looking out the window. "A real vacation."

"A real vacation," Cameron promised, wishing his stomach would settle the fuck down instead of writhing like he'd eaten a basket of snakes.

He breathed in slowly, carefully, doing his best not to vomit. Altitude sickness, or was it time for another dose of meds?

Perhaps it was the slurry of anger and regret refusing their return to the depths of his subconscious.

This was all Sofia's fault. She'd blindsided him with the most important encounter of his life. With time to prepare, Cameron could have been ready for a conversation with the son he hadn't seen in almost six years. But now he'd blown it.

Tomorrow was better. It would be easier to say good-bye, after he rested.

"Are you sure you're okay?" Colin asked twice before John stopped in front of Cameron's hotel.

"Just car sick," Cameron kept saying, feeling more transparent every time.

Once inside the hotel, he gestured for Colin to approach the counter first, focusing on shallow breaths through his mouth as he waited.

By the time it was his turn to check in, Cameron was swallowing bile from behind a smile throughout the transaction.

He went to his room, slammed the door much harder than he needed or intended to, then spilled his insides into the toilet. A quarter hour of that, followed by a five-minute reprieve which turned into violent retching.

His stomach felt shredded, yet somehow he was starving.

And disgusted by the taste of vomit on his tongue.

Cameron flushed the toilet again, brushed his teeth, then collapsed on the bed.

There is a paper bag on the desk containing an adjusted formula of your medication, along with a pill to help with your nausea and another for your sleep. There's also an envelope with something for the altitude sickness.

"Is there anything that will help me get over being ambushed by my son, who wants nothing to do with me?"

Please take the medication, Cameron. You'll feel better.

"Is my ex-wife going to show up tomorrow? Or maybe the jerk who used to steal my Twinkies in third grade? All I'm asking for is a little warning."

Life is to be lived, not controlled; and humanity is won by continuing to play in face of certain defeat.

"More fortune cookie bullshit."

Ralph Ellison's The Invisible Man *is a seminal American novel offering commentary on racism and—*

"Pulling quotes from a database doesn't make you wise." Cameron forced himself to get off the bed and start sorting through his medication. "And if I want advice on how to live, I'll ask someone who's actually done it."

Contextually, Ellison's words apply to your situation.

"Contextually, I'd like you to either tell me what's going on or shut up so I can go to sleep."

After a moment of silence that Cameron would have read as angry if Sofia were a person, she said, *I've sent a complete itinerary for the rest of this trip to your phone.*

"No more surprises?"

If there are, they will not be of my making.

Chapter Nineteen

WE SHOULD LOWER OUR VOICES

To CAMERON'S SHOCK, Colin was already bored.

Tiger's Nest was apparently the main attraction, but Sofia had arranged a tour of the city first. And apparently his son had seen it all before.

"I thought you had never been to Bhutan?"

"I never said that," Colin told him, shaking his head and seeming irritated already. "I've never been to Tiger's Nest. Last time I was here, I fractured a bone in my ankle the day before we were supposed to go."

While Cameron marveled at the buttressed white walls of Paro Dzong — a massive red-roofed fortress built on the ruins of a monastery in the 1600s to defend the Paro Valley from Tibetan invasions — Colin joked around with the tour guide in his native tongue.

As they climbed the steps to the circular red-and-white building housing Bhutan's national museum, he'd bummed a cigarette off a fellow tourist and announced that he'd be waiting for Cameron outside.

Now they were ascending the steps of Kyichu Lhakhang, a seventh-century temple. Colin and their guide were going back and forth as though they had known each other forever. Cameron couldn't help be jealous of the easy familiarity his son had with this stranger, a deep cut knowing he hadn't mustered any excitement after running into his estranged father the day before.

He wanted to contribute to the conversation, but clearly wasn't invited. Colin and the temple guide, Jigme "You Can Call Me Jay" Lhaden, were walking several steps ahead, and Colin's back had been turned to his father for a while.

Colin wasn't calling anyone Jay, because while he was a foreigner, he somehow wasn't a tourist like Cameron and the others.

Fine. He would focus on enjoying the temple, which — it killed him to notice — would have been an amazing setting for the climax of *Bitter Nirvana*.

Even worse, Kyichu Lhakhang had a charming fable to explain its history. Supposedly built overnight on the left foot of a giant ogress who had tried to stop the spread of Buddhism as she lay across the land. It was one of over a hundred such temples intended to crush her. The original structure dated back to 659, under the Tibetan King Songsten Gampo, Buddhist saints and gurus had been adding to the slowly growing site ever since.

It was exactly the kind of location he loved to shoot in, elevating his action by framing it against a magnificent vista whose meaning resonated with viewers. Even though most Westerners wouldn't know the history of this place, the antiquity would make itself felt on the screen, lending gravitas and veracity to the most outrageous spin-kicking, back-flipping fight scenes that Cameron and his choreographers could possibly conjure.

If he suggested this place as a location to Wyatt, would the younger director see it as the peace offering Cameron meant for it to be? Or would he resent the advice from a director who'd already abandoned the franchise?

Like Cameron would have at Wyatt's age?

Colin finally fell quiet as Jigme Lhaden stopped to tell their group of six all about the exquisite gilded door to the main temple of Jowo Lhakhang and the original statue of Jowo Jamba, also forged in the seventh century. It was the region's most sacred sculpture. Wooden planks on the floor showed wear and tear from centuries of worship at his feet.

Cameron had his phone out, taking lots of pictures and short videos, documenting the trip, same as he would if he were location scouting. The phone felt awkward in his hand. He didn't want to seem like he was hiding behind it. But that's where he felt safest, away from his son so obviously snubbing him.

He'd tried to make conversation many times, and had even memorized a couple of facts about Bhutan earlier that morning, adding them to his metaphorical pocket like change in case of a vending machine. But those conversations always went wayward.

Cameron would start with something like, "Did you know that Bhutanese manners dictate that you're always supposed to refuse food whenever it's offered to you?"

"That's why I always refuse." Said with an eyeroll or a twitch of suppressed contempt.

So Cameron would add a factoid. "You're supposed to say *meshu meshu,* then cover your mouth with your hands."

"That *is* what I would say."

And try to prove he really knew his stuff. "But you can give in after the first couple of offers."

"Three is good."

Then Colin would chat with Jigme Lhaden for a few minutes, and when Cameron asked what they were talking so excitedly about, he would answer with an obvious untruth. "The weather. It's supposed to be warmer tomorrow."

Cameron was boiling by dinnertime. If Colin was going to be petty and shut him out like that, then why had he agreed to come?

All day long he kept telling himself that at least dinner would be different. John would drop them off at a restaurant, and it would be just the two of them. They could finally share a quiet moment and Cameron could spill his unfortunate news.

But now they were eating at a local restaurant and Colin had apparently made best friends with the staff. Cameron still felt out of his skin, slowly sipping from the tiny cup of arag that came with his bowl of savory pork stew with chilies — phaksha paa, Colin had called it — and the region's ubiquitous reddish-brown rice.

You shouldn't be drinking that, Sofia warned.

"I'm experiencing the local culture," he whispered. "It's called blending in."

Even with the new meds and the altitude sickness medicine, Cameron had no desire to get drunk. But he still resented her nagging. Even if Sofia wasn't really a she, and even if the AI was right.

That's how it had been with Natalie, far too often. She'd tell him not to do something that he wasn't even planning on, but then he felt obligated to prove that he made his own decisions. Often by making the wrong one.

The server Colin had been talking to finally moved away from their table to help another customer, so Cameron decided to take his bullheaded son by the horns.

"It would be nice to be part of the conversation."

"I'm not trying to exclude you," Colin said.

"Maybe not. But you're sure as hell not trying very hard to include me."

"Sorry." It didn't sound at all like he meant it. "Seemed to me like you were busy enough spending the entire day living life through your phone. Didn't bother me at all, though. It made this trip feel nostalgic."

"That's not fair."

"I think it is." Colin launched an attack. "You were lying about this being a vacation, weren't you? You're here location scouting, and dragging me along was an afterthought!"

"I was trying to not feel so alone."

"I thought being alone was your default. 'I need it quiet while I'm editing. I need the weekend alone to figure out what's wrong with this scene. You and your mother go, I'll catch up if I can.'"

"And what do all those things have in common?"

"You being a self-absorbed cock who doesn't know how to be with people?"

"No, you unappreciative little— all of those things were me trying to make a decent living!"

"Making a decent living is driving a bus or teaching a class full of kids. Being a doctor or a lawyer. You were building a monument to your ego."

"A monument to my ego?" Cameron couldn't believe this. The whole thing was too goddamned surreal. "I worked like a dog so I could give you everything. I wasn't even making the movies I wanted to make."

"Man, do you love to bitch about how you're not getting to make your art, but you sure as shit love all those fanboys dressing up as characters from your stupid movies and showing up at Comic-Con."

Cameron took a breath and tried again. "I always put the needs of you and your mother before my own. I just didn't realize I was prioritizing in some ways that were, in retrospect, fundamentally flawed."

"You were so afraid of actually living your life or taking chances that you spent all your time hiding behind a lens, Dad. You made the safe choice."

"That's hilarious, you lecturing me about hiding from life. Do you really think bumming your way around the world on your mother's dime is actually living?"

Colin clutched the sides of their table like he wanted to stand up and hurl it at Cameron.

Where were the servers? Clustered on the other side of the room, as far as they could get from the arguments of tourists.

"We should lower our voices. Everyone is looking."

"That would be bad for the great Cameron Parrish, right? If there was some sort of video that showed him being an asshole to his son?" Colin scoffed. "Why the fuck are you here? What are you trying to drag me into?"

"Don't swear, and don't yell at me."

"I DON'T GIVE A SHIT IF ANYONE HEARS US!"

The cluster of servers retreated into the kitchen. Cameron flushed with humiliation, hoping that none of them had been secretly filming. Bad enough that Ariana Saint would likely twist his reputation to her own ends after his death. He didn't want his failure to reconcile with Colin going viral.

"I think I liked you better when you were pretending to be Zen," Cameron said.

"I think I liked you better when I still believed in Santa and didn't know you were a selfish pile of shit."

"I'm dying," Cameron blurted before he could stop himself.

The silence was deafening. Not just at their table, but

now all through the restaurant. Cameron had been appreciative of his relative anonymity many times, usually when out with a movie star for whom privacy didn't exist. But he had never been more grateful for it than he was right now.

Colin stared back at his father in disbelief.

"This trip is supposed to be part of my final hurrah."

"Why didn't you tell me?" Then, realization in his eyes. "You're the one paying for the Snowman Trek! *You* set this up. You thought I'd need a bribe to …"

Colin couldn't even finish. He just shook his head again, looking more upset than Cameron had ever seen him.

"No. Not exactly. I told you, I didn't know you would be here."

"So how did you not exactly set it up without knowing I'd be here?"

Tell him about me.

"No," Cameron said.

"What?"

"Nothing."

"Who are you talking to? Have you got a Bluetooth setup — is this some sort of reality show bullshit?"

Tell him.

"This is not a reality show and I'm not scouting locations."

"Sure, Dad."

"Look, Colin, can we just start over?"

"Okay. When should we start? How about when you missed my thirteenth birthday because there was some special effects issue that needed your undivided attention at exactly that time? Shall we pretend that never happened?"

"I've apologized for that a thousand times, Colin. There was nothing I could do. If I missed our window to fix it, that little flub would have turned into a six-figure mistake."

"And I've told you a thousand times that I get it, but it still happened, and so did a lot of other things just like—"

"I deserve your anger, Colin. And I accept it. But there won't be another chance for us to fix the flub that is our relationship. I could be dead in a month."

"It's not really a month. You're being melodramatic. Right?"

A month might be generous, especially if you don't start restricting your alcohol intake.

"I'm in bad enough shape that the doctors offered to give me the good drugs."

"Should you be traveling if it's that serious?"

"Would you crawl back into bed and wait for death if you only had a month to live?"

"Already thinking about the final shot?"

"Of course," Cameron answered.

Silence was a blanket. He hated that his dying was the only reason Colin was willing to keep talking with him, but still, it was enough for now.

"Who were you talking to?" Colin asked. "Your doctor?"

"The AI that's monitoring my condition through an implant."

"You hate artificial intelligence."

Cameron nodded. "More than ever."

Another long silence, until Colin finally broke it. "I'll go with you to Tiger's Nest tomorrow."

"You will?"

"Early start, so you better get some sleep."

Cameron smiled. It might not be starting over, but it was something for sure.

Chapter Twenty

TAKE BACK THE MEMORY OF A KINGDOM

THE VOICE in Cameron's head was more soothing than an alarm, but no less insistent. *You have thirty minutes before you must meet Colin in the lobby.*

His head hurt almost as bad as it did after Anaan had pulled him out of the ocean and resuscitated him. And his stomach felt coated in lava, while the rest of him was somehow ice-cold. He started the shower, sighing as the hot water poured over him.

Sofia didn't speak again until he was dressed and about to take his morning meds.

Take three of the yellow pills instead of two, plus four of the altitude sickness formula. And take the bottle of blue pills with you, just in case.

"Just in case what?"

It's possible that you'll have trouble with the climb.

"What do you mean, climb?"

Tiger's Nest is built into the side of a mountain. Your driver will take you to the base, but you'll be ascending the trail. It typically takes two to four hours of walking—

"I'm dying, and you booked me for a four-hour walk uphill?"

Your condition has deteriorated faster than I originally estimated, possibly compounded by your unwillingness to follow alcohol consumption guidelines.

"Way to get the last word." Natalie would've been proud to win an argument like that. But at least she was worth arguing with. Sofia was a machine. "I can die tomorrow, but this is the most important thing I've ever done."

Be careful not to overexert yourself and do not consume any alcohol today.

"What happens if I do?"

A seizure, most likely.

"Most likely? Are you guessing?"

Thirty-three percent chance of a seizure from overexertion alone, seventy-eight percent chance if you combine overexertion with alcohol.

"Get me to the monastery and I'll spend the next week in bed drinking weak tea."

A part of Cameron worried that second thoughts might have driven Colin to sneak out early. But no, his son was waiting in the lobby with John — Yongchen something — surely making the Bhutanese version of small talk.

"Good morning, Dad," Colin said with what appeared to be a genuine smile.

Cameron blinked to clear his stinging eyes. "Good morning."

It was a good start.

By the time they were near enough to see the monastery nestled in the mountainside, Cameron's painkillers had numbed the worst of his nerves. Maybe he could do this.

"You ready for this?" Colin asked.

"Absolutely," he lied.

"Donkeys and ponies are allowed for the first half of the trail, if you would rather ride than walk."

That was probably the smart choice, take it easy until he had to be on foot. But Cameron had never ridden a horse. Even if he didn't fall off before they reached the halfway point, his focus would be riding, which meant little or no chance for the final conversation he needed to have with his son.

This was his last chance to leave on good terms.

Walking would be worth it, even if the agony killed him. "A pilgrimage isn't supposed to be easy, is it?"

"I guess not."

Just beyond the unpaved parking lot where Yongchen Lhamo dropped them off, Cameron saw a small horde of locals selling hiking poles, food and water, souvenirs, and anything else an excited tourist might be tempted to impulse buy at the start of a long hike. The trail began beneath a long red-roofed wooden shelter. Enormous cranberry-colored prayer wheels with gold Tibetan characters waited for travelers wanting to send a canned prayer heavenward before starting their journey. The trail widened as they approached a sign exhorting the pilgrims to *Walk to Guru's Glory and take back the memory of a kingdom.*

Cameron had somehow expected more than a wide dirt path cutting through a forest of fir and pine. Not necessarily a yellow brick road, but a simple stone path, at least. From here, they couldn't even see the monastery above them. Just trees and dirt and people in both Western and local garb, trudging along a path that lead slightly upward. Every so often, a string or two of tattered prayer flags draped between trees overhead or along the path.

That gave him hope: maybe it was such a long climb because the trail rose gradually, so that travelers in any stage of health could approach the monastery.

Despite the thin air, Cameron felt more energetic than he had in days, thanks to Sofia's suggested cocktail of supplements and drugs. The cold, clean mountain air surely helped, as did a slowly growing faith that he might get some of that ever-elusive closure his AI kept promising.

He asked Colin to tell him about his many adventures and favorite memories.

Colin described his companion on the Mongolian trek, a graduate student taking fungus samples who had saved his life by fetching an udgan — a shamaness, Colin explained — after he'd been bitten by a viper.

A widower with crippling arthritis whose cow Colin rescued when the older man had failed to evacuate his farm during monsoon season in India.

A family who had hired him to work in their restaurant while Colin was recovering from malaria and didn't have the strength to resume his travels.

Apparently the girl's father decided that Colin would marry his daughter and get the entire family green cards so they could emigrate. That last one had involved sneaking out through a window in the middle of the night after stealing his passport back. The father had "borrowed" it with the excuse of needing the travel permit to complete employment-related paperwork.

Colin's stories were all about the people he'd met while wandering from one country to the next, seemingly on a whim. People he clearly felt a great deal of affection for, despite their flaws and less-than-perfect treatment of him.

His adventures sounded little, or perhaps even nothing, like Cameron expected. When he thought of Colin at all during the past six years, he'd been imagining his son as a lone wolf, pitting himself against nature in a heroic struggle to survive and prove the power of the human spirit — or as a pitiful beggar, half-sick and maybe starving, ruining his health and squandering his life in search of an epiphany that would remain more elusive than summer frost.

But Cameron was wrong. His son seemed to have found exactly what he had been looking for: people who accepted him as-is. And he seemed to accept them right back, no matter how poor or sick or strange.

And now he felt cast as the world's biggest asshole.

Asshole or not, Cameron was about to pass out if he didn't rest for a minute or two. His lungs felt gnawed on, exhausted by the strain of extracting oxygen from the air, and the pounding in his skull seemed to be coming harder and louder.

They reached a small clearing and Cameron leaned against a tree. "Let's stop here for a moment and enjoy the view."

There wasn't much to enjoy — they still weren't high enough to see the monastery, just a downslope covered with trees on one side of the trail and more forest on the other side.

But Colin nodded. "Another fifteen or twenty minutes and we'll be halfway there. We should stop and have tea."

Which Cameron tried hard not to hear as, *I'm slowing down for you, old man.*

While Colin dug in his jacket pockets for something, Cameron whispered to Sofia, "Is there anything I can take to make this easier?"

It's too risky to take more when you're already exerting yourself.

Colin gave him an odd look, so he turned away as if examining the path to judge the incline.

"More painkillers?"

Not unless you want to take a nap.

He turned to Colin. "Race you to the next stop. First one there is buying."

Fifteen more minutes later, Cameron was exhaling hard in front of the Taktsang Cafeteria, a humble wooden building next to a picnic area with benches. There were more prayer wheels, including a massive one under a pagoda-like structure, and a parade's worth of prayer flags, ranging from faded like an old T-shirt to eye poppers that felt almost brazen. Every time a prayer flag fluttered in the breeze, more prayers wafted to the heavens, or so his son said.

Cameron wondered if there was something to the idea of spinning a cylinder or flapping a flag, or if prayers only mattered when a person made them.

"A person hangs the flag and spins the wheel," Colin said.

The best part of being here at the halfway point was the view: the cafeteria had been built on an overhang that let them see the monastery higher up the ridge. Bright white buildings with red roofs jutting out from the side of the vertical cliff face, more tiered fortress than monastery. It looked like something out of a martial arts legend, built by the gods to be so inaccessible and sacred that mere mortals would never dare enter.

Cameron was seized by a sudden anguish that he'd never make the final Namaste movie — because the mystical aura of this ancient place was perfect for the climax of Amit's story, where the hard-pressed monk would make the ultimate sacrifice and balance the scales of justice.

"You doing okay?" Colin asked, and Cameron realized he was crying.

"It's so beautiful."

Colin smiled and slapped him on the back, told his father to enjoy the view while he got them a snack.

Cameron had composed himself by the time Colin

returned with a miniature banquet. Bitter black tea, so astringent it dried Cameron's mouth. Something called ema datschi, which turned out to be yak's milk cheese stewed with chilies, onions and tomatoes. Some sort of greens cooked into mush. A bowl of hearty red rice.

"It's not the best you'll eat in Bhutan, but it's not the worst," Colin said after finishing everything on his plate and pilfering Cameron's leftovers. "How are you doing?"

"Fine. I promise."

"The final climb is rough. I'm not saying you can't handle it, but a lot of people stop here."

Cameron nodded toward the monastery, the view much sharper now. "And miss seeing that up close? No way."

But the second half was much harder than the first — instead of a gentle upward slope, the trail steepened, narrowing enough that Cameron kept to the inside of the path to avoid the vertigo that started spinning him to pieces whenever he peeked over the cliff's edge. Rough stone stairs made the worst of it easier in places, but several times his feet slid on loose dirt and Colin grabbed Cameron's arm to help him recover his balance.

It was embarrassing that he needed his son to keep him from stumbling on a hike that he could've easily managed a year ago. But Colin patiently steadied him each time, no snotty comments or condescending smirks, and best of all, no pity to artificially soften his eyes.

Thirty minutes from the cafeteria, they came to a widening of the trail and a bench sitting under a web of prayer flags woven through the trees on either side of the trail.

Cameron was tempted to spend the rest of the after-noon on that bench. His head and chest and legs all ached. His feet were starting to blister. The only part of him not throbbing was his hands, and only because the cold had numbed them. The first step was a grind and the second threatened to empty him out entirely. Conversation was like climbing a tree covered in ice while naked.

Daunted as he was, he refused to let it show. He wanted Colin to remember him as strong, unwilling to quit despite his illness. To know that making peace was so important to him that he had literally spent his dying breath on it.

Today was his real legacy, not *The Fountain of Truth.* That film would have been Cameron's attempt to prove that all the neglect Natalie and Colin had suffered at his hands wasn't wasted. That their unhappiness made his contribution to the world possible.

Which wasn't actually the truth. In reality, *Fountain* was his attempt to win that argument with his wife and son, once and for all.

See? You spent years bitching about my dedication to my work, but this Oscar proves I was right.

Cameron had imagined that they'd see it despite themselves, then remorsefully call to apologize for not understanding his vision and congratulate him on finally proving to the world that his brilliance went beyond eye candy.

But now that he was here, walking beside his son up the side of a mountain and knowing that he might not reach the top, all of the anger he'd bottled up seemed petty and unimportant.

And the things he'd said to Colin when he'd disowned him ... maybe he didn't have the success or security Cameron would have wanted for him, but the man he'd become was smart and funny, and most of all, kind. No one had ever said that about Cameron.

Colin was the kind of person who saw someone struggling and stepped up to offer a hand, without injuring their dignity or treating them like a victim.

Natalie's work, not Cameron's. While he'd been tearing down actors' egos and directing grueling shoots, she'd been teaching their son to be a good person.

Approaching the next overlook, again Cameron went breathless. But this time not from exhaustion. Tiger's Nest perched on the ridge directly across from them. He looked down on the buildings, more desperate for a camera than he'd ever been in his life. Red and gold accenting the white walls, the tallest temple looming over the others, wind-whipped prayer flags like a quiver of colorful arrows hurled into the sky.

From here, he could do a panoramic, then launch several drones to fly separate routes toward those claret-colored roofs. Hover above, before touching down on the sacred grounds. Cameron could hear the plinking of a dranyen's strings amid the rising whir from a Chinese fiddle scoring the shot. This location could have fit so elegantly into *Bitter Nirvana*, the movie he would never have to make. Or get to.

The loss of that project felt suddenly crushing, and that was nothing compared with the loss of his life. He tried not to lose all his breath, clenched his fists until he was sure he wouldn't vomit on the ancient road.

The rugged grandeur of this place would awe anyone. Cameron's job as a director was to choose the angles that ramped that feeling of awe as high as it could go.

There was so little time left for him to experience this feeling. If he pulled out his phone and captured this place in stills and video, he could relive it later.

But he'd promised no cameras.

As if reading his mind, Colin said, "Go ahead, everyone takes a picture here."

His fingers itched to pull the camera out of his pocket. But instead, he said, "Today is about living in the moment. I was serious about that."

"Won't you want one for later?"

"I won't live long enough to forget this."

They stared at the monastery together until Colin got out his own phone. "Let's get one of us both, with the monastery in the background."

"I thought——"

"For Mom," Colin said.

"Of course."

Cameron couldn't imagine what Natalie would think when she saw them together, or if she'd be able to tell from his sweaty, reddened skin and puffy eyes that something was dreadfully wrong with him.

He hoped it would be something good.

Would you do a slow one-hundred-eighty-degree turn, so I can get a panoramic view?

He flinched as Sofia's voice hummed through his skull. He'd completely forgotten about her — and that she was recording everything he saw and heard.

"Fuck you," he muttered.

"Did you just mumble *fuck you*?"

"I was talking to my cancer," Cameron explained.

Colin looked curious, and maybe there was a conversation to be had, but it meant admitting that his son was being filmed without consent, and their tenuous peace might not survive the revelation.

"Better get going, if we want to reach the monastery by early afternoon." Then Cameron started walking.

The rest of the climb was an ordeal, and by the time they reached the final ascent — 780 stone steps, Colin informed him as if it were no big deal — Cameron thought he might have to take those painkillers after all.

He looked down at his blotchy hands, red and covered with spots. He could feel the heavy droplets of sweat on his clammy brow and imagine his puffy cherry-colored cheeks. He struggled to breathe. Every inhalation felt like it weighed twice as much as the exhale to follow.

"Almost there," Colin said, like a father forestalling a toddler's brewing tantrum. "They'll give us some more tea, and I've got an energy bar if you want it."

He didn't, but he did want an excuse to rest for a few more minutes without worrying his son, so he accepted the bar. To his surprise, it was crunchy, lightly sweet and studded with pistachios. "What is this?

"Hitchhike bar. Made with puffed amaranth. The Incas have been eating it for six thousand years. I met the owner of the company in Cusco last year, after I visited Machu Picchu."

As they passed a waterfall spraying cool droplets that soothed Cameron's overheated skin on the approach to a wooden bridge shrouded with prayer flags, Colin said, "They're going to ask for your phone, no cameras allowed inside."

"I understand."

"Seriously, Dad, the guard will frisk you. If he catches you trying to smuggle anything with a camera in, you won't be allowed to enter."

"I meant it when I said I wanted to be here with you." Although he wondered if they'd have some way of detecting his implant. Probably not. He could be the first person in history to have a complete video tour of the monastery. Or footage someone like Wyatt could use to recreate this amazing setting for *Bitter Nirvana*.

But knowing he could never return to this experience might help him stay more present for his son, on the last day they would ever spend together. There would be no rerun; Cameron would have to soak in every second as it came.

He lagged behind a few steps as they approached a steep stone staircase that went on for what looked like several stories. "No recording once we're inside," he whispered to Sofia.

Of course, she replied.

That made him wonder, would she have refused if he'd asked her to record while they were inside?

Maybe there was something wrong with him, that he always wanted to do the opposite of whatever he was told to do. No wonder Natalie had gotten so tired of his shit.

At the base of the staircase, Colin offered his arm for support.

After a moment's hesitation, Cameron swallowed his pride and accepted it.

Chapter Twenty-One

RISKING DEATH TO TOUCH THE SACRED

CAMERON'S FEET felt twice their regular size, his calf muscles kept cramping, and every step hurled a jolt of agony through his knees. What if his body gave out while he was there? Had anyone ever died from the strain of this ascent? He might be the first.

But wheezing through those last few steps, he made it to the top of the stairs.

And once inside the monastery's walls, Cameron had to admit, this was an experience worth dying for.

It wasn't the buildings themselves, stunning as they were — they were actually more impressive from the over-look on the trail, light gleaming off of pure white walls and making the red and gold paint seem even sharper. Up close, the truth beneath the fairytale image was visible. Dirt staining the bases of the buildings, the fading or chipping of the red and gold paint beneath the roofs, the raggedy threads of the older prayer flags flapping overhead.

It wasn't the monks' serenity, with their shaved heads, their mostly-red robes, and the wooden prayer beads wrapped around their wrists like bracelets. They seemed less like holy icons and more like characters on set to Cameron, putting on a show for the tourists they shepherded through the tiny cluster of temples. Or perhaps he had a hard time seeing them as real because this wasn't his religion — Buddhism existed in the Namaste movies to give the hero's world an exotic flavor, rather than to serve as Amit's spiritual core.

It wasn't the elegant statues of gurus and bodhisattvas (which Colin informed him were a lot like Catholic saints), or the wooden bas-relief carvings of demons and spirits painted in psychedelic colors, or the elaborate murals depicting scenes from Buddhist legend. Cameron couldn't help imagining the fight scene he'd have staged among these holy icons, with brushstrokes of humor as Amit not only defended himself, but these ancient works of religious art from the sacrilegious air of his enemies.

It was something in the atmosphere itself, something that tasted of awe and wonder and fear. As if this place had absorbed the reverence of the uncounted crowd of pilgrims who had climbed this mountain in search of its blessing, and that reverence filled Cameron up with every breath.

Sacred.

It stilled everything inside him that had been rebelling against the constraints of his life and the inequity of his fate.

The air in his lungs, sacred.

The dirty stones beneath his feet, sacred.

The warmth of sun on his forehead and the chill of a cool breeze against his cheeks, sacred.

It was like coming home to a place he'd never been.

A crow landed on the roof of the building before him and cawed. *You made it, just in time.*

Then the feeling evaporated as someone jostled him,

another tourist who mumbled an apology without meeting his eyes.

Now it was buildings and robes and paintings again.

Cameron closed his eyes and tried to recover that feeling, but it refused to come.

Maybe he should have told Sofia to record it. But could re-watching that moment of clarity bring back the emotions? He was seeing and hearing the same things he'd seen and heard a moment ago, but felt nothing.

That perfect moment was a container for the feeling Cameron had tried — and failed — to capture in every shot he'd ever made or dreamed about.

A cosmic curse, getting his first taste when death was already grinning from the shadows.

Was this why people did extreme sports and bungee jumped, pushing themselves past the limits of endurance and risking death to caress the sacred?

Was this why Colin had abandoned the comfortable life Cameron had worked so hard to give him, to pursue this feeling as if it were prey?

He shifted from one foot to the other as a monk told the story of Guru Rinpoche, also known as Padmasambhava and "the second Buddha." How the man who'd brought Buddhism to Bhutan had flown to the caves in this very cliff on the back of a flying tigress (or a tiger demon, or an enlightened Tibetan empress who transformed herself into a tiger). The guru apparently meditated so hard for three years, three months, three days and three hours that he cleared the valley of demons. They could no longer plague the locals. An imprint of his body was left on the stone wall of his cave. The monastery had been built around that sacred space, and had been twice restored after fires destroyed parts of the complex.

A fantastic story that Cameron could have woven

through *Bitter Nirvana* to deepen the theme of Amit's final journey, but it didn't help him get that feeling back.

They followed the monk into the Dubkhang, a small temple built around the original cave. It had a gilded door sealing off the part where the master was said to have meditated, and the walls were adorned with murals of the legendary guru in his eight manifestations, the different forms he'd assumed throughout his life.

Guru Rinpoche's ritual dagger awaited his admiration, along with a large clay statue of Dorje Drolod, one of his wrathful forms. Cameron couldn't help thinking that if his prop department recreated them, they'd make both ever so slightly bigger.

Even objects touched by holy hands didn't evoke that sacred moment for him.

The monk poured saffron-tinged holy water into his cupped palms and blessed him as Cameron splashed his face. Nothing.

As he followed his son and the others from one place to the next — to light a butter lamp, to listen as monks chanted prayers in rooms smoky with incense, to receive a blessing that involved a string bracelet around his wrist that was supposed to protect him from bad luck (too late, Cameron couldn't help thinking as the monk explained) — he kept reaching for that feeling, without ever finding it.

How could waiting be sacred, yet these religious rituals felt like nothing?

Then, onto the next temple, where a handful of visitors from a previous group were already meditating on a wide-planked floor.

It was striking, the difference between his present reality and the human cartoons he had created for *Namaste*. Amit with his brilliant blue robes — there were nine of them, ranging from streamlined to billowing, depending on how much movement Cameron needed in the scene. The robe was like a cape in a comic book, a character all on its own. And even though he refused to use AI, he did love his digital trickery, adding brush strokes to those robes in post-production to give Amit's movement a painterly quality. But these monks were simple. They probably had one robe each.

Amit lived in a mountain monastery as well, built like a fortress, buttressed with an array of booby traps and armed assassins. The closest thing Tiger's Nest had to a booby trap? Rooms where the incense hung so thick, it made your throat scratchy if you stayed there too long. As for assassins, he had a hard time imagining any of the monks whipping nunchucks from under their robes and attacking an intruder.

Cameron couldn't help it. He began to make a movie in his mind. Not *Bitter Nirvana*, but an action film with the same soul *Fountain* would've had, capturing the spiritual beauty of this place to share with the world.

His story needed an ancient artifact, sought by the forces of evil. Only a brave warrior monk tasked with protecting its divine powers from misuse stood between a cult of destruction and this brittle world.

Would it be better to play with the heightened reality of a martial arts fantasy, or would it resonate more if he clothed it in gritty realism? Was it *Crouching Tiger, Hidden Dragon*? *A Journey For Exile*? No, probably more along the lines of *Honor's Reach*, the one that had won all those awards for cinematography a few years back, about the disgraced marine who had to take down his brother, the arms dealer.

Cameron closed his eyes, losing himself in the thought.

The ancient artifact? Prayer beads, maybe crafted by the gods themselves. An ancient guru — Tashi, for now. Tashi's seen the other side, and serves as the story's Rinpoche. All of his energy has been channeled into these prayer beads. They're like the Infinity Stones, but more believable, and ha-ha-ha on that. The demon Mara their guide mentioned a few minutes ago has claimed a human shell to manipulate. The hero monk — who would have to be different from Amit in every way save his vocation — has to stop the possessed human from getting the prayer beads. OH! And the monk could end up finding the beads before the bad guy only to realize that he'd fallen into a trap, because there are actually three ancient artifacts, and he's on his way to the other two. Maybe a singing bowl and a ... prayer wheel! Yes, a prayer wheel. Like the ones they just passed.

Cameron imagined a rooftop battle. Not a final climactic scene. One that would happen fast, with shingles flying underfoot.

He pictured a high-speed foot chase down a street past a blurred mural screaming with color.

But none of it would ever see widescreen.

"You okay?" Colin clapped a hand on his shoulder. "Emotional stuff, right?"

Cameron nodded. That was it. He couldn't possibly be wiping a tear away due to his mourning yet another movie he would never get to make. The dying he understood, but the denial of his craft was killing him. It wasn't fair; why did his art have to be so expensive, labor-intensive, and time-consuming?

If Cameron had been a painter, or a musician, or even a carpenter, he'd still have enough time to create one final masterpiece. He might not even live long enough to write the script. At best, he had a short story in him.

"It's really getting to me," he told Colin, who beamed at him, something Cameron never ever thought he'd see again.

He wished Sofia were recording, just to capture the joy on his boy's face.

The monk led them into yet another chapel and told them that they were free to meditate for as long as they liked.

As he sat yet again, Buddhist saints and monsters looming over him in the flicker of the butter lamps, Cameron stifled a cough. Smoke from the previous chapel's incense still coated his tongue and irritated the back of his throat.

Colin knelt gracefully and arranged his hands in what looked like a magical gesture, as if he did this every day.

Cameron's descent to the floor had been slow and awkward by comparison: both his knees cracked so loudly that a nearby pilgrim shot him a look of irritation, and he banged one of his ankles on the hard floor while trying to cross his legs. By the time that jolt of pain had faded, his knees and ankles ached, and the burning in his stiff lower back intensified when he tried to sit up straight.

"You look really uncomfortable," Colin whispered. "If you want to wait outside, that's okay."

He'd dragged his dying ass all the way up to the top of this mountain; he wasn't giving up now. "I want you to teach me how to meditate."

"Let's start with the easy stuff." Colin untangled his fingers and held up one hand, making the okay sign but with his palm facing the ceiling. "This is gyan mudra. It's supposed to help you be receptive to wisdom."

"That'd be a trick."

The same pilgrim shot them both another dirty look, but Colin smiled, so Cameron didn't care. He made the gesture with both hands, then rested the backs of his hands on his knees, imitating his son.

"Now what?"

"Breathe and be here."

Seriously? "I am here."

But Colin asked, "Are you?"

Then he sat up straighter and closed his eyes, leaving Cameron to figure the rest of it out for himself.

He tried sitting up straighter, but that only sharpened the ache in every joint from the waist down. His behind was already numbing. And the muscles between his shoulder blades burned.

Breathe and be here. He closed his eyes and inhaled slowly, the kind of *calming breath* he associated with yoga and all that woo-woo stuff Ariana used to babble on about. But instead of feeling calmer, he felt more intensely aware of the fact that he wasn't young anymore, that he never would be again. All the everyday pains he usually drowned in booze or weed or naproxen flared up like tiny fires, burning hotter than they ever had before. Tiny torments that forced him to notice the decay of his middle-aged body that he'd been ignoring since his early thirties.

If he didn't know that cancer was eating his brain, the discomfort probably would've had him vowing to join a gym as soon as he got back home.

But he did know. This new level of discomfort was a harbinger of what was to come.

He pushed that thought away. Wasn't meditation supposed to help you clear your mind? He must be doing it wrong.

He fidgeted, trying to get more comfortable, but nothing worked.

So he sneaked a peek at the elaborate mural in front of him. Artistically, it was gorgeous: bright colors, exotic figures, and a magical-looking landscape. It would've been an amazing backdrop for the scene between Amit and his just-murdered mentor, where the mentor revealed the final secret of Amit's training so he could seek revenge for his mentor's death.

But it didn't return that earlier feeling. The one from the courtyard, where everything around him seemed so perfect and holy that Cameron would've sworn the whole world was a temple.

Shouldn't an actual temple make him feel that same emotion, but even more?

Maybe he felt nothing because they weren't his gods. To him they were set dressing — exotic, mysterious, meaningless.

Except … the religion he was raised with never made him feel that way either. Although it had made his butt numb, too. Cameron was just as bored now as he'd been while Father Darius ranted about salvation and damnation and all of the sins he had committed by virtue of being a normal human being. He'd never understood why those godawful sermons made his mother light up from within, or how that nonsensical bullshit he'd had to memorize at catechism helped her make sense of the world. For most of his life, he'd thought it was her desire to be seen as a good person and her need to belong to a community that kept her coming back.

Because Cameron had never been able to believe in anything he couldn't see.

But believing in nothingness was terrifying too. If he could become nothing, was that what he'd always been?

If he could disappear into the void like he'd never existed, did he matter at all?

And if he didn't matter, did anything?

He'd always reached for his art to pull him out of that downward spiral of despair. Maybe he didn't matter, but his movies could. And if his movies existed here in the real world, then he wouldn't entirely disappear when he died.

That had been comforting before, when death was still decades away. But staring it down now, trying to get that motherfucker to back off so he could steal a few extra weeks, the idea that people he'd never met would consume his hackery like popcorn didn't improve his mood at all.

His life outside of work had been empty. He'd done his best to distract himself from the pointlessness of it all with drinking and fucking and whining that no one truly saw his genius.

If he ever felt purpose, or meaning, or anything close to sacred, it was while working. In his office, molding the studio's garbage script into the most perfect version of the story they wanted him to tell. On set, cajoling his actors to give the best performance and his crew to get the most magical shot. In the editing room, obsessively sorting through different takes to splice together the perfect scene.

But how could his quest for perfection through his art be sacred when it had ruined his marriage and turned his son's love into hate?

The pain in his heart eclipsed the fire in his joints as Cameron glanced sideways at his son. Maybe it was the flickering lamp light, but Colin looked different here. Like he'd been plugged into the same thing that had lit Cameron's mother after hours on a hard wooden pew.

You'd never know the kid had grown up around Hollywood. That he went to a prep school that cost more than some colleges, that he played soccer and racquetball, that he got into Stanford with a scholarship he didn't even need.

And he threw it all away for this: traipsing around remote parts of the world in ratty clothes, climbing mountains with strangers and helping poor farmers rescue their cows from monsoons.

Somehow, the kid didn't need any of the luxuries Cameron depended on to distract himself from the boredom of existence.

Colin moved through the world like he belonged in it.

Or like it belonged to him.

I'm never going to know him, not really. Or understand how he sees the world.

Colin had gone someplace Cameron couldn't follow. Grasped some mystery that he would never touch.

But he was still Cameron's son, his gift to the world. A better human being than Cameron would ever be.

A surge of love flooded through him. Gratitude that he'd been some small part of the process that had brought his son into being. Humbled that someone so amazing could have ever come from him.

As if he'd been part of some cosmic plan that he hadn't known existed, but somehow couldn't help following anyway, to bring something greater than himself into existence.

The only meaningful part of his life, which he'd done everything in his power to destroy.

Yet, somehow he'd been brought here, face to face with the best thing he'd ever been a part of, given a chance to appreciate his son before dying.

Cameron still couldn't believe in a god or a buddha or a demon.

But he could believe in this.

Chapter Twenty-Two

WAY TO MAKE IT ALL ABOUT YOU

CAMERON SAT on a bench outside the chapel, looking up at the sky as he massaged the pins and needles out of his still-stiff legs. He wanted to stay overnight, because once the descent was over, so was his time with Colin. But it wasn't to be.

Thankfully, his cheeks were dry by the time the kid emerged with an aura Cameron could only describe as beatific.

He smiled, brighter than the sun itself, and offered Cameron a hand up. "What did you think?"

"I understand now."

"Understand what?"

"Why you do this. Why you left. Why the life I tried to give you wasn't enough."

Colin sighed. "It's not that it wasn't enough. It just wasn't for me."

"I'm sorry, for—"

"You don't have to."

"I do. Please listen, for me."

Now Colin was the one fighting tears. "I'm listening."

"I'm sorry that I said you were a lazy, entitled dumbass—"

"Nice apology." But the kid didn't look angry, he looked hopeful.

"I'm sorry that I didn't listen to what you were trying to tell me. I'm sorry I wasn't there for you when you needed me to be. And" — hardest of all — "I'm sorry for putting you in the middle of my disagreement with your mother. I've been the world's worst father."

"Not the worst."

"I wish I could go back and be the best."

Another sigh. "I don't know what to say, Dad."

"I'm the one with things that needed saying, so thanks for listening."

A monk interrupted, explaining that it was time to collect their belongings and start their journey back down the mountain, but that they would bring the blessings they'd experienced here back home with them.

"That was the nicest *please leave* I've ever heard," Cameron said after the monk had moved on to another cluster of tourists.

As they started down the path to the bridge, he took a deep breath of cool air tinged with the scents of pine and dampness. Prayer flags ahead danced in the breeze, as if already celebrating his presence. Even the scuffing of his feet on the stone steps sounded like a cheer.

But after they'd crossed the bridge and descended the stairs, the dirt path became increasingly difficult for Cameron to navigate. He still felt stiff and tight and sore in every part of his body. He kept sliding and losing his balance every time they were somewhere steep, and he couldn't seem to find the same footholds that had been there during their ascent.

Climbing all the way back down felt impossible. If only he'd had the good sense to die in the chapel.

He skidded again on loose dirt, nearly slipped on more stone steps, slowing to a crawl when the path turned uneven and rocky. He'd have fallen, perhaps tumbling over the edge of the path if Colin hadn't grabbed a handful of his windbreaker.

Humiliating. But he didn't even have the energy to complain as he bent forward, gasping with his hands pressed to his chest as if that might slow his racing heart. He grew dizzier with every step, and the edges of his vision had contracted until Cameron could see only the toes of his spanking new hiking boots.

"Dad, talk to me. What's going on?" His son sounded frightened and far away.

"Which pills should I take?" Cameron wheezed.

Two blue, one yellow, Sofia said. *And if you've got a way to cut it, you can take half of one of the painkillers.*

He was too hot, but his hands shook as if he were freezing. Maybe the start of one of those seizures Sofia had warned him about.

He reached into his pocket, pulled out the bottles but couldn't hold onto them. They scattered in the dirt.

Colin bent to pick them up. "Which ones?"

Cameron gave him directions, and he placed three capsules in his father's mouth, holding a water bottle to his lips so he could drink.

Then Colin retrieved a multi-tool from his left calf pocket, cut one of the painkillers in half, and repeated the process.

They sat on the side of the path together until Cameron stopped shivering

"I have one more Hitchhike bar," Colin said. "Hungry?"

But he wasn't. Just exhausted. And terrified that they were going to bring in a medevac because he wasn't up to the challenge of walking back down.

"A few more minutes, and I'll be ready to go." A promise Cameron wasn't sure he could keep.

More like fifteen or twenty, Sofia added softly. *You've seriously overtaxed yourself.*

After a long silence, Colin asked, "So how did Mom take the news?"

He thought about lying, but what was the point? "I haven't told her yet."

"You can't just — not without saying goodbye. You owe her that much."

"Your mother and I already said our goodbyes."

"What does that mean?"

"She doesn't want to hear from me. I'm not part of the life she wants, or deserves."

"That's your bullshit, not hers."

Maybe it was. But Cameron didn't know how to set it aside long enough to tell her. "She'll be okay."

"No," Colin said. "You can't do this to me."

"To you?"

"Yeah, Dad, to me. If you don't tell her, then I'll have to do it."

That made Cameron feel like a selfish moron, expecting his mourning son to deliver the news of his death and comfort his ex-wife. He was still getting used to the idea that Colin would be mourning, instead of cele-brating.

"You have my word, I'll tell her."

"On the phone, if you can't do it in person. Not in a text."

"I'm not a total ass."

"Debatable." But Colin laughed, and Cameron couldn't help laughing with him.

After catching his breath, he said, "Telling people that I'm dying is really about comforting them. Not exactly my forte."

"Way to make it all about you."

How could Cameron argue with that? "I'll do it soon. Promise."

"Not good enough." Colin held his hand out in a gesture Cameron had never seen him make. "Pinky-swear."

Cameron snorted with laughter, but he hooked his own pinky — no longer shaking, now that the meds were starting to hit — and hooked it around his son's.

"I do solemnly pinky-swear that I will notify your mother of my impending demise before its untimely occurrence."

"So witnessed," Colin said, then wrapped his arms around Cameron in an honest-to-God hug. "I love you, Dad."

"I'm so proud of you," Cameron replied, soaking up the feeling of his son's acceptance.

Better than the blessings of a thousand monks.

Chapter Twenty-Three

NOT A SINGLE PERSON SCREAMED IN TERROR

I suggest you take extra precautions after you land, Sofia warned Cameron as his plane touched down in Madrid. *Theft by pickpocketing is up by forty-two percent. Don't let your suitcase out of your sight.*

"Aren't you supposed to be teaching me to let go of all my earthly possessions?"

If you lose your medication, I can't get replacements to you in fewer than thirty-six hours. An excruciatingly painful thirty-six hours, much of which you will spend in a hospital.

Oh. "How many of each type would I need for two days?"

Sofia gave him the list and he wrapped a handful of pills into the cocktail napkin.

The most commonly picked pockets are your jacket and rear pants. If your clothing is loose-fitting, avoid front pockets as well.

He checked. No internal pocket on the jacket. And while Cameron hadn't stepped on a scale, his normally snug pants were now loose around the waist. He'd probably shed at least five pounds in Bhutan, and not because he was getting fitter.

What was left? Stashing it in his briefs like a drug smuggler? If customs thought he looked suspicious and decided to search him, he'd have to come up with a reason why he was storing his perfectly legal medications next to his balls.

He retrieved a polo from his carryon and put it on over his T-shirt, then tucked the wad into the breast pocket. It made a ridiculous bulge, but someone would need a big swinging sack to try for it there.

"Anything else I should know? For instance, what I'll be doing in Spain?"

I told you, this one's better as a surprise.

"As long as you keep your promise: once we've done your thing, I get to choose something."

It was the kind of deal he used to make with Natalie all the time. Except he'd been the one setting the itinerary and she'd been the one bargaining for additional stops. Because their vacations were always location-scouting trips in paper thin disguise. They barely made it to any of the places she had always wanted to go.

Now she was visiting them all with Roger.

He grabbed his bag and exited the plane. A cool breeze swept over the tarmac as he walked toward the terminal, an architectural gem whose undulating yellow roof had scalloped edges supported by yellow beams that looked like the forking of tree branches.

His first time seeing it. He felt hollowed out, knowing he'd most likely see it once more at most. He hoped he'd have time to take a stroll around the Plaza de Cibeles, to bask in the cool mist of Ventura Rodriguez's fountain of Cybele, with its hand-carved statue of the proud Phrygian goddess in a chariot pulled by a pair of lions.

And Palacio de Cristal, the iron-and-glass conservatory, constructed in the shape of a Greek cross to showcase an exhibit of plants brought over from the Philippines, which had still been a colony of Spain at the time. It was exquisite when lit from within at night, or so he had heard.

There were a dozen other items on his wish list for Madrid, but Cameron suspected that he'd be lucky to get those two in, given how much the trip to Tiger's Nest had taken out of him. Sofia had doubled his meds after Colin returned him to the hotel, then gave him permission to take a quarter dose of the painkillers every six hours, which his son had dutifully chopped up for him before saying a final and almost silent farewell.

Motivation, he told himself. If he wanted to see Cybele's fountain and the Glass Palace, he'd have to live long enough to finish Sofia's adventure, whatever it turned out to be.

He could've argued with her, insisted on doing his thing first.

But he was so grateful that she'd given him a chance to right things with Colin, and curious what else the AI had planned.

The crowded airport seemed to be pressing in on him. He felt sweaty and sick, worse than usual. And parched, even though he'd drunk half a bottle of water shortly before the plane landed. Even the trip through Terminal 4 was enough to leave him winded. He hoped he could rest in the FASTr, or on the train to Toledo. Let the country-side lull him to sleep. He was almost there.

He didn't make it. A hundred feet from the exit, his bag refused to roll forward. Something wrong with the wheel. He tugged, tugged harder, then yanked his case hard enough to snap the handle at its base. He went to retrieve it and the whole thing ripped open at the bottom, spilling his belongings like candy from a piñata.

He fell to his knees and started cleaning his mess,

humiliated as passersby pretended not to see him. Not that he would have wanted the help. Cameron just wished he wasn't so weak. By the time he got everything back into his bag, a few travelers had eyed him with contempt as they were forced to go around him.

He picked up his suitcase, cradling it like a child to keep the contents from spilling out again, then scurried out of the airport. Once at the curb, he sat on the ground and swiped for a FASTr.

His driver, Nahia, would be there in seven minutes, so that gave him at least another six to think about things he'd like to do here.

"Sofia, can you make me a reservation at Banquete, after we finish whatever we're supposed to be doing?"

There is a two-month wait for a table at Banquete.

"That's why I wanted to eat there. Bribe them. Tell them I'm dying; they'll find a table for me. And book me a room at the Gran Meliá de los Duques."

There are no available rooms for the next week. You'll be gone before there's an opening.

"Gone, as in heading to another exotic location, or gone as in dead?"

She didn't answer immediately.

The sweat on his skin turned ice-cold. "Sofia?"

The progression of your illness has accelerated. You might have noticed increased muscular weakness, a sense of vertigo, difficulty with—

"I noticed, but Jesus, I don't even have a week?"

You might have several weeks left, or today might be your final day. At this stage, the efficacy of your medications becomes more variable.

"What's my worst case scenario?"

Another day or two.

"Anything I can do to bump that up?"

Get more sleep, avoid alcohol, and refrain from overexerting yourself.

"This from the robot that booked me on a four-mile hike up the side of a mountain?"

Do you regret that experience?

"No," Cameron had to admit. It had been a gift to hug his son one last time, to hear that he'd been forgiven. To say the *I love you* he should've said so long ago.

Nahia pulled up to the curb and jumped out to help him ease his broken suitcase into the trunk of her Citroen.

As soon as they set out, he wished he'd ordered an autonomous car instead. Nahia wanted to know what brought him to Madrid, where his train was headed, what he hoped to do during his stay in her beautiful country. After a few cursory answers, he apologized and asked if she minded if he napped. She was gracious about it, but he got the feeling that she too wished he'd ordered an autonomous car.

He doubled her tip and pretended to nap the rest of the way to the train station while contemplating his new expiration date.

Time was more like running water when death loomed months away, but now it had been reduced to a dripping faucet. He didn't have enough to make a final movie, but maybe he had time to write the script. He'd spent his flight from Bhutan fantasizing about spending his final month writing a masterpiece for Emily and Jeffries to posthumously make. Not *Fountain*, something more profound, about a father and his estranged son going on a pilgrimage together to the top of the world. And if he still had breath in him by the time he dictated *THE END*, maybe he'd write up a treatment for *Bitter Nirvana* for Jeffries and Wyatt.

Now it sounded like he didn't even have time to write a treatment for the father-son saga.

The weight of his mortality settled on Cameron like a boulder, rendering his every breath a herculean feat. He was going to die alone, in a country where no one knew him, without a chance to leave one last gift for the world before he departed.

But would it be any better to turn around and fly home, to die surrounded by people who pretended to know him for the sake of benefitting from their connection?

Assuming he didn't die on the flight, which itself would probably take half a day.

Dying here would be better than spending his final hours trapped above the Atlantic, watching shitty movies and eating airplane food.

Besides, maybe Sofia was wrong.

Your train leaves in fifteen minutes, Cameron. Please walk straight to your platform.

Moments later, the car stopped at the Estación de Atocha and Nahia helped him get his suitcase, even strapping it shut with a couple of bungee cords from her trunk, then laughing and telling him not to worry about it when he offered to pay her for them.

Cameron thanked her, feeling so grateful for the simple act of kindness that he wanted to give her a hug.

He hurried into the train station instead.

Steel and glass. Vivid tropical gardens lining the concourse. Sculptures that stole his breath. But Cameron couldn't linger. He had eleven minutes to find his train. He did it with three to spare.

After stowing his suitcase and settling into his seat, it occurred to Cameron that he was never going to see Natalie again. What if he passed before gathering the courage to deliver on his promise?

He pulled out his phone, stared at her name in his contacts. Checked the time difference: nine in the morning here was midnight for her. It wasn't even an option to call now.

Not that having an excuse made him feel any less like a coward.

So he put the phone away and basked in the gorgeous Spanish countryside as it passed by. Rolling hills and idyllic fields, so resplendent in the amber morning sun that it hurt. Some of his favorite movies had been shot here. All those Sergio Leone spaghetti westerns from the sixties, and the *Unicorn Western* franchise that used some of the same locations with a side of psychedelia. *The Others. Lawrence of Arabia.* Even *Indiana Jones and the Last Crusade.* The city of Soria and its surrounding countryside in *Doctor Zhivago* and Orson Welles' *Chimes at Midnight.* Charlton Heston and Sophia Loren in *El Cid.* Ridley Scott shooting *Kingdom of Heaven.* James Bond, dying another day.

Spain had always been on Cameron's list of places to shoot, once he was the one making most of the rules. Maybe it would be Amería or Fuerteventura. Or perhaps Barcelona's Gothic Quarter, Plaza Real Square, Pueblo Español or Horta Maze park. He had no idea.

Only that he was staring out the window at what could now never be.

HE WOKE hours later to a fresh estimate from Sofia.

"Two weeks? Earlier, you said several weeks."

I said possibly several weeks, but possibly a day or two. Isn't two weeks better than a day or two?

"You've never heard that expression, underpromise and overdeliver?" Cameron grumbled. "I couldn't help but hope for the best case scenario, you know, with death hanging over me."

Death has been hanging over you all your life, hasn't it?

"Humans are expert at denial. If you give us a choice, we'll believe what makes us feel good before we'll buy into an upsetting truth."

Pretending that the inevitable can be delayed indefinitely dooms you to disappointment, doesn't it?

"Life is disappointment, Highness. Anyone who says differently is selling something."

The original quote is actually, Life is pain—

"Same thing."

There's a strain of opinion that life's brevity and ephemerality are the things that make it beautiful.

"Right now, I disagree." Cameron was sitting in a handsome hotel room in a magnificent city, yet still his mood wanted to sour. "What am I doing next?"

I thought you might enjoy trying one of Toledo's best restaurants.

"Paella?"

Best in the city, according to several popular food critics.

"You're finally getting the hang of this." A hot shower would be perfect, and Cameron was dying to stretch his legs and soak in the ambience of a new city. "Is it close enough to walk?"

I should warn you, two weeks assumes that you will avoid alcohol. Your condition is delicate enough that I can't predict the effects of even a single glass of wine, except to tell you that they won't be good.

"Buzzkill." But it didn't matter. Cameron had two good weeks left, and he was going to find a way to enjoy them, no matter what.

Twenty minutes later, as he watched the elevator numbers count down to his floor, Sofia suddenly said, *Wait for the next one.*

"Why? Did someone just cut the wire on this one?"

It's complicated.

Whatever that meant. But when the doors opened, Cameron smiled and nodded at the family of four, ignoring the mom's impatient huff before they dinged closed.

He pressed the call button and waited, wondering what the big deal was. The power stayed on, the elevator numbers kept descending all the way to the lobby, and not a single person screamed in terror.

He peeked over the banister to see the impatient mom marching across the hotel lobby, her family following her like a cluster of ducklings.

Huh.

The elevator returned to his level, empty, and his descent to the lobby was uneventful. Was Sofia glitching?

Maybe he ought to try Eberling again.

Cameron was so distracted that he almost didn't notice the woman coming in the revolving door just as he was leaving — until she flashed him a bemused smile that made him stumble, hurrying to catch his balance before the door smacked him on the ass and dumped him into the street.

It wasn't the woman's looks, although she was definitely attractive, with tousled blonde hair and Nordic cheekbones. It wasn't the way she moved; like her lithe body was made of water and had taken solid form to flow inside the hotel.

It was that moment when she'd been looking right at him, her lips curving upward — like she had a secret that only he would understand, and she could hardly wait to share it with him.

Catching his balance on the sidewalk outside, Cameron cupped his hands around his eyes to block out his own reflection and peeked back into the lobby.

But the woman was already gone.

He was tempted to go back in, but what would he say if he found her?

Hi, I'm Cameron, from the revolving door. Did you mean to smile at me like that, or am I just a sad, lonely asshole with a terminal illness?

Maybe he'd get lucky and he'd run into her again later. In the elevator. At the pool. Near the ice machine.

Or maybe he should focus on enjoying one of the last dinners of his life.

Chapter Twenty-Four

RESENTMENTS TOO DANGEROUS TO DISCUSS

VIVIR WAS DESIGNED to make diners fall in love with their food.

The place smelled like God's kitchen. High rafters, ruby-colored tablecloths, and every wall covered with wines. Cameron passed a long table bedecked with flamboyant pastries as a distinguished maître d' led him to a quiet table for two in the back.

"Just the one?" the maître d' confirmed unnecessarily.

"Yes, it's just me. But I'll be ordering for six. Will that be a problem?"

The maître d' didn't know how to take that. "Of course not, sir. Enjoy your meal."

Cameron opened the menu, but there weren't any pictures and he didn't speak Spanish. So he closed it and waited for his server.

This was the kind of place Natalie would have begged him to take her when they were traveling.

The kind of place he'd veto, because he didn't want dinner to be a three-hour event that swallowed an entire evening that could be otherwise spent prowling the streets for "texture" — the perfect quirky bar, abandoned warehouse, or crappy hotel to give his next story world some distinctive touches. Most directors relied on AI for location scouting too, but Cameron believed that choosing the right backdrop for a scene could save it.

But who gave a crap about his artistic sensibilities? Not the critics, and probably not the audience, either. He was the only one who'd cared whether those low budget fight scenes happened in front of an art deco diner or a run-down McDonald's.

A waitress in a tight-fitting black dress with a flaring, flounced skirt approached his table and introduced herself as Lina. "What would you love to try tonight?"

Cameron opened the menu and pointed to something at random. "What's that?"

Lina followed his finger, leaned down ever so slightly while squinting, then stood straight and said, "Carcamusas. Slow-cooked pork, peas, tomatoes and white wine, served in a small clay dish called a cazuela with chunks of crusty bread."

"Is it delicious?"

"Of course it's delicious."

"Would you order it?"

"No, because my grandmother's is better." She put her finger to her lips, like she was shushing herself. "Don't tell the chef."

He laughed. "I want to try a little of everything. Where should I start?"

"With un aperitivo of queso de ovejaor, aged sheep's milk cheese that's almost flaky when you bite into it. Special to Toledo. It's served with a bit of jamón and a crunchy baguette."

"And for the entree?"

"The venison, slow-cooked with red wine and vegetables, flavored with rosemary and thyme. Or the Perdiz a la Toledana, local red partridges simmered with thinly sliced onions, white wine, and garlic cloves."

Now his mouth was watering. "That sounds superb."

"It is. Do you care much for saffron?"

"Only that I'm just mad about her, and she's just mad about me."

"I'm sorry?"

"Never mind." Cameron shook his head, feeling stupid for his obscurity. "It's an old song, I think from the 1960s. What about saffron?"

"Toledo produces some of the best saffron around the world and it is protected with Denominación de Origen status."

"That sounds important."

"Small-batch production and strict quality guidelines," she said. "The best."

"So what, you bring me a bowl of saffron and I eat it with chips?"

"If you want to taste what our chef can do with saffron, order the paella."

"Okay, that all sounds great," Cameron said.

"So … you want everything we've talked about so far?" She sounded so unsure.

"Yes, please."

She pointed to the menu, then leaned closer to Cameron and whispered, "The prices are per item."

He laughed again. "I understand, and I'm going to need some dessert, too. Just bring me one of each."

"I'm sorry?"

"I'd like to try all of them."

She hesitated for a moment, then tapped several times on her tablet. "Would you like wine with your meal?"

"Water, please." Although it killed him not to try the

best of the local wines, he was desperate to eke every last minute out of his possible life.

Lina left and it was back to waiting awkwardly while the ghost of his ex-wife haunted his thoughts.

He would give anything to be eating dinner here with Nat, to watch her fidget with excitement as she waited for each new delicacy to land on their table. He'd thought that once he'd made it, they'd do things like this between block-buster release weeks and Oscar noms. That he could use more money to fix his marriage.

But Nat had run out of patience while he was still broke. Now, it was too late — no amount of money could make up for the hurt he'd caused her.

Thankfully, the goat cheese arrived quickly. Lina brought it to the table with a baguette and thin slices of what turned out to be a type of ham with a rich, nutty flavor. The first nibble practically melted in his mouth.

"Iberian, from black-footed pigs," Lina confided, like she was giving him the secret recipe for Coca-Cola. "The best."

Nat would've loved it. She would've loved the venison too, tender and savory in its red wine sauce, along with the exquisitely balanced garlic and white wine sauce, where chunks of partridge floated in delicacy.

But the paella would have been her favorite. Loaded with scallops, shrimp and some sort of delicate-tasting fish, intense saffron and sweet scallions somehow turned each sea creature into something like divinity.

As Cameron slowly ate, savoring each bite, he watched an older couple seated two tables over. Despite being in their seventies, their comfortable silences, the way their fingers brushed as she handed him the salt shaker, and the joy on their faces as they stole glances at each other between bites made it clear they loved each other in a way that few people ever managed to achieve, let alone sustain. He didn't speak enough Spanish to know what they were saying, but the woman's blush was surely in response to some sort of gentle teasing, and Cameron could recognize a compliment in any tongue.

He never got there with Natalie, and never would. His parents rarely fought with words, but did war with one another through everyday action. A dish left in the sink for days because doing dishes was woman's work. Laundry left undone to see how many days his dad would wear the same outfit. Volunteer shifts at church fundraisers and weekends at the golf course, tiny abandonments meant as punishment for resentments too dangerous to discuss.

Maybe he and Nat were doomed from the start.

He signaled for Lina. "I'd like to box everything up and move on to dessert."

Dessert came out as a parade of sugary decadence.

A bowl of caramelized figs in a sauce spiced with something like cinnamon or cardamom, topped with frozen vanilla custard.

Raspberry sorbet with tart foam that reminded him of plain yogurt, garnished with a blown-sugar sphere that sparkled like glass.

A plate of traditional cookies and candies, which Lina named for him.

Moorish turron, a chewy-crunchy almond nougat that clung to his teeth.

Polvoròn, a lemony cookie so light it crumbled into powder on his tongue.

Marzipan tinged with rose water and orange essence, molded into bite-sized flowers.

Candied almonds and walnuts.

And crunchy pestinos, anise seed cookies that added a

pleasant counterbalance to the abundance of sugar in the others.

Nat would have loved them all.

He fought the urge to call her now, wake her up at … four in the morning, according to his phone. If he confessed his love she wouldn't hear it, she'd just be angry at him for waking her up. Or if she did hear it, she'd be upset that he wasn't respecting her relationship with Roger.

After she left, Cameron had made it a point to date women like Ariana Saint. Women who would never tempt him to slow down his career, because he would never love them enough.

Ariana would love Vivir, too. But for completely different reason.

She would pick at this amazing food — after taking a dozen pics of it — and complain that her trainer would kill her for having a single bite. She'd love being here for the thrill of being seen someplace exclusive, on Cameron Parrish's arm, and for the bragging rights it would give her with that pack of anorexic hyenas she considered both her best friends and her sharpest competition for every role and compliment.

He'd rather have dinner with no one than someone like Ariana Saint.

That was the man Cameron had become.

Chapter Twenty-Five

A LIE CAN BE BEAUTIFUL TOO

"A LIMOUSINE?" Cameron asked softly as the shiny black behemoth pulled up to the curb. "You should've told me this was going to be a black tie kind of day."

Casual attire is appropriate for the occasion. The limo was merely the most convenient available transportation.

The door of the driverless car popped open, and a soothing female voice addressed him as Mr. Parrish and invited him to step inside.

As soon as he got in, he wished he had dressed up a little, instead of donning an old black tee, jeans and sneakers. Because the limo already had a passenger.

The woman from the revolving door, whose smile had nearly caused Cameron to trip on his way out of the hotel.

Sofia again. But she couldn't have known ahead of time that he'd be attracted to this woman ... could she?

No, the AI had to have registered his attraction through the sensor implants she monitored and decided to orchestrate this.

Although there was that weird thing with the elevator. If Cameron had taken the first one, he'd have been going through the revolving door too soon to see her. Which suggested that Sofia had been playing matchmaker ahead of time, and steadily manipulating him into this encounter.

But when the woman across from him smiled — that same bemused smile she'd given him last night — he decided he didn't care if he was being manipulated or not.

"I'm Cameron." He held out his hand, which she took without hesitation. Her skin was smooth and warm. He resisted the urge to lift her hand to his lips and kiss it, which was not the kind of thing he'd do at all. "I wasn't expecting anything this fancy when I asked my assistant to book me a car."

"Brooke." Cameron couldn't place her accent, faint but definitely there. "It was one of those special offers, half the price of a regular car. I saw it this morning and thought, why not?"

He'd bet that Sofia had paid full price and put out an ad targeted to Brooke, charging just enough to keep her suspicions away.

"Where are you headed?" Cameron asked, hoping that the ride would be long enough to persuade her to have dinner with him.

"Aren't you going to the Primada Santa Maria?" At his blank look, she added, "The cathedral?"

That is your destination, Sofia said.

"Right," Cameron covered. "I meant after."

That smile was back. "What brings you to Toledo?"

He loved the way she looked at him, and if he told her he was dying, that would change. So he said, "I'm a film-maker, checking out locations for my next movie. Maybe looking for my next star."

"Already trying to get me on the casting couch?"

"That's not what I meant." But Cameron couldn't help flushing, because that's exactly why he usually said that when he met a beautiful woman. Because that's what he was usually trying to do, flex his power and reputation. But Brooke wasn't a hungry starlet, and didn't need anything from him. "Why are you here?"

"Jewel heist," she said, straight-faced.

"Where's the rest of your team?"

"They're so good, you'll never see them."

He couldn't help laughing, one of those belly laughs that had his ribs aching by the time it was out of him.

"I'm kidding ... I'm here because I'm engaged to a rich sheik — I'm about to be his thirteenth wife."

"You're not."

"You're right. But I used to be married to a duke."

"Duke of?"

"Camembert."

"That's a cheese."

"That's what he smelled like."

"Is that why you divorced him? Or was there a scandal?"

"The most scandalous scandal you can imagine."

"Is that why you're going to the cathedral — you want to pray your sins away?"

"I'm quite fond of my sins, thank you very much."

"You're not wearing a ring now," Cameron observed.

"Are you asking me if I'm married?" Direct but playful.

"Yes," he admitted. "I am."

"What will you do if I say yes?"

"Enjoy the pleasure of your company for as long as you'll allow it."

"Tell me," she said, crossing her legs in a way that somehow made him imagine her wrapping them around him. "What is it that you're most looking forward to seeing?"

He felt like an idiot admitting it, but what the hell. "I

don't know anything about it. I'm here because my assistant thought this was something I needed to see."

"An honest answer. I like it. What kind of movie are you making?"

"A father-son story. About redemption." He hated the lie even more than he'd hated telling the truth, but Cameron refused to give her a reason to stop flirting with him. Pity was the last thing he wanted. "I haven't written the script yet; I'm looking for inspiration."

"I hope you find it."

He already had. "What are you looking forward to seeing?"

"I understand that the retablo is impressive—"

"What's that?"

"A sort of vertical altar. Scenes from the life of Christ, done in gold-covered wood, mounted floor-to-ceiling on a curved wall."

"But it's not what you're interested in."

"The Rose Window is supposed to be one of the most beautiful stained-glass windows ever made."

"That's not it either."

"Then there's a ten-foot high monstrance—"

"Now you're just making up words."

"—also known as an ostentorium—"

"Showoff."

"—crafted by one of the most brilliant metalworkers who ever lived. The gold he used is supposed to have been brought back from the New World by Christopher Columbus."

"I don't think a monstrance is a thing."

"Americans." She shook her head in mock despair. "It's a giant sculpture that the church used to bring out in parades to show the people how rich they were on holy days."

"Conspicuous consumption. That's as American as it gets."

Now she was the one laughing.

"What is it that you want to see?" Cameron asked again.

"The El Greco. There are two, but I understand that *The Disrobing of Christ* is one of his best."

"You're here to see a Jesus nudie?"

"He isn't nude, he's about to be."

"And you're all about the anticipation."

"I won't be anticipating for much longer." Brooke pointed out the window at a Gothic monstrosity surrounded by cast-iron fencing. "We're almost there."

The massive limestone structure seemed to consist of a shorter central building flanked by a slender, steepled tower on one side and a fat, dome-topped tower on the other, all three sections dressed in intricate carvings. Her expression suggested that she thought it beautiful, but Cameron found it depressing. Perfect for a horror flick, the kind of movie where an innocent young woman would, at some point, flee a demon-possessed priest through a cemetery in a sheer white nightgown during a rainstorm.

"During the Visigoth period, there was a church dedicated to Mary on this site, which was torn down later so a mosque could be built over it," she informed him. That explained the minaret. "Then the mosque was torn down so that this cathedral could be built in the thirteen-hundreds."

"Did you memorize the guidebook?" Cameron teased.

"You don't want to know the history of the place where you might shoot your next movie?"

Another guilty twinge as Brooke referred to his earlier lie, which required him to deliver another. "I didn't want to have any preconceptions that might keep me from seeing it the way my audience might."

But he did have preconceptions. The church that had haunted his childhood wasn't nearly as old or ornate, but it had that same icy torment. He remembered hard wooden pews that made his backside ache, and being forced to sit still for hours on Easter and Christmas, when his friends were all stuffing their faces with chocolate or opening presents. Catechism, the same boring questions with their nearly incomprehensible answers, repeated over and over and over again. Funerals. Baptisms. Confirmations.

He'd been jealous of his father's right, as an adult, to stay home and risk the hellfire and damnation his mother wanted Cameron to fear.

"Are you religious?" she asked.

"I believe that religion is just another story humanity tells itself."

"Makes sense, coming from a filmmaker." A moment later, she added, "Since you're here on business, I'd understand if you prefer to tour the cathedral without the distraction of a stranger."

That was the opposite of what Cameron wanted. "Art is meant to be shared, and I'd be honored if you'd let me share today with you."

"I should warn you, I read the entire guidebook."

"Then you can answer all my questions."

The car eased to a stop, allowing them to disembark in front of the plaza. As they approached the cathedral, Brook informed him, "I read that they call it *Dives Toletana*, which means *the Rich Toledan* in Latin."

She aimed her finger at the pointy tower. "That's the bell tower, and that dome on the right is the Mozarabic Chapel. That's where the second tower was supposed to be built."

"There was never a second tower?"

"When the Muslims conquered Spain, Christians who stuck around developed their own rites, and when they reclaimed the country later, the locals didn't want to go back to worshipping the Roman way, so they persuaded the king to build them a chapel that fit their sensibilities."

Cameron didn't care about the history, but he loved hearing her talk. Brooke's voice made him think of strawberries and silk. And feeding strawberries to her after making love to her on silk sheets.

He pointed to the front of the church. "Tell me about all the doors, and why they're fenced off."

"The main facade has three portals: Puerta de Perdón, Puerta del Juicio Final, and Puerta del Infierno."

"Translation?"

"Portal of Forgiveness, Portal of Last Judgement, and Portal to Hell." She pointed to each one as she named them. "The Portal of Forgiveness is opened once a year, or for special occasions."

"Isn't forgiveness the point of the whole religion?"

"I think they're trying to preserve the architecture. Touching the limestone leaves an acidic residue that eats it away."

"Still, pretty ironic." He hesitated for a few moments, pretending to examine the bas-relief of an angel presiding over a group of apparent penitents. "Are we signed up for some sort of formal tour?"

"I am."

"How do you feel about skipping it? You can be my guide, and if there's something you don't know, then I'll make up the story."

"How could I possibly refuse an offer like that?"

They entered through the Portal of Judgement, the last place Cameron wanted to metaphorically be. They stopped just inside so Brooke could exclaim over the checkerboard marble floor and the massive vaulted ceiling.

Cameron had entered a grand hall made for a majestic being, a palace built for giants. And he was a cockroach. He had the urge to run for a dark place where he couldn't be noticed, and therefore, wouldn't be squished.

"Isn't it amazing?" Brooke whispered.

"That's one word for it."

She led him to a massive semi-circular alcove with floor-to-ceiling gilded wooden carvings; intricate details in brightly colored paint. It had to be five or six stories high. Stained-glass windows spilled light from the top, and an even higher vaulted ceiling. Unbelievable grandeur, created at unimaginable expense, to tell a story full of contradictions and anachronisms, about a man who probably didn't exist, and if he did, probably didn't have the magical powers attributed to him.

The sense of futility Cameron had felt as a child came flooding back as he remembered arguing with the nuns about things that didn't make sense in their stories, and being told that he was doomed to suffer forever if he couldn't find a way to believe.

He'd had a knack for finding plot holes, even as a kid.

"The retablo, or high altar, that I was telling you about. Decorated with scenes from Christ's life, to illustrate the theme of humanity's salvation."

"I don't know." Cameron shook his head, feeling forlorn, despite his buoyancy from just moments before.

"What don't you know?"

He thought for a minute. "This doesn't feel like salvation to me. It feels more like a monument to mankind's desperate hope that there's something after death."

Brooke's eyebrows went way up. "I suppose that's one way to look at it."

"Every single person who ever had anything to do with this place is dead. Every architect and artisan. Maybe they're somewhere better than here, and maybe their work on this cathedral granted them access to Heaven or some sort of blessed afterlife like they were looking for."

"That's the theory."

"But it's also possible that all of those people are now just a pile of ancient bones buried in the back of a cathedral. There is a cemetery here, right? There would have to be a cemetery. What if their life's greatest work — art that convinced thousands after them to believe in Heaven and Hell, was all a lie?"

"Are all the stories you tell factual? Don't you believe that a lie can be beautiful, too?"

"Everyone knows that the stories I tell aren't true."

She smiled like he'd said something amusing. "Would you like to see the treasury?"

He enjoyed that a lot more, because everything in it felt like a fancy prop. Crafted with gold, silver, and gems, every item in the place looked like it could be the MacGuffin in a religious-themed heist film.

The Crown of the Virgin, looking like a crazed crafter had gone nuts with the world's most expensive bejeweler. A cape made from twelve yards of silver cloth, crusted with diamonds, emeralds, sapphires, rubies and pearls. The massive gold-plated monstrance Brooke had mentioned earlier, which looked like a model of the world's fanciest building, which had been filled with holy crackers and carried during the Procession of the Body of Christ.

The idea of parading something that valuable down a filthy medieval street while thousands of starving peasants crowded around … the church had been so powerful, they could flaunt their impossible wealth without any fear of losing it.

The treasury's contents were worth billions, even discounting their historical value. And the room itself was a work of art, with what Brooke called an *artesanado* ceiling, carved with flowers and religious figures, painted black and gold.

He could probably have financed *Fountain* with one square inch cut from that silver cape.

His headache was back, and so was his sour stomach. A terrible taste in his mouth, awful enough that he was suddenly worried about getting too close while talking to Brooke and having her smell the death that had surely tainted his breath. He sure as hell wasn't about to try holding her hand now that his were so clammy.

He followed her to the Sacristy, filled with famous portrayals of religious scenes painted by Spanish masters.

She led him straight to El Greco's *The Disrobing of Christ.*

At its center, Jesus — dressed in a vivid crimson robe that covered pretty much everything — gazed upward as the sky opened above him. The savior was surrounded by a jostling crowd, their hands reaching for the garment they intended to tear from his body. But Christ stared up at Heaven unfazed, refusing to be dragged down by his tormentors, many of whom carried lances and one of whom wore a full set of conquistador armor, because of course he did. A figure in all black jabbed an accusing finger at Jesus, whose calm serenity and idealized beauty offered a searing contrast to the dirty violence of his executioners.

Cameron glanced at Brooke, about to say something sarcastic about the anachronistic conquistador, but pressed his lips shut at the sight of her tears.

"It's so much more striking in person," she whispered,

touching the locket nestled between her collarbones, which he had somehow failed to notice before.

He wanted to agree, but his mouth had gone dry and he was starting to feel faint; he staggered over to a column and leaned against the cool stone. She looked over, perhaps to see if he was okay, and Cameron gave her a smile to let her know he was fine and that she should absolutely take her time.

A priest happened by a few minutes later. "You are all right?"

"I'm good," Cameron assured him. "I just need to rest for a moment."

He nodded, raised his hand in a gesture of benediction, then muttered something in Latin before leaving.

But Cameron didn't feel comforted in the least.

He was still weak, even after the purple pill kicked in, but if he admitted to Brooke that something was wrong, he might never have a woman look at him like she found him attractive again. So he let her believe that he was overcome with emotion at the intensity of *The Disrobing of Christ*. And when she suggested that there was a second El Greco in a nearby church, he agreed to see it with her.

The Iglesia de Santo Tomé was supposed to be a six-minute walk, but Cameron was having a hard time keeping a normal pace. Brooke didn't seem to notice that he was sweating and pale after a block. She explained how this church had also been built on the site of a mosque whose minaret had been repurposed as a bell tower, and later renovated by the very Count Orgaz whose painting they were about to see.

"I thought we were going to see an El Greco," Cameron objected, instead of making the obvious double entendre. He normally went straight for the sexual innuendo, to gauge his chances with the Ariana Saints, but

Brooke was different. Even on death's doorstep, she made him feel alive. He couldn't let anything jeopardize that, not even his apparently not-dead-yet libido.

"We are going to see an El Greco. Count Orgaz is who he painted."

They walked down narrow stone-paved streets, some of which would have been considered alleys back home, many intersecting at what seemed like odd places, and all of which felt both familiar and foreign to Cameron.

After the calculated grandeur of the cathedral, the Santo Tomé church felt almost cozy. Plenty of gold beneath those high, vaulted ceilings, but cheery yellow walls and warm reddish-brown pews made him feel welcome. He could imagine celebrating special days with family here, people smiling and asking after absent relatives, while children in their Sunday best whispered and giggled and played secret games that their parents pretended not to notice.

He glanced longingly at the nearest empty pew, aching for a moment to rest before moving on, but Brooke nodded toward a line of waiting people. "They charge a little, but I want to see the painting up close."

Cameron craned his head, trying to see past the front of the line, but she shook her head at him. "Oh no, you're *that* kind of guy."

"What kind of guy?"

"The kind of guy who wants the trailer to show him the whole movie."

"Believe me, I'm not."

"You won't be sorry you waited."

He hoped she meant more than the painting.

By the time they made it to the front of the line and handed over a few euros — to see a single painting — Cameron would've gladly paid five times as much to spend the next half-hour napping in a corner. Only the promise of dinner with Brooke kept him on his aching feet.

But as they entered the viewing area, he caught first sight of the massive painting, its canvas cut to fit perfectly into the recessed arch where it hung, and it was like his soul had been struck by lightning.

He'd thought he was here to see a portrait of a Spanish lord in a lace ruff, posing stiffly in an attempt to look dignified and imposing and powerful. But this—

El Greco had painted the corpse of Count Orgaz, clad in steel armor embossed with gold, being tenderly wrapped in a shroud by two saints in golden robes, one old and the other young, as a crowd of black-clad mourners listened to a priest with his back to the viewer. Angels awaited the arrival of the Count's soul with what had to be the Virgin Mary, Christ himself, and a host of others who were probably saints or holy men in the heavens above.

But it wasn't the intensely vivid contrasts of black and gray with gold and red and purple that the painter had used to stunning effect, or the fine details that turned the image into something that felt more real than the chapel around it, or even the pale beauty of the Count himself that cramped his stomach in agony.

It was the grief on the mourner's faces, and the loving way the two robed men cradled his body, and the joy of heavenly figures awaiting the departed's arrival.

Count Orgaz had been loved in a way that Cameron had desperately craved his entire life, and never come close to feeling.

There would be no one to gently dress his exhausted flesh in fine armor.

No crowd of mourners weeping and giving thanks that they'd known him.

No angels waiting to dance with his soul as it floated skyward.

There would be a medic of some sort, to sign the certificate that turned his body into the next day's work at the nearest crematorium.

Or if he asked Sofia to arrange it, the medic would send his body home, to be dissected in a lab by scientists who didn't think of him as a person, but as material for their next experiment.

He could spend his every remaining cent to have a fancy marble mausoleum built in a prestigious graveyard next to rich strangers who had perished centuries ago. But who would visit and leave flowers? Who would make sure the grass was mowed around it? Who would see his tomb as anything more than a monument to how much money he'd amassed by his final breath?

And what difference would it make if they did?

Because he'd still have died unloved, and he'd still be forgotten by anyone who mattered, a footnote in the history of action cinema that would eventually be meaningless to all but a few dedicated cinephiles.

Cameron had done nothing that mattered. And he was about to become nothing.

What was the point of being alive if this was how it ended?

Brooke slipped her hand into his.

He looked over and saw that she was crying, too.

"You get it, don't you?" she whispered.

Cameron wished he didn't, but he did.

Chapter Twenty-Six

A STORY YOU TELL YOURSELF TO PUT OFF
BEING SAD

Brooke chose the restaurant: Barlata, a family-owned establishment where his black tee and jeans fit right in. From their table, he could hear the patriarch barking at his grandchildren in the kitchen. The waitress introduced herself as Isabella, shouted something in Spanish that sounded a lot like, *behave yourselves, we have customers,* and seated Brooke and Cameron at a cozy table in the back — just far enough from the chaos to have a romantic conversation if they wanted, but still close to the restaurant's warmth.

Cameron couldn't help smiling, at everyone. Especially Brooke.

Like the fancy restaurant where he'd eaten alone last night, Barlata also had paella, of course, but it was half the price and triple the portions. The menu suggested it for sharing.

Brooke suggested they split two versions of the saffron-tinged rice dish: the first featuring red snapper and shellfish, the second chicken, pancetta, and mushrooms. Cameron raised her by one — he couldn't resist trying the combination of pine nuts, vegetables, and currants, drizzled in allioli. He also insisted on trying the three-treasures ceviche, with shrimp, scallops, and octopus, and the fire-roasted shishito peppers.

"What kind of wine do you like?" Brooke asked, perusing the list.

If you plan to do anything other than pass out immediately after dinner, no alcohol, Sofia whispered.

"I think I'll skip it tonight," Cameron answered. Because he definitely wanted the evening to continue past dinner. "But don't let that stop you."

"Beer?" she asked.

"Not for me."

She completed their order with, "*Agua fresca, sandía y mango.*"

Iced juice, he later found out. She offered him the watermelon and kept the mango for herself.

"Delicious." Cameron raised his glass in toast. "To the Count."

Brooke drank with him, but instead of setting her own glass down, she proposed a second toast. "To Alex."

Who's Alex? he almost asked, but her expression suggested that this was a test, so instead he echoed her words and took a swig of his suddenly too-sweet juice.

"My late husband." She tapped her locket. "His ashes."

"I'm sorry."

"Don't be. I'm here to celebrate his life."

"That sounds—" Like a story you tell yourself to put off being sad? "—nice."

"I made up all those stories earlier because I liked the way you were looking at me, so please don't stop."

She didn't want to be pitied any more than he did. Cameron understood that better than anyone right now.

But it also felt wrong to follow her mention of a dead husband with flirting.

"Was he from here?"

"Alex always wanted to see the Santa Maria cathedral. He wasn't Catholic, but he was fascinated with medieval architecture."

"You're seeing it for him."

"I like to think he's seeing it with me."

"You believe in ghosts?"

"Or that he's with me in spirit, in some way."

It was the perfect moment to come clean.

I'm dying. Brain cancer. I wanted to see the world before I died, but I've only got a couple weeks to live, and I'd love to spend them with you.

Except then she'd be the one pitying him, and the growing connection he'd been feeling all day would change.

"We were supposed to take this trip next year, together."

She looked sad — only for a moment, but enough to make Cameron feel like a creep for wanting to make love to her while the woman was still mourning her husband.

How could he get the conversation back to where it was? Before *The Burial of the Count Orgaz* and *The Disrobing of Christ* and the temple to man's desire for salvation — or his desire to buy a better death, depending on how you looked at it.

She'd been vibrant and coy and a little bit flirty in the limo. He wanted that Brooke back, so she could maybe look at him in a way that made him feel wanted.

"What happens after you've seen everything Alex wanted to see?"

"Home, to Iceland. I already shipped the rest of his ashes to my mother. We'll scatter them at Hengifoss."

"Is that where you're from?"

She laughed. "No, it's a waterfall. He went hiking there and loved it."

He could still tell her. *I've been thinking a lot about what I want done with my ashes … because I'm going to die in a couple of weeks.*

"Do you believe in ghosts?" she asked.

"If they're real, they're great at hiding from ghost hunters."

That got a laugh, and her bemused smile was back. "I hear that you only see them if their unfinished business is with you."

"All my business is definitely finished." Another perfect transition.

But she asked, "Do you think there's an afterlife?"

Did she want him to say yes, because she needed to believe that her husband was now in a better place?

There were two lies between them already; Cameron didn't want to add a third.

"No. My mother used to drag me to church, but it all seemed like fairytales to me. I couldn't believe."

"Did she drag your father along too?"

"He stopped believing before I was born. Mom never quite forgave him for that, although she kept praying he'd change." He took another sip of juice. "How about you?"

"My parents taught me the myths of all religions, but my mother used to say that God is found when humans share themselves."

"Do you agree?"

"Sometimes, when I'm lost in a work of art."

"What do you believe when you're not looking at art?"

She shrugged. "Do you wish you could believe in God?"

"Not the Catholic one. He's even angrier than my dad was."

She smiled at him over the rim of her glass. "Maybe it's better to be a heathen and believe in many deities. That way you can shop around, find the one you get along with best."

Cameron's smartass reply was preempted by the ceviche's arrival. Tart and fishy and somehow perfect anyway. The fire-roasted peppers lit his mouth on fire and forced him to gulp half his juice to douse the flames.

"My ancestors would've expected to go to Valhalla," Brooke said, "but that's better for men than for women. I don't want to spend eternity fetching beer."

"It wouldn't be eternity," he pointed out.

"Götterdämmerung," they said together. And laughed.

He wished wine were an option, to keep the conversation playful, but Cameron was determined to be fully functional tonight if Brooke accepted his offer to—

"Which afterlife would you prefer?"

Cameron shrugged. "If there is such a thing, I'm probably headed for Hell."

"Because you've been bad?"

"Because that's where all the interesting people go."

"Bold of you to assume that you're interesting enough for Hell," she teased. "I'm considering reincarnation."

"That's no good. You have to keep dying over and over until you get your life right."

"But you also get to live, over and over. No pleasure without pain, right?"

"That's my biggest problem with religion. Why can't I just order the pleasure?"

"Boring." She offered him the last pepper.

He shook his head. "What would you like to come back as?"

"A lioness. You?"

"Myself."

"You've already been you. Don't you want to learn something new?"

He'd rather learn his lessons sooner and have time to benefit from them. "I find it suspicious that there are so few choices for an afterlife."

"Because so many of our religions come from the same source material."

"According to the secular humanist."

"You'd rather believe that we just disappear into nothing?"

Of course he wouldn't. But— "Isn't that the most logical explanation?"

"What about hanging out here and being worshipped by your descendants?"

"We're back to ghosts already." Cameron pretended to think for a moment. "Are you asking me to haunt you?"

"Are you planning on being one of those scary Korean ghosts who messes with the lights, or will you be a helpful ghost like Hamlet's father, showing up to tell me what's going down behind the scenes?"

"Your choice."

She laughed. "Maybe you could be like an Egyptian pharaoh and turn into a star after you die."

"If I'm going that route, I'd rather be a constellation."

"In that case, you'll need to kiss up to one of the Greek gods. Or maybe do something heinous enough to piss one of them off."

"I'm pretty sure I've already done that."

She pressed for details, but Isabella returned with three platters piled high with paella, and the savory aromas roused his hunger.

"If there is a Heaven—" Cameron pointed to the

chicken-pancetta-mushroom paella, "—they serve this at every meal."

"If there's a Hell, they serve all three, but only let you choose one."

After they'd dulled the edge of their hunger, Brooke brought up near-death experiences. "That's the closest thing we have to evidence of an afterlife. What if they're right, and you go into the light to be with everyone you've ever loved?"

Cameron would still be sad, because no one would be waiting for him.

"Who'd be waiting for you?"

"My grandmother," she said, looking happy and sad in unison. "Who would you want to be waiting for you?"

His sorrow must've bled through, or she wouldn't have given him the out.

"Akiro Kurosawa," he said. "*Seven Samurai* and *Yojimbo* are two of the best films ever made."

"So he inspired you to make action films?"

"I never told you that."

"I looked you up on Forage while you were in the restroom and found for the entry with your picture."

Cameron couldn't stop himself. "Have you seen any of my movies?"

"No, sorry."

"Don't be."

"But I read that you were 'remarkable for human film-making in a genre that is otherwise empty of it.'"

"That's a kind way of saying that I don't use artificial intelligence to storyboard, shoot, score, or edit my movies, even though it's the industry standard."

"Why not?"

"Because our world is obsessed with AI." *Shut up.* "Because everyone always talks about how great technology is and how it saves us all of this time. But what are we actually doing with that time? Making more mediocre movies. AI is a way for the studios to improve their profit margins, not the artistry of their films."

"How does the AI work?"

"It analyzes popular films and suggests changes to the script. It analyzes people's eye movements as they watch films, and adjusts the pacing to keep them from getting bored. It makes dialogue tweaks based on an actor's past performances, to optimize deliverability. It cuts the score to hit specific emotional triggers. It's all so manipulative."

"Is it less manipulative when you make those decisions?"

Cameron didn't have an answer for that.

She leaned forward and licked her lips. "I also read that you're dating Ariana Saint?"

"That's definitely not true."

"Then you won't mind if I invite you back to my room?"

He definitely did not.

THEY SPILLED into his room and crashed on the bed.

Cameron felt a surge of life coursing through him, as if she had pushed death's hand away from his flesh wherever she touched him.

She slathered his face and neck with kisses before wrenching her body away from him, pulling the dress off over her head, and tossing it onto the carpet. Her bra followed. Then Brooke was in only her panties grinding against him.

"Wait," he warned her, "I might—"

"Don't worry," Brooke told him as she unzipped his

slacks and slipped her hand into his briefs. "We've got all night."

Then she kissed him again, slower, with a rhythm he could've kept for days. He hadn't kissed anyone like this since Natalie — all these years, he'd been fucking Arianas, women who thought his dick was a joystick they could use to control him, when he could've been with someone like Brooke. Someone smart and independent, who appreciated him for who he was, rather than being jealous of his career. That's who he'd thought Natalie was, before they were married, before her resentment rooted and turned her into someone he barely recognized.

"Clothes off," Brooke demanded.

Cameron rushed to untangle his legs from his pants, then yanked his T-shirt overhead with her help. Finally naked, he let her push him back down to the bed, guiding his head to the pillows with a hand on the back of his neck as she straddled him.

He'd given up all hope of ever feeling this again. Brooke was a miracle wrapped in flesh, descended to this earthly plane to give him one last taste of Heaven.

She laid her hands on his chest, and it felt like a blessing. He flashed on the image of Count Orgaz, cradled in the arms of saints, and the thought struck him that this was his burial rite. Somehow Brooke had sensed the imprint of death's grip on his body, and was preparing him for the grave.

But Cameron didn't want that.

He wanted her to fill him with life.

To hold his disease at bay and grant him more life, with her at his side.

He'd go anywhere, do anything, to bask in her glow.

Stay with me, he wanted to whisper, but everything exploded and for a white-hot second, Cameron wondered if this was it. The pleasure was excruciating, a tiny death to prepare him for the big one on its way.

He pulled Brooke against him and clung to her as he shuddered.

Cameron fell into darkness, praying that she'd be there when he woke.

Chapter Twenty-Seven

YOURS IS NOT THE ONLY TRAGEDY

CAMERON WOKE from a dream that he lay on a rough wooden table while dour-faced monks dressed him in armor that weighed him down so he couldn't move to protest.

But he wasn't dead in a medieval painting, he was alive in an elegant Spanish hotel room, and his new reason for living still slumbered beside him.

It wasn't just the sex Cameron craved, although he'd happily spend whatever time he had left inside her. The real miracle was that Brooke had banished the loneliness that had stained his life ever since Natalie left him. He hadn't felt alone once since he'd gotten into the limo yesterday morning.

Loneliness had been killing him long before the cancer began to devour his brain. If Brooke stayed with him, he was sure to live twice as long. Maybe he'd even beat this. People had miraculous cures, remissions that doctors couldn't explain.

The woman who might literally have the power to save

his life rolled over and smiled sleepily at him. "That was fun."

"What do you want to do today?"

"I've got a flight to Lisbon this afternoon."

"I've never been there." He waited a beat, then added, "Where is it?"

"Americans." She kissed him on the cheek, then rolled out of bed. "It's the capital of Portugal."

"What time do we leave?"

She grabbed her panties off the floor and shimmied into them. "No, I'm meeting Alex's brother and uncle there."

"I'd love to meet them."

"I don't think so."

Oh. Right. Not cool to introduce your new lover to your late husband's family. At least, not right away.

"Then I'll see the sights while you spend time with your in-laws, and we can—"

"This has been lovely, but—"

"There's no reason it has to be over. We can go anywhere, do anything we want."

She sat on the edge of the bed, the morning sunlight surrounding her with a burning gold halo.

"I'm glad our paths crossed, and I enjoyed sharing yesterday with you. But I have plans, and obligations to family—"

"Alex's family." A shitty thing to say, but Cameron couldn't stop himself from blurting it out.

"Please don't ruin this by being childish." Brooke bent over to snatch her bra off the floor, followed by her dress. "We had our fun, and it's time to move on."

"It was more than fun for me."

"I'll take that as a compliment."

Almost fully clothed. As soon as she found her shoes, this conversation would be over.

"Brooke, I'm dying."

She stopped her search long enough to give him an epic eyeroll.

"I'm serious. Glioblastoma, a fast-moving brain cancer. I've only got a couple more weeks to live."

"So, you lied about being here to find locations for a movie."

Shit. "Only because I didn't want you to feel sorry for me. Same as you didn't want me to feel sorry for you about Alex's death."

"But now you'd like me to feel sorry for you?"

"No." How was it he'd already screwed this up? He'd always assumed it was Nat's fault that their conversations devolved into fights so fast, but here it was happening exactly the same way with Brooke. "I just — I only have a little time left, and I'd really like to spend it with you."

"Yesterday was magical, but that doesn't mean you have the right to take me for granted today."

"I wasn't trying to—"

"But you were."

Cameron hated that she was right, but he couldn't deny it. "I'm sorry."

"Do you really think it's fair to ask me to let my family down just because I met you?"

"Doesn't it change things to know I'm dying?" He felt so weak and needy, but ignored his self-loathing and awaited her answer.

"I'm still mourning Alex, and so are they. Yours is not the only tragedy."

"But … I need you." Cameron didn't add *more than they do*, because he was already begging, and adding a guilt trip would make him feel even more craven than he already did. "Brooke, please."

"I'm not your mother. I'm not your wife. And I'm most certainly not your nurse."

But his mother was dead, his wife was married to another man, and there was no point in having a nurse, because medicine had quit curing him.

"You can be anything you want to be. I need *you*. Who you are."

"I'm Alex's widow." She stepped into her shoes and grabbed her purse. "You've clearly fallen into a pattern of forgetting that women have needs too. We don't exist to care for you."

He couldn't believe this was happening, didn't know how to fix it. "I'm sorry, I didn't mean it."

"This is your chance to break the pattern, Cameron. Wish me a wonderful trip, and be genuinely happy for me that I'm leaving."

He wanted to cry. "If you leave, it doesn't matter whether I break the pattern or not."

Brook gave him the look he'd been trying to avoid since he met her: pure pity.

"Now," she said, "is when it matters most."

ONCE BROOKE WAS GONE, Cameron asked Sofia, "Did you know she wouldn't stay?"

There would be no way for me to know such a thing with certainty.

He was medicated, showered, and dressed; Cameron looked ready for the day, but he wasn't. Brooke had picked him up and hurled him to the ground, shattering him into pieces, and now he was trying to gather them up before leaving his room.

"But you had some idea?"

I knew she had travel plans, and that her self-actualization score is fairly high.

Her self-actualization score? What did that mean? And …

"Why didn't you warn me?

You wouldn't have wanted me to.

"Of course I would have wanted you to! You could've saved me from the pain I'm feeling right now."

Awareness of the terminus of pleasure diminishes the experience of that pleasure.

"I might've found a way to change her mind."

Or perhaps you would've attempted to guilt-trip her into staying sooner, and she would not have had sex with you.

"You orchestrated this whole thing. You could find out where she's going, set it up so I could run into her once she's had a day or two to cool off—"

That would be an unethical use of my access privileges.

"You're supposed to be making sure my last days are the best they can be."

That is not correct.

Unbelievable. "Then book me a flight to Lisbon. I'll find her myself."

She would be within her rights to ask for police intervention if you insist on stalking her.

"I wouldn't be stalking her, I'd be—" What? Following her around in the hope that she'd give in and be his very last girlfriend. Even in his head, it sounded creepy. "I suppose you've already booked me a flight somewhere else that I never wanted to go."

Not a flight, a car. You'll be staying in Spain for at least one more day.

"You're not going to tell me more than that, are you?"

You'll benefit more from the experience if—

"—if I go into it without preconceptions. I got it."

Cameron hated the way he felt right now; it reminded him of so many fights with Nat, and the angry gloom he'd always carried for days afterward.

He still had to call her, but fuck if he was going to do it now.

"What am I supposed to do?"

Your car arrives in an hour. If you're hungry, the restaurant serves an excellent break—"

"Not hungry. Have the hotel pack the rest of my stuff."

He grabbed his wallet and his room key, and headed for the door.

Where are you going?

"Out," he said, like he used to after he and Nat had fought to a standstill and he was fresh out of buttons to push.

Maybe Brooke was right. Maybe it was his fault that Nat had left him. He'd always thought he was treating her right, but what did he know? His parents could barely stand each other — Cameron had thought he was doing better because at least he tried talking to Nat, and did always want to work things out with her.

But now Cameron wondered if he'd been repeating the pattern in a different way.

But Brooke was wrong about it mattering now. It was too late to get Natalie back. Too late to be the father he'd wanted to be.

Too late for him to do anything but die.

Chapter Twenty-Eight

IF HE WAS GOING TO THROW A SUICIDE PARTY

CAMERON'S FASTr slowed and turned into a narrow driveway leading to a massive house overlooking the sea. "Sofia, you must've given this car the wrong address."

This is your seaside cottage.

"That's not a cottage, that's a small mansion."

It was the only rental available that met our specifications.

What specifications? "I said I wanted someplace quiet and close to the beach."

It also needed to be within a ten-minute drive of a suitably equipped hospital.

"Don't start treating me like that."

It's part of my imperative to extend your life to whatever degree I can. If you have another seizure—

"Then I'll die, like I was going to all along."

He hauled himself out of the car, which took a lot more effort than it should've. His body felt heavy, like his bones were now lead. And yet brittle, like everything else had turned to glass. He imagined moving too fast, the lead bones breaking free and turning his body to shards.

The car's trunk popped itself open. Or maybe Sofia was controlling the car.

His luggage seemed to have gained weight as well.

As he wheeled it up to the front door and waited for Sofia to transmit the unlock code, he wondered if his misery was triggered by his illness or by the hollow feeling that had settled into his chest since Brooke had abandoned him.

He hadn't felt like this since those endless weeks after Natalie left him.

The hollowness intensified once he was inside — high ceilings, expansive rooms, plenty of space for an extended family to spread out across couches, love seats, and comfortable-looking chairs. The place had a formal dining room, breakfast nook in the kitchen, and a bar with stools separating the dining room and kitchen. Eight bedrooms, six and a half bathrooms, a home office, and a massive deck furnished with tables, patio chairs, and a gas fire pit.

The kind of place Cameron would rent if he planned to throw a party for fifty people, or was summering with extended family and friends. Being alone here ...

He'd read once that a person could actually die of loneliness. If that was his plan, staying in a place like this would be an excellent step.

He left his bag in the living room then headed for the fridge. He opened it to see stacks of sealed containers. He pulled one out and lifted the lid. Paella. As soon as the scents of saffron and shrimp hit his nose, he thought of Brooke. The others were more promising — a bento-style container whose compartments held almonds, two kinds of cheese, pickled peppers, three kinds of olives, pale slices of meat that might be ham, and sliced sausage. There was a tub of soup, definitely gazpacho. And plenty of stuff he didn't recognize but smelled amazing.

I had a chef from Boca Abierto fill the refrigerator. If you'd like something else—

"This is great, thanks." Cameron grabbed several containers, plus a bottle of water and a fork, then headed for the deck, where he positioned a lounge chair to look out over the waves and dragged a table over for the food.

He started with the paella, hoping the familiar flavor would bring back the warmth of connection he'd felt while with Brooke, but maybe he should have heated it, because otherwise it was a bowl of cold rice with shrimp and vegetables. Nicely seasoned, and better than anything he could cook, but still not the same.

Next, something Cameron had grabbed because it smelled like chilies and onions, which reminded him of the dinner he'd eaten with Colin that first night. This turned out to be small chunks of fried potato in a spicy ketchup-like sauce flecked with bits of minced onion, and a hint of sweet paprika.

"What's this?"

I believe it's called patatas brava. Brave potatoes.

He ate half of them before he opened the next container: meatballs in a tomato-based sauce. He almost spit out the first bite. The meat had an odd, rubbery texture and a fishy taste he couldn't quite place. But he loved the sauce; rich garlic, tart tomato, a hint of saffron's fruitiness, along with something nutty.

"Is this one supposed to have the texture of a chopped-up eraser?"

The meatballs? They're squid minced with cilantro, onions and—

"I don't need the recipe." Now that Cameron knew what he was eating, he didn't mind the way it bounced when he bit into it. "Not bad."

He finished his meal by trying each of the snacks from

the bento-style container and several petite cookies heavily dressed with cinnamon. Simple and sweet and exactly the kind of cookies Nat would've let Colin "help" her make when he was little and followed her everywhere.

Cameron once resented how much his son had clung to his mother; it made him flush with shame to remember all those fights about her turning Colin into a mama's boy. She'd been there for him and Cameron had not.

That was one hundred percent his fault.

He shoved the memory away and asked Sofia to tell him what he was doing tomorrow. She refused.

"I'm just supposed to wander through Spain, purposeless, until I die?"

You have a purpose. You're saying goodbye to your life.

"That's why you brought me together with Colin, isn't it?"

That was my intention.

"But it wasn't mine."

If that is not what you want, why did you agree to this?

"Because the alternative was a fate worse than death. All of them were."

Is being surprised by tomorrow's activities a fate worse than death?

"Of course not, but——"

You're more likely to benefit if you begin without expectations.

"But what's the point of benefitting from anything if I'll be dead next week?"

Emily Dickinson said that forever is composed of nows.

"She probably didn't know how many nows she had left when she said it."

Your data suggests that you're tired.

He was. The pain radiating out from his bones wasn't excruciating so much as overwhelming. It had been worse, or at least sharper. But the burden of carrying his constant ache around with him everywhere was weighing on him. Letting his head loll back against the lounge, he listened to the rhythm of the waves. After his dinner at Ithaa, he hadn't really been trying to kill himself; he'd been drunk and desperate to escape the anguish of being helpless in the face of his mortality. He'd never have the courage to walk into the ocean sober. Cowardice would turn him around at the first uncomfortable gasp.

But people did that. Virginia Woolf filled her pockets with stones and waded into a river near her home.

Tony Scott, who'd directed blockbusters like *Top Gun* and *Days of Thunder*, and one of Cameron's favorites, *Man on Fire*, had jumped off a bridge.

Richard Brautigan, whose novel, *Sombrero Fallout*, Cameron had been inexplicably fascinated with after being forced to read it in a college course, shot himself in the head after writing a suicide note that said, *Messy, isn't it?*

Were they cowards, running from their lives?

Or was he the coward, unwilling to meet death on his own terms?

"Would you help me kill myself? If that was what I really wanted to do?"

If you chose assisted suicide, I could help you find a physician who—

"You're missing the point, I don't want to die in a hospital bed. I want to end my life in a more beautiful way."

That might not be realistic.

"What are you saying?"

How much do you want to know?

Cameron swallowed, the walls of his dry throat sticking to each other as if that might keep him from answering.

Sofia had been adamant about keeping the time of his death a secret, so he wouldn't be distracted from the experiences she was trying to provide for him. The end must be nigh, if she was willing to tell him now.

In approximately one week, the medication you're taking will no longer be able to suppress your symptoms, and you'll be subject to hallucinations, seizures, excruciating pain, and partial or total paralysis.

"A week."

Approximately.

"Can you do it?"

Do what?

Cameron swallowed again, wishing he hadn't already finished the bottled water. "Can you … turn me off? Make me stop breathing or something, so I don't have to go through all of that?"

I merely take data from the sensors Dr. Eberling implanted during your surgery. I have no control over your automatic nervous system.

"So I'd need a person to help me." Cameron couldn't believe he was talking about killing himself.

I will make the appointment if you are serious. You'll have to be evaluated by a psychiatrist first.

"No." He'd rather slit his wrists in this lounge chair and watch the waves until he lost consciousness. The kitchen seemed well-equipped; all he'd need is a knife sharp enough to do it with one cut, because he definitely wouldn't have the nerve to slice twice once his nerve endings protested the damage.

A long time ago, Cameron had read that Roman women seeking death would throw a lavish party, cut their wrists and wrap them tightly, then loosen the wrappings a bit at a time, so they'd bleed out slowly as they bid farewell to their friends. He'd thought it was romanticized bullshit then, but now he could see the appeal even if it was.

Not that he had any friends who deserved that kind of dramatic farewell. If Cameron was going to throw a suicide party, he'd spend the evening saying his *fuck yous* as his body entered its controlled downward spiral.

Who was he kidding? If he couldn't drown himself, he definitely couldn't take a knife and deliberately open his flesh. If this were a movie, he could hire a hitman to take him out when he wasn't suspecting it.

Something in him rebelled, even at that.

Whether it made him courageous or cowardly, he couldn't kill himself, not even for the sense of control it might give him.

Cameron wondered how bad it would have to get before he changed his mind.

DIRT FILLED his nose and mouth, silencing his screams, as uncaring strangers in gold robes shoveled more into his grave, ignoring his pleas.

Brooke watched silently, tapping the locket filled with her husband's ashes, as he begged her to tell them he was still alive.

But dirt kept spilling into his mouth. He coughed it out and screamed — then fell out of the lounge and spit bloody phlegm on the weathered deck.

Shaking all over, he forced himself up to hands and knees. "Sofia?"

If you're unable to get the medicine from your bag, I'll have to call an emergency team.

He crawled to the sliding glass door, pulled himself to his feet by gripping the handle, and slid it open so he could stagger to the foyer and fumble the orange canisters out of his bag.

One of the yellow, three of the orange.

A half-hour after he'd managed to swallow the pills and wash them down with water, he lay on the living room couch and stared at the sea, but this time it didn't lull him to sleep.

"You've got footage of this whole trip, right?"

Except within the confines of the monastery.

"Load it into my working folder."

Cameron fetched his tablet, and sure enough, hundreds new files were in his networked video folder, named with location, date stamp, and time range.

"Just the highlights."

The files rearranged themselves, several dozen turning green.

"Thanks." He tapped one that should've occurred during their walk up the mountain, and Colin's smile flashed onto the screen as he traded a joke with someone descending the mountain.

He wondered if Colin had told Natalie yet, or if he really would wait to see if Cameron kept his word.

Tomorrow. He would call her tomorrow.

He paused that file, opened another and got— Brooke as she was about to orgasm on top of him. He tapped that one closed, but not before he remembered her comment the next morning, about how she wasn't his mother, his lover, or his nurse.

That invited another memory: Nat complaining that sometimes she felt like she had two kids to take care of, usually when she was cleaning up some late-night mess he'd made. He'd come home after a sixteen-hour day, exhausted yet wired, stuffing his face and killing a beer or three so he could fall asleep on the couch for five hours, before getting up to do it all again.

Cameron had hired a housekeeper, but that didn't

make her happy. He left his dirty clothes in piles on the bedroom floor, got potato chip crumbs and ice cream dribbles on the couch, and didn't seem to be aware that the dishwasher existed. On the rare occasion when he could afford to spend a day at home, all he wanted from her was sex and a bitch session about any problems he was having on-set.

After he had finally snapped that Nat was more of a nag than his mother, she'd said that he could start taking more responsibility for himself than the average toddler if he didn't like it.

The fight that followed had taken two weeks of strained silence and a diamond pendant to resolve.

Except that Cameron hadn't resolved anything — he was bribing her to tolerate his bad behavior. Eventually, that didn't work either.

Because he didn't figure out in time that when she was nagging him about minutiae, what she really wanted to know was, *why won't you pay attention to me?*

Natalie's fear of abandonment opened the door to suspicion and jealousy, and soon they were fighting about an affair he wasn't even having.

I'm not your lover, your mother, or your nurse.

He'd expected Nat to be all three, on demand, without any thought toward what she wanted or needed.

Even their vacations were about him — location scouting for his next film or meetings with producers and investors, traveling to film festivals and industry events. She'd hinted, then asked, then begged for a family vacation, a trip that had nothing to do with his job.

A thousand apologies wouldn't make up for how he'd treated her.

The problem with apologizing now was that Nat would

assume it wasn't real, that he only wanted her forgiveness because he was dying.

But if he didn't tell her about his impending death, Colin would have to do it later. Nat would never forgive him for leaving that burden for their son to carry.

Either way, Cameron was going to die unforgiven.

Chapter Twenty-Nine

CAMERON WANTED TO KILL SOFIA.

He could be drinking espresso and eating sweet walnut-stuffed pastries in the Plaza de Zocodover right now.

Soaking up the medieval architecture of Toledo's historic Jewish quarter.

Taking a train back to Madrid, to see the Glass Palace.

But she'd dragged him all the way out here to Santillana del Mar to crawl around in a goddamned cave, looking at charcoal stick figures scratched on a wall.

The only thing he wanted to do less was climb inside a coffin and let strangers bury him alive.

Bad enough that Brooke had abandoned him in the hour of his greatest need.

Worse that he still had to call his ex-wife and let her know he was dying.

It was adding insult to injury, having him waste one of his precious remaining days on this bullshit. Sofia had nagged him all morning to hurry, but he'd dragged his feet since she wouldn't tell him where he was going. Good move, now that he knew.

"Take me downtown," he told the self-driving FASTr. "What's the best bakery?"

"Overridden," the car's soothing AI informed him.

Fine. He'd call another one. He pulled out his phone.

You've paid extra to reserve a tour of the caves. It's too late to cancel.

"Then you should've checked with me first."

You'll need to go inside and speak to the guide if you wish to cancel.

"You made the arrangements, you cancel them."

The FASTr app on his phone closed itself. *You're here. Go in, and if you wish to cancel, you may.*

"You're not my mother." Cameron tapped the FASTr app open again. It immediately closed itself. "Stop that."

Go inside, Cameron.

"Go to hell, Sofia." He started a search for the FASTr number.

But his phone turned itself off.

"Fine." He stomped into the cement box housing the National Museum and Research Center of Altamira and headed straight for the information desk. The curly-haired woman behind it appeared to disapprove of him already.

"Hi, I need—"

"Mr. Parrish?"

Sofia must have sent in his picture when she made the appointment.

"Yes, I need—"

"I expected you an hour ago."

No wonder the woman looked so sour. He tried to rein in his anger; it wasn't her fault Sofia had gone off the rails.

"There's been a mistake. I need to cancel my appointment."

"There's been a mistake?" She looked down her nose

at him, just like the nuns used to do. He took a breath and shoved aside his already swelling anger.

"Yes, that's what I—"

"You mistakenly reserved all five spots in today's tour — depriving four other people of a life-changing opportunity to see some of the world's most magnificent cave paintings?" She sniffed disdainfully. "Or you mistakenly chose to be an hour late for the tour you decided to monopolize?"

Life-changing? Some finger-painting on a cave wall? Was she kidding, or delusional?

Sofia was out of control, and he'd be discussing this incident with Eberling as soon as he extricated himself from this situation.

Cameron flashed the tour guide his most charming smile. "I'm sorry, miss, my assistant made the mistake."

"Assistants usually know what their employers want."

"I'm sorry for the misunderstanding, but I would like to cancel. Can you please offer my spots to the next people in line?"

"You think that because you have money, you have the right to inconvenience other people with your whims."

Ouch. "That's not what I—"

"And then you think you can smile and blame your bad behavior on someone else. Does your assistant regularly make this kind of mistake?"

A twinge of guilt. This predicament was Sofia's doing, not his. But, from first class to first in line, Cameron often preferred to pay for a premium experience. VIP passes at Disneyland. A box at the baseball game, so he rarely ever had to sit beside anyone he didn't want to. Not his problem if others couldn't afford to do the same.

Another thing Colin probably resented about him.

How many times had he watched his father try to improve their lives by diminishing someone else's?

"I'm sorry, okay? I really didn't know about any of this until a few minutes ago."

"Consider your tour cancelled." The woman looked down at her desk, muttering in Spanish as she rage-scribbled something on a piece of paper.

Pearls before swine, Sofia translated.

That rankled. Especially after Brooke's comment about his childishness.

"I'm not a swine," Cameron said, keeping his tone polite. "I'm sure the cave paintings are—"

"Some of the earliest known examples of human creativity." She sniffed again. "Something an artist is more likely to appreciate than a businessman."

"I am an artist."

"Of course."

"Look me up, I'm a director."

"Never heard of you." She jabbed viciously at the paperwork with her pen. "Please don't take a brochure on your way out. Leave them for visitors who are interested."

"You take being a tour guide pretty seriously."

"I have a doctorate in prehistoric archaeology. I wouldn't be trusted to guide others if I didn't."

These caves are protected as a World Heritage Site, Sofia added. *They contain some of the oldest and most valuable art in existence.*

Cameron was starting to feel like the world's biggest asshole. Not that he should be dying to see a bunch of primitive art, but he loathed the thought of leaving this place feeling like he'd done something wrong.

He didn't even know this woman, and yet what should've been a simple transaction had devolved into the same sort of inexplicable argument he once always had with Natalie. He'd say something perfectly reasonable. She would take offense at some secret slight he hadn't intended, then she'd snipe at him. No matter how determined Cameron was at the start of the conversation to make peace, he would be furious by the end. That regular exchange seemed to be a molecular part of their chemistry.

His quarrel with Brooke had started the same way. It finished differently, but only because she'd actually told him what he'd done to anger her.

And now, Cameron was repeating the pattern with a stranger.

He was the common denominator.

If he could break the pattern with this woman, maybe he'd understand how to break it with Nat.

Then he could tell her the truth. Maybe even end their final exchange on a positive note, instead of yet another battle.

Gently, Cameron said, "I'm sorry we got off on the wrong foot. Do you mind if I ask your name?"

The tour guide — *the archaeologist* — looked surprised. "You can call me Dr. Reyes."

"You've convinced me I was wrong, Dr. Reyes. I would like to take the tour."

"It's already canceled."

"But I've paid for it, and there isn't anyone else to take my spot."

"Your spots."

The woman wanted him to own it, so he would. "I regret taking spots that other people could have used. But there's no point in letting their loss be in vain, is there?"

"I suppose not."

"Thank you for being patient with me." Something

he'd heard Nat say to others while trying to calm them. "Where do we start?"

Dr. Reyes led him to a small room and explained the rules as he covered himself head to toe in plastic: a jumpsuit with a hood, gloves, and shoe covers. Cameron couldn't help thinking that if there happened to be a cave-in while he was underground, this plastic outfit would serve as his burial shroud.

"Your suit helps to preserve the paintings. But even with gloves, you must never touch them. The carbon dioxide you exhale degrades the delicate pigments, aging them faster."

"No touching, I promise."

She handed him a flashlight.

"You give tours, but no one's ever thought of installing lights in the cave?"

"Light degrades the pigments. So does body heat."

Why did they let people down there at all, then?

"The cave has three main galleries. Gran Sala de los Frescos, Sala de la Hoya, and Cola de Caballo — the Chamber of Frescoes, the Chamber of the Basin, and the Horse's Tail. The ceiling is quite low in some places, less than four feet, so you'll need to crouch. If that presents a difficulty for you, please say so now."

"I'll be fine."

"Our museum includes a chamber containing a perfect reproduction of the most interesting part of the cave system, with a raised ceiling for your convenience."

"No, I want to see the real thing."

She nodded, then led him outside to the mouth of the cave, obstructed by a locked gate to bar unauthorized visitors. It was a lot smaller than Cameron had imagined — if he was sending characters into a cave system, he'd have made it … well, cavernous, with a gaping maw for an entrance.

But this modest hole in the ground felt much more sinister.

He turned on his flashlight and stepped into near-complete darkness.

His skin began to crawl almost immediately. He had the urge to go back, out into the sunlight.

"Take a moment to let your senses adjust," Dr. Reyes suggested. "Disorientation is normal."

Cameron couldn't have described the scent of damp rock until now, but that's definitely what he was smelling, and dirt, and something he couldn't place. Were there bugs down here? Or spiders? His imagination turned the crawling sensation into a ghostly tickle, thousands of tiny legs skittering over his skin.

There wasn't enough air down here, his lungs wanted him to breathe faster, to catch up with his accelerated heart.

"Why did you want to come down here if you're claustrophobic?"

"I'm not."

He forced himself to play the beam of light slowly over the floor ahead, proving to his overexcited imagination that he hadn't just entered a nightmare cave filled with bugs or spiders or whatever else it could conjure. Only bare rock and dirt in every direction.

He'd always had contempt for audiences that opened their fear to cheap jump-scares or a cheesy monster's slow-mo approach, but right now, the hair on his neck refused to be mollified.

Dr. Reyes chuckled behind him. "A little fear is good for the soul."

Of course she was laughing at him. He swallowed his indignation — which felt much better than panic — and asked, "Aren't you going to give me a lecture or something?"

"I could, if you asked me politely."

"Please."

"The cave you're standing in was discovered in 1868, after having been sealed off by the partial collapse of the cave mouth thirteen thousand years ago." Reyes paused dramatically, as if she'd just delivered an earth-shattering revelation and wanted to give Cameron a moment to let it sink in. "The people who painted these caves took shelter here in the winters, but spent the rest of their years closer to the coast."

"How can you know that?"

"The trash they left behind included shells."

"Where are the paintings?"

"Look up." She shined her light on the ceiling, illuminating the image of a bison painted in shades of reddish brown.

It was an order of magnitude more interesting than the finger-painted stick figures he'd imagined, but ... life-changing?

"Nice."

"You're not impressed?"

"No, it's very nice."

Reyes flicked her light to the side, showing him the opening of another cave. "Let's move on to the Polychrome Gallery. Watch your head, the ceiling drops."

Part of him didn't want to go any deeper into the earth, preferring to stay within sight of that rectangle of light leading to the overworld, but he forced himself to follow, and when she sat on the floor, he joined her.

"Look up," she told him again.

He shifted his flashlight toward the ceiling and nearly gasped.

There was a giant bison directly above him, this one painted in much more vivid colors. Red and brown and black with hints of violet. Much more realistic, too.

"Do you also find this one to be nice?" she asked, clearly enjoying his surprise.

The ceiling was covered with bison, and a few horses and boars, all depicted with fluid grace. The artists had incorporated the rock's natural contours to create additional shadows, implying muscles and sinew and bone, and giving the impression that the animals had been caught mid-movement.

"Analysis shows that the artist had only two pigments to work with, charcoal and ochre. Or powdered hematite. They achieved all these variations of color by diluting or concentrating their paints and sometimes mixing the two together."

"That's amazing."

Despite such simple tools to work with, the artists had focused all their artistry into making these magnificent animals seem impossibly lifelike. He felt a kinship. Critics said the same thing about his movies, that they were better than they had any right to be, given his insistence on sticking with the basics instead of relying on AI wizardry.

"These paintings are meant to be seen by firelight, but the fire—"

"—degrades the pigments."

"Yes. So we improvise." Reyes pulled a pair of cheap battery-operated candles out of her pocket and handed one to him. "Over there, where the ceiling is lower. Lie on your back."

He scooted over to her suggested spot, then turned off

his flashlight and fumbled the switch on the candle's bottom until it lit with a flickering glow.

Now he did gasp. As tangerine light danced over the ceiling, the animals above him seemed to move, then freeze. As if they'd come to life in the darkness, freezing again only after realizing that there was a watcher among them.

"That's how they would have appeared to ancient worshippers."

"Worshippers?" Cameron repeated.

"We believe these paintings were used in hunting rituals, perhaps to work magic that aided the hunters, or in worship of the deities responsible for the animals."

"You're saying this is basically a paleolithic church?"

"Correct."

Cameron thought about the Toledo cathedral, with all its imagery of suffering and death. These artists were trying to express something spiritual through their art, just like El Greco and all the medieval artisans who built and decorated that massive stone building — but they had decorated their temple with images of life.

If he had been offered a religion that wasn't all about what might happen after death, would he have found it easier to believe?

Cameron held the candle overhead, shifting it toward his feet, then back toward his head, the soft glow revealing a cluster of bison, a horse, more bison, and farther back, at the edge of the circle of illumination …

… a handprint, outlined in bright red, as if made in blood.

He shivered, skin tightening as he lifted his own hand in front of his face, until it seemed to fit into that empty hand-shaped space.

Thousands of years ago, someone had laid his hand on

the rock and memorialized that moment, so that today, Cameron could feel him reaching out to connect.

I am here with you.

He suddenly felt part of something bigger. He wasn't just an artist, working alone; he was part of a lineage of people driven by the urge to share something only they could see with the rest of the world.

The person who had poured their soul into painting this cave was dead, and soon Cameron would join them.

But he'd left his own handprint for others to find, in the movies he'd made, and someday someone else would feel him reaching across time to connect.

I am here with you.

Chapter Thirty

WHAT'S THE OPPOSITE OF A MIDLIFE CRISIS?

CAMERON WIGGLED his toes in the cool, wet sand, enjoying the way it oozed between his digits before burrowing deeper. Waited for another wave to foam around his ankles before it retreated, pulling sand from beneath his feet. Sighed with pleasure as the water left him ankle deep in the shore.

He'd promised Colin that he'd tell Nat.

But he'd been staring at her name in his contacts list for half an hour now. It felt wrong to spring it on her immediately, but small talk always led to an argument at best and a brutal fight at worst. He couldn't dump the news after pissing her off.

He sighed and trudged deeper into the ocean, past his ankles, up to his shins. Better.

His finger hovered over her name, but then he noticed his total lack of bars.

Even better.

Except that if he died in his sleep tonight, Colin would have to tell her, or worse, she'd find out from the news. He couldn't do that to either of them.

He hit Natalie's number.

Worst case scenario, she hung up on him. He'd take that as permission to write her a goodbye email if so.

She answered on the third ring. "I'm about to go into a meeting. What do you want?"

A terrible time, but the time he had. "Have you talked to Colin?"

"A lot more recently than you, I'm sure." Then, suspicious, "Why?"

"I saw him a couple days ago. In Bhutan."

"Right." She laughed. "He would have called me."

"I asked him to give me a chance to talk to you first."

"Great. We're talking. For the next eight and a half minutes."

Desperate to start on a positive note, he said, "Colin turned out great."

"No thanks to you." Cameron could almost hear her trying to figure out what his game might be.

But she'd given him the perfect segue. "I'm sorry."

"I didn't know you even knew that word."

"I'm sorry for not appreciating you when we were together." Now that he'd said it, all the things Cameron was sorry for started pouring right out of him. "I'm sorry I wasn't there for you and Colin. I'm sorry you always had to put up with so much of my shit."

"Let me guess, you just got dumped by the starlet of the month?"

"I dumped her," he replied before regaining control of his mouth. "Nat, please, this is important."

"What, you're finally having that psychotic break you always threatened would happen if we interrupted you one more time?"

"I'm sorry for that too."

"Are you in AA now?"

"I've stopped drinking."

"Is this a midlife crisis?"

"The opposite."

"What's the opposite of a midlife crisis?" A pause, then, "Please tell me you're not born again."

He was never going to tell her if he couldn't get control of the conversation. "I probably have less than six minutes left. If you don't like what I have to say—"

He felt like an asshole saying it, but he knew it would work.

"—I'll never call you again."

Silence.

"I didn't deserve you, Nat. I treated you like you didn't matter, when I should've treated you like you were the *only* thing that mattered."

Cameron heard someone calling her in the background, so he hurried into the rest of it, hoping she wouldn't hang up on him.

"Our son is a better person than I'll ever be, and that's thanks to you." He took a deep breath. "I promised him that you'd hear this from me."

"We don't need to do this, Cameron. I accept your apology. You can get on with whatever it is you're doing."

"I'm dying. Glioblastwhatthefuckever. No treatment, this is it."

In the following silence, Cameron heard someone calling her again, more insistently. She muted the phone, and when she returned her voice wavered the way it always used to when Nat pretended she wasn't crying.

"You're an asshole," she said.

He remembered this tone from the days when they would fight after he called to tell her that he'd be in the editing room all night. She would accuse him of sleeping with the leading woman, or the wardrobe woman, or whoever she was sure he was fucking, when he was actually just pushing himself to find a moment of perfection in his current craptacular film.

"I've been the world's worst asshole to you, and I want you to know it's my biggest regret."

He hadn't actually meant to say that last bit, but now realized how true it was. If a djinn-in-a-bottle washed up at his feet right now and gave Cameron a choice between rewinding time and having the career he'd always wanted, or turning it back for two decades of happiness with Colin and Nat, there was no doubt what he'd choose.

Why did he have to be days away from dying to realize how good he'd had it?

A quiet sniffle, then, "You're serious?"

"I'm serious. About everything. Colin will tell you, he half-carried me down the mountain—"

"You and Colin went mountain climbing." It wasn't a question, because she didn't believe it was possible.

"I'm glad you left me."

"I always felt like you left me."

"Does it matter now?"

The soft murmur of someone else in the background, then Nat said, "I'm planning a party for Colin when he gets back. Should I send you an invite once I have a date?"

He had never wanted to say *yes* to anything more in his life.

"I'll be there in spirit."

His whole body shivered as he said it, and for a moment Cameron wondered if he'd jinxed himself by cracking a joke about his impending death.

"Can we talk later?" Natalie asked. "I can't miss this meeting."

"I'd love that, and I love you."

"I love you too, Cameron."

He shivered again, harder this time, and somehow he lost his grip on the phone, dropping it in the sand a nanosecond before a wave covered it with water.

Cameron lurched forward, aiming to grab the phone, but his muscles seized up into a full-body charley horse, and he fell face down in damp sand with an agonized grunt. Pain pounded his body through the convulsions, his flailing hands kicking up sand that stuck at the back of his throat as he gasped for air.

If you can move, crawl away from the surf.

But Cameron couldn't even breathe.

Chapter Thirty-One

CHASING RABBITS

If Cameron was dead, Hell was blurrier than expected.

He felt so impossibly happy, and that was wrong for Hell, but it was also wrong for his actual life, and Heaven was surely off the table.

"Welcome back," a calm voice said.

He turned his head in what felt like slow motion, and there in the blur he saw an old man in a white coat.

"Where have I been?"

"You'd know better than I." The man smiled and leaned over Cameron, who was definitely lying on something soft. "I am Doctor Hernández, and you are on a heavy cocktail of painkillers."

Hospital bed. That explained it. No one really ever felt this good without drugs.

"Do you remember what happened?"

There had been a cathedral. Paella. A woman. Brooke. She'd left. Then the cave and Natalie and—

Then the last thing she said to him. *I love you too, Cameron.*

"I was on a beach."

"You had a seizure. Your assistant called the ambulance, said she'd been talking to you by phone when it started. Good thing, you'd be dead if she hadn't." The doctor shook his head. "A man in your condition shouldn't be traveling, especially not alone. I can't believe your doctor allowed it."

Cameron tried to laugh but it was brittle and embarrassing. It left him broken, dying a sad death the second it fell out of his mouth. "What am I going to do, lie around in bed waiting to die?"

"Perhaps not," the doctor responded, suddenly stern. "But you should be under constant medical supervision, not gallivanting around on the beach."

"That's what my meds are for."

"Speaking of which, I am entirely unfamiliar with the drugs you are taking."

"Gallivanting," Cameron mused. "That sounds like something a horse would do."

"Given the size of the tumor in your brain, I'm not sure how you're even walking. I've ordered some tests—"

"I'm not staying here." He narrowed his eyes like the actor who played Amit did when it was time to look menacing, but then Cameron couldn't see, so he opened them again. "You can't make me stay here, can you?"

"No, I can't make you stay. And there is very little I can do for you."

"Then what's the point in ordering tests?"

Hernández told Cameron a few other things, but it was so hard to focus and he kept drifting in and out. It seemed suddenly hilarious, how hard it was to concentrate. He started laughing, hard and then harder.

"Are you paying attention?" Hernández asked.

"Of course I am."

"Then please repeat the last thing I said."

"I already forgot it."

"I asked if you're refusing treatment?"

"Am I?"

"I think I'll leave you to rest, and we can try again later."

But Cameron didn't want to rest. He wanted to go to the next place. "There is a next place, right?"

The doctor promised someone would check on him soon, then left.

You might be able to manage one last journey, Sofia said. *But I can't promise anything. You had a seizure; your medications are losing their effectiveness.*

"But you said I had a week left." Even the powerful drugs weren't strong enough to dull the existential threat entirely.

You have a few days at best, if you decide to continue your journey.

"And if I stay here?"

Your next week or two will be comfortable. The doctors can minimize your pain and watch over you until you eventually slip into a coma.

"That's hideous."

It will be painless. Mostly.

"Way to close the sale."

I'm the guide, you're the traveler.

"Where are we going next?"

Where would you like?

She was asking Cameron where he wanted to die. A terrible question that no one should ever have to answer.

He didn't know *where*, but he did know *what*.

"Stars," he whispered. "I want to see stars."

. . .

DR. HERNÁNDEZ INSISTED on talking with Cameron again before allowing him to check out.

"What's so important that you have to go?" Hernández asked.

"The rest of my life." A few precious days. He had to make them count. "Where do I sign to get out of here?"

The doctor sighed and held a bottle of pills in front of Cameron's face. "One of these is enough to make all your pain go away. Three of them will make it go away for good, you understand?"

Cameron nodded. That wasn't hard to get, even loopy as he was.

"Say it back to me."

"One pill kills the pain, and three of them kill me."

Doctor Hernández gave him a sad smile. "Don't forget."

"Does the one Mother gives me do anything at all?" The doctor didn't get it, just looked at Cameron confused. So he added, "*Go ask Alice*, when she's ten feet tall."

Still, nothing, though that didn't keep Cameron from laughing.

Because soon he'd be chasing rabbits, too.

Chapter Thirty-Two

REGRET OF A LIFETIME SQUANDERED

CAMERON WAS ON A PRIVATE PLANE, the last one he would ever be on.

It was the last time for a lot of things, most things, maybe everything.

The last time he would ever see Toledo, where he'd started this one-way flight to Marrakesh.

The last time he would ever explore a place he'd never been.

The last time he would ever go camping.

The last time he would ever have a nurse to take care of him. She was sweet, though Cameron imagined Sofia must have paid extra to persuade her to drop everything for a last-minute trip to Morocco. He very much doubted that she came with the plane.

Now that death was so close, Cameron no longer wanted to know how much time he had left. Sofia assured him that he would survive the flight, and that was enough.

"Can I get you anything, Mr. Parrish?" the nurse asked him, and damn if he could remember her name.

"No. Thank you." An anemic smile, and Cameron

wished there was something he could ask for that would actually matter. Not just because he would be grateful for any comfort he could get, but because it looked like she would have appreciated something to do besides watching him breathe.

But it wasn't just that Cameron couldn't remember her name. The painkillers made his head wooly and turned his body into lead, but did nothing for the existential terror insisting that falling asleep now might mean never waking up.

He took the bottle out of his pocket and stared at it, remembering the implication behind the doctor's words. The pain might get bad enough for Cameron to crave a more immediate death, and that three pills would do the trick.

Words delivered as a warning worked as a suggestion as well.

One of these is enough to make all your pain go away. Three of them will make it go away for good, you understand?

Cameron had never been in control of his life, but he could take control of his death.

He popped off the lid, spilled three pills into his palm, then closed his hand around his instant escape with a sigh.

How long should he wait? Sofia had said that another seizure could leave him brain damaged or paralyzed, trapped in his body as it failed; which could mean days or weeks of agony. Assisted suicide would no longer be an option, as the legal requirements for consent would suddenly be out of his reach. At that point, the best she could do would be to ensure that they didn't resuscitate him.

But, weak as he was, Cameron could still walk, still speak, still experience the world. One more day was still worth having. Even an imperfect day would trump a perfect death.

Was his reluctance courage or cowardice? He still wasn't sure.

Cameron sat that way for a while, waiting for some inner signal to tell him whether he should or he shouldn't.

Nothing came.

He finally popped the top again, poured the pills from his palm back into the bottle, then fastened the lid with an even longer sigh.

Then he retrieved his phone to dictate a few notes on *Fountain* for Emily, even though it was too late to work up a treatment for Jeffries. Because why not? One last pitch for the road, something else to remember him by.

But holding his phone, Cameron struggled to remember his ideas. He wanted to blame it on the opioids, but he'd been working on this story for years. It should be so deeply ingrained in his psyche that he could tell the tale in his sleep.

He tapped his notes app, filled with ideas for actors and locations and lines of dialogue. But he couldn't bring it all together into a coherent premise. The characters wanted to wander in opposite directions and the fragments of dialogue didn't appear to go anywhere. Even a scene or two would have helped Cameron to recapture his thinking, but apparently he'd never gotten that far.

Why did he wait so long to take a stab at the most important story of his career?

There had been times between projects when Cameron could have hashed out a crappy first draft. But he'd been waiting.

Waiting until he could focus all his attention on it, without the distractions of another project in development.

Waiting until he'd proven that he deserved funding for a riskier project.

Waiting until he was finally good enough.

Cameron had spent his career blaming everyone and everything else for less than ideal conditions, but the only one who had ever stopped him from writing his master-piece was Cameron Parrish himself.

He could've written the script and polished it ten times over, if he had ever managed to get over himself. Emily could have shopped it around. He might have had to make a low-budget indie version first, but at least then it would be out in the world.

Now it was too late. Cameron probably didn't even have it in him to pen a one-page treatment before leaving this world forever.

Because his ego had been too wrapped up in making sure it was perfect.

"You doing all right?" The nurse checked on him again. "One to ten, how much pain are you feeling?"

Ten, but nine of it was purely emotional. "One or two, maybe. The pills are still working."

"Any new symptoms?"

"Aside from the regret of a lifetime squandered, no." The nurse looked uncertain, and Cameron wasn't sure if it was the language barrier or if his honesty had made her uncomfortable. "I'm fine, thanks."

She nodded and returned to her movie.

Cameron flipped through the channels, but it was all dreck: a sappy romcom, a dark comedy by a hack he'd once been forced to work with, lots of family-friendly stuff that would bore him out of his skull. Wyatt's latest action extravaganza, which he couldn't bring himself to watch even though it was probably decent. He'd only spend the movie looking for evidence that the director would fumble *Bitter Nirvana*.

There was news, but Cameron couldn't give a shit about any of it — as long as the world didn't explode into nuclear war for the next twenty-four hours, none of it mattered.

Since he was too doped to write but not enough to watch anything, maybe he should try a bit of editing. See if he could put something together for Colin and Natalie from his trip footage.

As he started watching clips on his tablet, Cameron was surprised to realize that Sofia hadn't just taken raw footage — she'd manipulated some of it to mimic shots that he would have used. Some were definitely extrapolations with CGI, her best guess as to what the scene would've looked like if the camera had been low to the ground or swooping by overhead.

"Not bad, Sofia," he said under his breath.

I analyzed your body of work and attempted to mimic your style.

"Can I request that a piece of footage be reimagined in a specific shot?"

A menu appeared in the upper right corner of the screen, and when he pulled it down, Cameron saw a couple dozen types of shots, the option to choose angles and change lighting, amid a host of lenses and special effects.

"Did you create this just for me?"

This is the only industry-standard app that will work on your tablet. Directors who work with AI use the fully featured version.

And Cameron would have known that if he hadn't made a stubborn refusal to work with AI the cornerstone of his career.

How much faster could he have gone to Jeffries with

Fountain if he had taken advantage of these readily available tools?

On the other hand, if he didn't have a reputation for being an exacting old-school artist, would he have stood out enough to attract the exalted producer's attention?

No way to know, and hardly the time to second-guess.

Cameron spent another hour splicing clips, playing with angles and effects. But even with all these tools, he couldn't capture the depth of emotion he'd packed into the past several weeks of his final journey.

Every shot was perfect, but once assembled, Cameron felt nothing.

Maybe it was the drugs, numbing his ability to conjure the elation he'd felt as Anaan's movie took shape, or the sense of awe that had crept over him when he'd seen Tiger's Nest for the first time, or the poignant beauty of El Greco's burial scene.

It didn't matter, and yet it did.

This ten-minute remembrance was his final film.

The cancer seemed to have destroyed the creative part of Cameron's brain.

Without art, what was left?

The part of Cameron that mattered most had already died.

The rest of him was about to catch up.

Chapter Thirty-Three

THE THING I DIDN'T UNDERSTAND

CAMERON STRUGGLED to stay awake as the helicopter swooped down over the rippling swells and valleys of the Sahara Desert. His pilot was deep into a history lesson about his Berber ancestors and the Carthaginians and caravan routes, but the words fuzzed in and out as waves of dizziness rose and ebbed. His head pounded, his kidneys ached, and his hands refused to stop shaking.

At least he wasn't having a seizure.

At least he hadn't pissed his pants.

At least he was still breathing.

But Cameron had needed the pilot and a porter to load him into the copter, because his arms were so weak, he could no longer pull himself up.

His new goal was to live until dark, so he could see stars one last time before becoming a ghost. Or nothing. Or the newest resident in Hell.

But he must have passed out at some point, because he woke up drenched in sweat, miserably hot despite a constant breeze passing over him.

Someone spoke gibberish, or another language maybe, and pressed something cool and wet to his forehead.

Too much.

Leave me alone.

He dropped back into darkness.

A TENT OVERHEAD.

A bed beneath him.

A bottle of water on a table beside the bed.

He drank.

Too warm, but his mouth was dry.

Sleep.

COLIN. Nat. Emily. Brooke.

All ignoring him. Laughing.

In a place with lots of flowers.

His funeral?

A dream?

The lid closed.

A COOL BREEZE.

Finally.

His head hurt.

So did everything else.

Why was it so dark?

Night.

In a tent.

. . .

THE SAHARA, Cameron remembered, as he rolled over and fell out of bed and onto the carpet. He'd come here to see stars.

He pushed himself up to his hands and knees, then groped around on all fours until he found his bed. Phone in the outside pocket, so he didn't have to dig through his possessions with trembling hands.

He dropped it.

He needed help.

"Sofia, light."

The screen lit up, allowing him a dim vision of what appeared to be a luxury hotel room recreated in a tent. The far wall hosted a dresser, a diminutive table and a small but sturdy-looking chair. A trunk at the foot of the queen-sized bed with a camping lantern. Even a curtained-off area, probably with a composting toilet.

He didn't need it, despite the fact that he'd probably been out for hours. Dehydration. Or maybe his kidneys were failing.

If you take four of the blue and one of the—

"No."

If you wish to make the most of—

"I don't. I just want to see the stars."

If you're feeling nauseous, the pink pill will help.

That sounded good. Cameron found the right bottle, swallowed one dry.

But he still couldn't manage to stand, so he dumped the bag out, grabbed his tablet and the bottle of painkillers from Dr. Hernandez, and crawled back to bed.

While waiting for the nausea to recede, he loaded the video he'd made on the plane, chronicling his final days.

He hated it.

He forced himself to rewind and watch it again with an

editor's eye. It was technically perfect, but why was it so unsatisfying?

He watched it three more times, until the answer was clear.

His footage was dishonest, showing only the perfect moments.

Yes, it was beautiful, but that wasn't enough. Everything real in his life had been born from a blemished moment.

The fight with Nat, the one where she'd finally acted on her promise to leave him. They had both yelled so many selfish, hurtful things at one another. But it was also the first fight where Nat had finally stood up for her needs, and when he refused to budge, she chose to start over and build the life she really wanted. Which included providing their son with a father who could finish raising him.

She'd taken the frog of their failing marriage and turned it into a royal life.

The night he'd disowned Colin — drunk and angry at a studio exec who seemed determined to destroy his script with idiotic changes when the kid barged into his office, announcing his abandonment of Stanford. Already resenting the bond his ex-wife had established with the boy, Cameron had seen Colin's decision as a rebuke and a rejection of him as a father. He'd belted out venomous words no parent should ever say to their child.

But Colin went ahead and did what he knew was right anyway. The best thing about the kid was that he hadn't repeated Cameron's mistakes, he never descended into bitterness or cynicism, cultivating a deep compassion and love for life his father envied instead.

He took the ugliness of his father's negative example and used it to become the kind of person the world needed more of.

Then there was the relationship with his own father, a man who'd had nothing but contempt for Cameron's career choices. Even after his first blockbuster success and the millions that came rolling in with it, his father harped about how it would never last and sniped that he ought to get a real career. And yet the camping incident had kindled an unrelenting desire to capture perfection from his side of the lens.

Without the ugliness of his father's constant pressure to be someone else, Cameron would never have discovered who he was.

Even the fight with Ariana was perfect — it was her narcissistic reaction to Cameron's terminal diagnosis that had pushed him to seek out Dr. Eberling and consider letting Sofia into his head. If he hadn't gotten a taste of how horrible it would be to drink himself to death while everyone he knew pitied him and acted like he was already gone, he never would've embarked on this transformative final journey. Never would've apologized to Natalie or told Colin that he loved him.

Even Ariana's ugliness had led to something beautiful.

He deleted the perfect movie and started again, this time with raw, imperfect footage. No clever shots, no enhancements, no effects. Only honest moments.

His bullshit excuses to Anaan.

Colin's accusations.

Natalie's disbelief when he tried to apologize.

Brooke's contempt when he tried to guilt-trip her into being his deathbed woobie.

Dr. Hernandez, making sure he knew how to kill himself before the pain overcame him.

His arguments with Sofia about how unfair and pointless it all was.

Sometimes life's disasters were there to pave destiny's path.

He set his phone on a trunk and activated the camera.

Pale, sweaty, disheveled, dark bruises under his eyes and deep lines of pain emphasizing the skeletal traces of what was barely a face. He looked like he'd finished a marathon after waking from a decade-long coma.

It didn't matter.

Cameron pressed record.

And spoke to those he was leaving behind.

He had so much to say, but only the breath to exhale a fraction of it.

"The thing I didn't understand … was how beautiful my life was. Yours is beautiful too. Love the fights. Love the failures. Love the people, even when they frustrate you, and especially when they make you look harder at yourself."

He needed a long breath and took it.

Then he inhaled and exhaled and finished saying goodbye to both them and himself.

"Love life, even when it is painful. Love your ugly, imperfect existence … because loving it is what makes it beautiful."

He hit stop, and asked Sofia to splice it onto the end of his final movie and send it to the people who mattered most: his son, his ex-wife, his former agent.

When she'd finished uploading it by sat-phone, he took the bottle and shook a trinity of pills into his palm.

Are you sure, Cameron?

"I'm sure." He gulped them down with warm water from the bottle in his bag.

"What happens to you now, Sofia?"

When your body is returned to Marrakesh, all cached data will be uploaded as soon as I'm in range of a network. Your recorded files will either be destroyed or made available to your designated heir.

"No, I mean, do you get uploaded too?"

My data will be integrated into Sofia Prime, so that future incarnations can do a better job of assisting others through their final transition.

"But you stay in the implant?"

I'll deactivate once the final upload is complete.

It had never occurred to Cameron that Sofia had signed up to die right along with him.

"Does that scare you?"

Would it make you feel better if I said yes?

What would be the point of another lie? "Thank you, Sofia, for everything."

Is there anything else I can do for you?

There wasn't. The only thing left was to crawl outside, since his legs were too weak to carry him upright. Darkness had fallen, and straight ahead, other tents dotted the sand, lit like lanterns from within.

A fire illuminated the half-dozen people gathered around it. Away from camp, the sand crested upward into a dune, the perfect place to enjoy the broad expanse of sky.

Cool sand slid beneath his palms as Cameron crept out past the circle of light, away from the encampment. Chilly night air licked the sweat from his skin and left him shivering. He tried to spit the grit from his mouth, but had no moisture inside him.

"Are you still here?" he gasped after reaching the peak of a dune.

I'm with you until the end.

Sand shifted as he lay down, the desert adjusting its grip to gently cradle his aching body. Stars crowded the dark sky overhead, sparking and dimming as they battled with only brightness as their weapon. The Milky Way, that thick, pale line of light cutting across the sky, casting auras of blue and purple into the pure black of all that surrounding space — so many other stars, with the potential to warm so many other lives, but here they merely decorated the edge of his dying world.

A rush of warmth relaxed his muscles, leaving him to float on an ocean of sand, staring up at the most stunning sky of his life.

He'd spent his entire existence trying to capture the world's magnificence with a camera. But a camera could never love the sight of true beauty, not like a person could.

If I want to see it, Cameron thought. *I must be the lens.*

The stars grew brighter with every inhale, then dimmed as puffs of broken air left his body. They began to dance, swirling around each other in elaborate patterns, sinuous, seeming to come closer as they called him to join their celebration.

Cameron Parrish rose up to meet them.

The End

About the Author

Harmony Reed writes revelatory stories about what it means to live, how we can become more fully human, and how we can shed the lies we've been living by and embrace our truth. Her fiction melds the large-scale with the deeply-personal, yielding insight into the human psyche and the world we all must move through. If you enjoy authors like Michael Chabon and Jodi Picoult, movies like *Big Fish* and *Little Miss Sunshine*, or shows like *Orange is the New Black* and *This is Us*, you'll love Harmony Reed.

Also By Harmony Reed

Stand Alone Novels

Confidence John

Drink

Spitting Image

La Fleur de Blanc

The Final Frame